What people are saying about
TRISKELLION

"Fantasy and history thrown into one by Will Peterson – the result? Nothing other than a bone-chilling read that won't let you go."
JJ, aged 12

"One of the best books I have read for ages."
Dominic, aged 12

"Exciting, gripping and kept me wanting to read more… It is a real page-turner which will captivate you to the end."
Jack, aged 11

"Wow! Step aside Harry Potter … make way for *Triskellion* and my new heroes, Rachel and Adam. Gripping edge-of-the-seat, page-turning brilliance! *Triskellion* is total unput-downable fiction. Fantastically exciting and really scary too. Pure magic!"
Holly, aged 10

"A magical read with a mysterious paranormal setting. All the characters are highly believable, each with a strong indi-vidual personality… The only bad thing that can be said about the book is the agonizing wait for the next two."
Freya, aged 11

TRISKELLION

WILL PETERSON

WILL PETERSON is an award-winning novelist and acclaimed television writer. He lives in London and Kent. This is his first novel for children.

TRISKELLION

WILL PETERSON

WALKER
BOOKS

This is a work of fiction. Names, characters, places and incidents are either the product of the author's imagination or, if real, used fictitiously.

First published 2008 by Walker Books Ltd
87 Vauxhall Walk, London SE11 5HJ

2 4 6 8 10 9 7 5 3 1

Text © 2008 Mark Billingham Ltd and Peter Cocks
Cover design by Walker Books Ltd

The right of Mark Billingham and Peter Cocks to be identified
as authors of this work has been asserted by them in accordance
with the Copyright, Designs and Patents Act 1988

This book has been typeset in Fairfield

Printed in the UK by CPI Bookmarque, Croydon, CR0 4TD

British Library Cataloguing in Publication Data:
a catalogue record for this book
is available from the British Library

ISBN 978-1-4063-0709-2

www.walkerbooks.co.uk

For Katie, Jack, Rusty and George

prologue: new york

The creature drove its body again and again into the glass, unable to understand why the air had suddenly become impossible to move through, desperately searching for some way out.

The girl turned away from it and watched her mother opening and closing cupboards on the other side of the breakfast bar. She stared as her mother furiously polished the appliances, buffing up the surfaces of the kettle, the juicer, the coffee-maker that her father had bought the Christmas before.

Rachel opened her mouth to speak, but with a small wave of her hand, her mother silenced her. A gesture that said, "No, I'm busy and I can't think. No, I can't discuss it right now. No, please, I need to finish telling you these things before the tears come again."

Then, still talking, she was moving across the kitchen to start work on the stainless steel of the worktop, rubbing and rubbing at the metal, until she could look down into it and see her own drawn and determined expression.

As she went through arrangements for the rest of the summer.

Rachel stared across the table and tried to get the attention of the boy sitting opposite her. He glanced up briefly, looked over at Rachel with eyes that were the same as her own, then let his head drop again. Grunted to himself.

Adam. Forty-three minutes younger than she was. But he was a boy, right? So it felt like it could have been a whole lot more.

Rachel hissed at her brother. His head stayed down. He shook it slowly, and continued to push the cereal around in his bowl.

The two of them jumped simultaneously at the explosion of a door closing hard upstairs. The boy looked up at his sister, suddenly pale and afraid, and they turned together to watch their mother, her gaze fixed on the doorway, her arms stiff against the worktop. She stood frozen mid-sentence and mid-movement, wincing at the footsteps that thundered down the stairs like a series of rumbling aftershocks. Tensing for the noise that they all knew was coming.

The front door slammed shut, its echo died slowly, and there were just three of them.

Rachel felt as if the seconds were thickening, as if time was slowing down, though it was probably no more than a few moments before she and Adam pushed their chairs away from the table.

The scrape of the metal legs against the floor was terrible, like a hundred pieces of chalk being dragged down a blackboard.

Rachel's mother rubbed at her eyes and did her best to smile as her children moved towards her. She opened her arms and Adam walked into the embrace. He pressed his head against her chest, sobbing silently as she stroked his hair.

Hearing the buzz and the tap, Rachel glanced across again, oddly disturbed by the small drama at the window.

The bee was still flying headlong into the glass, though a little slower now, with much less enthusiasm as it tired.

Zzzzz ... dnk. Zzzzz ... dnk. Zzzzz...

She walked quickly across to the window just as the insect spun and dropped, exhausted, on to the sill.

The voice in her head was not her own. It was a male voice ... a boy's voice, and it spoke in a strange accent she didn't recognize.

Open the window, the voice said.

Rachel did as she was told, and watched as the bee crawled slowly up on to the edge of the window, then waited for a few seconds before taking flight.

When the bee rose up fast and flew back towards her face, she remained completely still and unafraid of being stung, as though the voice in her head had calmed her. As the bee circled twice round her head she followed its movements: seeing the gold and black fur on its back revealed in astonishing detail; clapping her hands across her ears at the deafening beat of its wings; and watching as it finally veered away out of the window.

Rachel Newman stared, almost hypnotized, as the bee

part one:
the chalk circle

1

Rachel came to with a start as the carriage door slammed. The clattering rhythm, the heat and the plush interior of the old train must have lulled her to sleep for ... seconds? Minutes? She didn't know how long.

She'd caught a little sleep on the plane, but now the lag was starting to catch up and she felt strangely floaty. The reassuring bleeps and electronic melodies of Adam's PSP were still there as they had been on the night flight from New York, on the high-speed shuttle from Heathrow and on the 9.32 a.m. train out of Paddington. It felt odd: such incongruous, modern noises as they rattled along an antiquated branch line, deep into the West Country. Rachel couldn't help but wonder what their next form of transport might be on this seemingly endless journey.

Steam engine? Pony and trap? Donkey?

Rachel smiled wearily at her brother as he looked up briefly from under the peak of his Yankees cap, eyes momentarily off the game, but ears still plugged with his Pod's white earbuds. Adam seemed happy enough in his self-contained world, alone with his computer game and the thrash metal pounding in his ears.

They had been alone in the carriage for the last hour, but now they had been joined by someone else. As the old lady perched a large wicker cat-basket on top of the luggage rack, Adam widened his eyes at his sister. The lady turned and nodded at Adam, who shifted awkwardly to one side as she shuffled her expansive bottom into the dusty red seat next to him and took out her knitting.

The only other person Rachel knew who knitted was Granny Root. Every year a misshapen sweater or cardigan made from scratchy wool would arrive from England. It would be five sizes too big, with one sleeve longer than the other, or tiny, with a neck hole too small to accommodate a human head. When none had arrived last Christmas they were almost disappointed, but by then Rachel and Adam had grown out of Gran's sweaters in every way.

Celia Root was the grandmother they had met only once, when they were babies; Mom's mom, who, in all the twins' fourteen years, had only managed to make a single trip to New York. They'd spoken twice a year on the phone, Gran's posh-sounding voice crackling down the transatlantic line on Christmas Day and on their birthday, sounding like something from an old radio play. There were photos, too, and Rachel had loved to look at those old black and white shots of a trim, striking woman in lipstick, with smart clothes and elegantly styled dark hair. The hair was still immaculate, but white in the more recent pictures and, though the clothes were softer, in earthier colours, the bright red lipstick was still in place. It was difficult for Gran to get around these days, though that wasn't the only reason she'd never been to visit. As she'd got older, Granny Root had developed a terrible fear of flying.

Mom, on the other hand, enjoyed flying all over the place, but had never seemed all that keen on getting them to England before now. She had told them that she hated the place, that it was stuffy, class-ridden and strangled by its own sense of history, whatever that was supposed to mean. Even if she'd wanted to go, her work had never seemed to fit in with their holidays anyway, and so summers were mostly spent in Cape Cod, in a regular rented house near the beach.

Now though, with the stuff going on between their parents, a trip to England had finally seemed like a good idea. Naturally reluctant to see them go, but with no other choice, their mother had announced that spending the rest of the summer in a quiet little village might be the best way for the twins to cool their heels. Somewhere for them to chill out, while things settled down a bit at home.

Somewhere calm, stable, unchanging...

The old lady smiled at Rachel and Rachel smiled back. She was not the kind of woman Rachel was used to seeing in the street or on the subway. In Manhattan most women were either wearing shabby sweats or else were decked out in a

couple of thousand dollars' worth of DKNY and designer
sneakers. This lady was something else entirely. She wore a
small straw hat held in place with a long pin, and brown
leather shoes that looked as if she hadn't taken them off for
fifty years. It was a boiling summer afternoon, but she was
dressed in a suit of something thick and dark green (closer to
armour-plating than clothing) with a dainty lace collar
sprouting from her neck, which made her look like she'd
stepped out of some historical portrait. Rachel tried not to
stare, taking in the details as the old lady concentrated on
her knitting, her needles clicking at a ferocious rate.

The cat in the basket mewled and the lady looked up,
catching Rachel watching her. They exchanged another prim
smile.

"He has been to the veterinary surgeon to have his stitches
removed," the lady said. She pronounced every vowel sound
and consonant with great care, as though she were practising
her English.

"Oh. Right," Rachel replied, really none the wiser.

"I have six cats," the old lady continued. "This is Danny
Boy, like the song, then there's Ozymandias, Marmalade, Mr
Kipps, Orlando, and Rum Tum Tugger. You know, from the
T. S. Eliot...?"

Rachel smiled and nodded, confused by the list and its
mysterious associations.

"We can't have cats. It's against the rules of our building."

The old lady nodded, equally uncertain of Rachel's

meaning, and cast her eyes back to her knitting.

The ice had been broken, but the heat in the carriage was becoming almost unbearable. The air blowing in through the open wedge of window felt like a hairdryer. Adam pulled out his earphones and lifted his cap to reveal a mop of thick brown hair plastered to his head with sweat. Rachel smirked, causing him to urgently ruffle his hair into a semblance of its normal, shaggy style – simultaneously pushing out his lower lip with his tongue as a rebuke to Rachel.

"It's terribly close…"

Adam almost jumped. The lady was speaking to him and had turned her pointed nose in his direction, catching him pulling faces.

"Excuse me?"

"It's terribly close," she repeated, dabbing at her cheeks with a tiny lace handkerchief.

Adam was stumped. What was close? Their destination? Christmas? He looked at Rachel, who immediately developed a keen interest in grazing sheep and looked out of the window, containing a smile.

"Is it?" Adam asked the old lady.

"It is." The lady nodded to him and returned to her knitting. Adam felt the need to reply. He thought he ought to be polite to this old-fashioned person who spoke like the queen.

"Um. Thank you."

The lady nodded and her needles clicked on in time to the clatter of the train wheels over the track. Sensing the

conversation to be over, Adam plugged his earphones back
in, back to his world where a thrashing guitar quickly lulled
him to sleep in the afternoon heat.

For the second time, Rachel was shaken awake by the crash
of the carriage door. Looking across, she saw that Adam had
dropped off too, but knew it would take something a lot
louder than that to wake her brother.

The old lady and her cat had gone. This must have been
her stop.

Rachel looked out of the window at an empty platform
and craned her neck to see the name of the station. A little
way down the platform a red, enamelled sign announced
itself.

Rachel's heart lurched. The name had so much resonance. A
place their mother had spoken of since they were old enough
to understand. The place where their mother was born, the
place she had left, but a place that Rachel and Adam had
never seen.

She leaned across and began to shake her brother awake.

2

Adam heaved his backpack on to his shoulder and stood blinking in the afternoon sun, eyes still puffy from sleep. Rachel watched the small train rattle off into the distance, then turned and looked along the empty platform. There was no sign of the old lady with the cat, or anyone else for that matter. Someone must have been there to pick the old lady up. So, would anyone be…?

"No one meeting us?" grunted Adam, reading Rachel's thoughts, as he often did.

"Let's try the parking lot," Rachel said. "Gran *must* have arranged *something*." She shouldered her bag and they walked along the platform towards the sign that said *Way Out*.

"Way out," Adam read, putting on a drawling Californian accent, extracting as much meaning from the two words as possible.

They walked past a red-brick waiting room with clapboard walls and thick, burgundy and cream paintwork. The etched glass windows and doors were detailed with an odd-looking symbol of some sort. Rachel thought it was an unlikely logo for a rail company. She decided it was probably a crest, or whatever one of those things was called; maybe the coat of arms for some local aristocratic family. She knew that kind of thing still went on in England, with whole estates, towns even, belonging to a single duke or lord or Sir Whatever.

"Everything's so clean..." Rachel looked at the spotless platform and the gleaming brass of the unoccupied ticket desk.

"Could always tag it." Adam took a thick, black marker from the pocket of his backpack and waved it at Rachel.

"Don't even—"

"Just kidding." Adam waggled his pen between finger and thumb like a cigar.

They turned the corner into a gravel car park with enough parking spaces for three cars, all vacant. They dropped their bags and stood there, silent in the heat, neither keen to admit their disappointment, their confusion, and the fact that they hadn't the faintest idea what they should do next. Rachel stared out beyond the car park at the lane, at the canopy of trees that hung over it and the lush hill beyond, still green despite the months of sun. She stood on tiptoe, willing a taxi, or a tractor, or *anything* to come.

"You got Gran's number?" Adam said. "Let's call her."

Rachel took her phone from her backpack and switched it on. Waited. "No signal," she said.

"Great." Adam studied the scuffed toe of his Vans, wishing he'd brought his skateboard after all. He kicked the gravel, scuffing the toe a little more and felt a fraction better.

He looked at his sister staring into the middle distance, chewing her lower lip as she always did when she was nervous. Rachel's slight overbite stopped short of making her look goofy – of course, she'd worn braces, but her teeth were still not completely regular. In fact, Adam thought they made her look pretty, though he'd never tell her that. With her heavy ringlets of dark chestnut hair and freckles, Adam thought how old-fashioned his sister looked. She didn't seem out of place in this environment, and although, as her twin, he shared some of the same characteristics, he imagined that somehow they conspired in him to look more ... well, modern.

Rachel sensed her brother's gaze and turned to face him, looking into his eyes, reading *his* thoughts, which, despite their inevitable rows, was always a great comfort to her. As one, they turned and walked back towards the station house, then immediately stopped in their tracks again. Propped against the front of the station wall was a pair of old-fashioned bicycles, and pinned to the noticeboard above them was a large, brown envelope.

On it was written: *Rachel and Adam Newman.*

Rachel tore down the envelope. "At least we're expected. And the good news is we have transportation."

"Bad news is ... this is it," Adam said. "Check out the

dorky baskets on the front," he moaned, testing the rusty handlebars of the old bike.

Rachel unfolded a piece of paper from the envelope. "We've got a map. Everything's going to be OK."

Rachel studied the hand-drawn directions. In large letters across the bottom was written "Triskellion". Above it, along with various other landmarks, a simple route was drawn from the station to their grandmother's house, Root Cottage, which had been marked on the map with a bold, red "X".

Rachel and Adam's spirits lifted. Things were definitely looking up.

Ten minutes later, they were forcing the heavy bikes up the last metre to the brow of the hill above Triskellion. Panting and pouring with sweat, they stopped for a moment to get their breath and survey the village below. It was exactly as described on the map and, from Rachel and Adam's viewpoint, it appeared on almost the same scale: the church there, above the village green; the big house on the opposite hill; the plain, dotted with scrub and dry-stone walls; the woods; and the moorland stretching into the far distance beyond.

The lane was completely quiet, save for the faint buzzing of bees. Rachel took a swig from what was now a bottle of warm spring water. She screwed up her nose and offered it to her brother who, rather than drink it, poured the remainder over his head, shaking his hair at her like a wet dog.

They looked down at the lane below, where the trees

overhung the road to such a degree that they almost formed a tunnel down into the village. Shafts of sunlight sliced through the gaps in the foliage and cut through the shade like lasers.

Rachel studied the map for a few seconds then looked up and pointed. "Gran's place is down there on the other side of the village," she said. "You ready?"

Adam, his face dripping with water, stood high on his pedals and edged the bike forward until gravity took over and forced it over the brow of the hill. The old machine gathered speed quickly and Adam freewheeled into the cool, green tunnel.

"Geronimooooo…"

It was exactly what their dad would have said, Rachel thought.

She grabbed tight on to the handlebars, and followed her brother down the hill into the cool darkness.

3

They cycled slowly past a sign asking drivers to take care, past another that *told* them to, and a third welcoming them warmly to Triskellion, and announcing that the village was twinned with somewhere unpronounceable in Germany.

"We should come back later with a camera," Adam shouted. "Get someone to take a picture of us under the part that says 'twinned'."

They came into the village alongside the green, a lush expanse of closely cut grass that must have been five hundred metres across. Geraniums and pansies crowded the beds at intervals on every side, and hanging baskets overflowing with flowers hung outside each shop on the narrow High Street, and from every one of the old-fashioned lampposts.

"Someone's got green fingers," Rachel said.

They pedalled sedately past a butcher's shop, an ironmonger's and a small general store. They stared into the window of the post office as they went by, and the green-grocer's, before slowing to a virtual stop when they arrived at a dead end at the bottom of the High Street.

They freewheeled in circles for a few seconds, looking at each other, both thinking the same thing; thinking that it was so incredibly weird, and both equally afraid to say it.

It was only ten minutes, but still in the time since they'd first ridden into the village, they hadn't seen anyone. Not one single soul.

Triskellion was deserted.

"Maybe it's lunchtime," Adam suggested.

"Or teatime. Or something."

"Don't they have half-day closing? Maybe that's it."

"You're right." Rachel nodded in an effort to convince her-self as much as Adam. "That's probably it."

The day seemed to be growing hotter by the minute and by the time they leant the bikes up against a bench on the edge of the village green and dumped their backpacks, the sweat was pouring from both of them.

"I need a drink," Adam said. He pointed towards the butcher's shop and began to walk towards it. "Maybe I can get a Coke in there."

"Duh! They sell meat," Rachel said.

Adam shrugged. "You drink Coke with a burger, right?"

As they neared the shop window, Adam pointed back to where they'd left the bikes. "Hey, we don't have locks for those," he said.

Rachel laughed. "Relax, we're not in New York City any more."

The shop was shut, the interior dark, so they could do nothing but stare at the shocking array of dead things displayed in the butcher's window. There wasn't a single piece of raw meat; nothing had been processed or prepared. Instead the animals were strung up, or laid out as if each had been freshly killed. Pigs' carcasses hung in rows from large hooks, while rabbits had been lined up underneath, as though they were chasing each other across the bright green butcher's grass. Each strand of fur looked bright enough. Only the eyes were flat and dead.

"You're right," Adam said.

Rachel looked at him. "About what?"

"We're a long way from home."

"It's so gross. Oh…"

They stepped back together as a tall figure loomed out of the darkness and moved quickly across a halflit doorway at the rear of the shop. The face was indistinct, but Rachel and Adam had both seen the knife in the man's hand, and the bloodstains, dark, wet against the white of his apron.

Rachel took a deep breath and put a hand on her brother's arm. "Well, at least we're not alone."

"Why don't I think that's such great news?" Adam said.

They moved away from the shop in unison and fell into step. Rachel laughed, leaning playfully into Adam as they walked. "He's a butcher, right? That's what butchers look like."

Adam managed a weak smile. "Only in movies when they have chainsaws and keep heads in the fridge," he said.

A cloud had begun to slide rapidly across the sun and the line of shadow moved behind them as they went, chasing them along the pavement and catching up with them as they reached the post office a hundred metres further up the street. Inside, it was dimly lit, but at least there was a sign on the door reading *OPEN*.

"We can probably get some candy in here," Rachel said.

Adam almost barged his sister out of the way. "I'll take everything they've got," he said. Laughing, they lunged for the door together, only to see a pale hand emerge from the gloom inside and flip the sign over.

CLOSED.

They turned round and leant back against the door. "Well, there're definitely people here," Adam said. "But I'm not sure they're very friendly."

Before Rachel could say anything, they heard footsteps along the pavement. They stepped out of the doorway to look, but saw nothing but the flap of a brown jacket, as whoever had been coming towards them veered suddenly down a narrow alleyway. Hearing a low growl they turned the other way and watched as a sleeping dog, that neither had noticed before, roused itself from the gutter and loped quickly away.

"I know it's been a while since we showered," Rachel said, "but this is ridiculous…"

It had been a few years since the two of them had walked

anywhere hand in hand, but Adam was happy to feel his sister's hand slide into his own as they continued to look round the village. They were wary, now. Each of them was ready to protect the other if it came to it, or to grab hold of them and run like hell, if that seemed the cleverer thing to do. They were geared up for whatever else the village had in store for them.

They were prepared for shocks, and though neither of them said anything, each had the feeling that unseen eyes were watching.

As they walked, they continued to catch glimpses of people, to see shadows moving behind closed doors and to hear vague snippets of conversation, as though a giant radio were being tuned in near by. Halfway across the village green they stopped, both convinced that they'd heard the voices of children singing, but the music seemed to have drifted away on the breeze as soon as they'd begun to listen for it.

They stopped at the centre of the green. Worn out suddenly, Rachel sat down heavily, then lay back on the grass. Adam took off his cap and, as he fanned his face with it, he turned slowly round on the spot, taking in the entire village as he did so.

"That's it," he said. "I am officially freaked out."

Rachel stared up at the sky. "Thanks for the update."

"What about you?" Adam dropped down next to her.

"What about me?"

"You happy about all this? You feeling nice and *chilled out*?"

"Right now, I just want to go to the bathroom," Rachel said. "I want to get something to eat and I want to go to sleep. I want—"

"I want to get back on that stupid little train." Adam was suddenly raising his voice, sounding like he had when he was younger and he couldn't get what he wanted. "I want to get the hell out of here."

"We can't," Rachel said softly.

"Why not?"

She turned over on to her stomach and put her face down. A few metres away, she could see a discarded ice lolly lying on the floor, bright red against the green. It was melting fast as she watched, the scarlet colouring running into the grass, while a bee hovered a centimetre or so above it, dropping down every few seconds to dip its feet into the sugary juice.

Rachel raised her head and shielded her eyes against the sun as she looked round. There was nobody to be seen, anywhere. Who could have dropped the ice cream?

Behind her, her brother spoke, sounding every bit as wiped out as she felt. "It sucks," he said. He sounded defeated. "This. All of it…"

"It's just different." Rachel sat up and tried to catch her brother's eye. "It's not what we're used to. It's bound to feel strange."

"Big time."

"Yeah … like it was so great at home."

"I know, but at least it was home."

Rachel thought about that, and though it was nothing more than a simple statement of fact, it hit her hard. She felt as though something were squeezing her insides. "I hope Mom's OK," she said.

Then for a while there was only the gentle buzzing of the bee and a distant hum from an aircraft passing high above them. Rachel and Adam sat a few metres away from each other, picking at blades of grass and each of them thinking about the life that, for the moment at least, they'd had to leave a long way behind.

The parents they loved, but who no longer loved each other.

"Race you," Adam said, suddenly.

"What?"

Adam could sense that Rachel's mood was darkening, that she was sinking into sadness. It hadn't been easy, but over many years he'd learned the best ways to snap her out of it at moments like this. He pointed across to the far side of the green. "I'll race you to that statue, or whatever it is, over there."

Rachel raised herself up, flapped at an insect in front of her face. "Too hot," she said.

"Too chicken, more like."

"Whatever…"

"That's a shame, 'cos I was going to give you a head start. I don't know, maybe twenty-five yards, something like that, but, you know, if you really don't want to—"

And suddenly Rachel was on her feet and past him.

They were fit, athletic kids, and they tore hard across the green, each as keen on beating the other as they had been since the day they'd first learned to walk, and tussle, and race each other to the refrigerator.

Adam had just about caught Rachel up by the time they'd reached the far side of the green. They argued for a minute or two about who'd won, and tried to catch their breath, before looking up together at the stone monument with the wreaths of faded poppies at its base.

The grey column rose several metres to a cross, with a symbol carved into the stone at its centre. Rachel looked, then turned to her brother.

"I know," he said. "It's the same thing we saw at the station. Your guess is as good as mine."

Rachel stepped forward and read the inscription at the monument's base.

To remember the men of Triskellion, who fought in two world wars.

"It's a war memorial," Rachel said.

"So where are the names?"

Rachel looked at Adam, then back at the obelisk. There were no names at all carved beneath the inscription. "I guess they're round the other side." She walked round the column and stared up, her expression as blank as the granite itself.

"Maybe nobody died from here," Rachel said. "Maybe this place is a lucky village."

Adam scoffed. "It's a *freaky* village," he said. "Seriously freaky."

Rachel leant back against one of the wooden benches alongside the memorial. "I'm not so sure," she said. She could hear a buzzing as she spoke, but couldn't decide it if was from somewhere close by or inside her head. "I think it just seems that way, you know? Because we've never been anywhere like this place before. It just feels strange to us."

"You've got that right."

"Plus, we haven't slept properly in God knows how long. Jet lag can make you feel really weird, you know? It can make things seem kind of … blurred, and jumpy. Like a dream."

"Like a nightmare you mean."

Wherever it was coming from, the buzzing grew louder suddenly, and they both flinched as a flock of crows rose up suddenly from the trees to the left of them. When they turned, they saw two young men stepping out from behind the war memorial, and coming quickly towards them.

Rachel looked at Adam. His face made it clear that he sensed the danger every bit as much as she did.

The boys were maybe fifteen or sixteen and both were heavily built, with short, spiky haircuts. One wore stonewashed jeans and a grubby T-shirt, while his mate was bare-chested with tattoos of some sort on both upper arms.

"Freaky, are we?" said the one with tattoos.

"That's not what we meant," Rachel stammered, but it was clear that the two boys were in no mood to discuss anything.

When Adam tried to speak, all he saw was a fist, like a great lump of meat with gold rings, and then everything went black.

4

"**K**eep your head back," Rachel said. "It's almost stopped."

The wad of tissue, which she'd dug out ten minutes before from her pocket, was soaked in Adam's blood and both of their tears. His nose had bled so much that Rachel was starting to wonder how there could be any of the stuff left in her brother's body at all.

She pressed the tissue against his nose. He moaned, but he wasn't in too much pain, so she was fairly sure there was nothing broken. Adam eased her hand back from his face and gingerly removed the tissue. His eyes darted around. "Are you sure they've gone?" he asked, sniffing cautiously.

The two thugs hadn't run off right away. Once Adam had fallen to the ground, they'd stood around jeering and pointing. Every time Rachel had pleaded with them to leave her and her brother alone, they'd laughed, mocking her by repeating what she'd said in a stupid, fake-American accent.

Once Rachel had stopped trying to reason with them, they'd quickly got bored and wandered off.

"I can't see them anywhere," Rachel assured her brother. "It's going to be all right now."

Adam nodded, but he didn't look convinced. For a few minutes the two of them stood in shocked silence, letting what had happened sink in. It was certainly not how either of them had imagined their arrival in England.

"Come on," Rachel said eventually. "Let's get out of here."

They trudged away from the war memorial, and back across the green towards the High Street.

"I want to call Mom," Adam said.

Rachel nodded. "OK." She'd been thinking the same thing. They quickened their steps a little, both eager to get back as swiftly as they could to the backpacks, which contained their phones. "That's if we've got a signal."

"It'll be morning at home now, right?" Adam said.

"Right. We're five hours ahead," Rachel said.

Adam managed a weak smile. His nose, which had already reddened dramatically, was now beginning to swell. "*Ahead?* I think this place is at least a couple of centuries behind, don't you?"

Gratefully, Rachel seized the chance to laugh and they walked even faster, their sombre mood beginning to lift.

"We'd be having breakfast if we were at home," Adam said.

"Uh-huh…"

"Waffles and syrup." Adam said it slowly, groaning with

pleasure at the thought of the food. "Oh, God, blueberry muffins."

"Pancakes and sausage," Rachel said.

"Scrambled eggs."

"French toast and crispy bacon…"

"Look," Adam said, pointing. "Siesta must be over."

Rachel looked, seeing what her brother meant as they walked on down the High Street into a different village.

At least, it *appeared* to be a different village from the deserted one they had left just twenty minutes before. People carrying shopping bustled back and forth in front of them and a rusty delivery van pulled up outside the greengrocer's opposite, which now displayed a stall overflowing with abundant fresh fruit and vegetables. A cheery, suntanned man, carrying an enormous cauliflower, crossed the road walking towards the twins. He saw Rachel standing on the kerb with her mouth open and winked at her.

"Lovely day, miss…"

Rachel closed her mouth and smiled back feebly, and they watched the man stride vigorously away down the busy street, whistling and nodding at his fellow villagers.

Adam was every bit as shellshocked as Rachel. "Let's get to Gran's place." He stepped out into the road, looking left after the whistling man, only vaguely aware of a bell ringing near by.

"Adam!" Rachel shrieked. She all but pulled her brother off his feet, as a vicar in a fluorescent tabard and cycling helmet sailed past on a black bicycle, missing Adam by a whisper. The bell jangled again. The vicar looked back and, seeing that nobody had been hurt, cycled on, waving a vague blessing in the twins' direction.

"Remember, they drive on the other side," Rachel said. "Let's stick to the path."

They collected their bikes and rucksacks and walked away from the shops to where the village thinned out a little, and the houses started either side of the main road. Set back behind a mesh fence and beyond a small playground marked with yellow, red and blue tramlines, sat a squat, stone school-house.

They walked on round the other side of the green, where children, clearly enjoying every moment of their summer holidays, kicked footballs and chased one another noisily. On the far side of the green was a cricket pitch, and opposite, just before the line of buildings gave way to one of trees and thick hedges, stood the village pub.

"The Star" looked to be one of the oldest buildings in the village, with timber beams visible on the outside, white-washed walls and a thatched roof. A trickle of smoke rose from a chimney that leaned so far to one side it almost defied gravity, and a painted sign of a shooting star hung from an ornate iron bracket above the door. The building, shadowed by a massive oak tree hundreds of years old, appeared so at one with its surroundings that it could have grown out of the soil itself.

Rachel and Adam had never seen a building so ancient. They had once stayed in an old whaler's cottage in Cape Cod that was over a hundred years old, but this place was prehistoric. A blackboard outside advertised the food on offer that day and also claimed that "Children Are Welcome".

"Yeah, right," Adam snorted, wondering what on earth a "Lancashire hotpot" was and whether or not you could eat it.

Rachel suddenly looked at him. "Can you feel it?"

Adam paused, cocking his head to one side. Yes he could. Once again, Rachel and Adam had the overpowering feeling that they were being watched.

They wasted no time heading back towards Root Cottage, pausing only to let a large vintage car pass them in the narrow lane. The car was the colour of red wine and highly polished, and it honked its thanks with a deep, rasping horn. The reflection of the trees on the windscreen made it impossible to make out the driver clearly but, as the car rolled past, Rachel and Adam could see a grey dog the size of a small horse sitting upright in the passenger seat.

The air was still heavy and humid, but the heat had gone out of the day, and as they walked up the garden path, their grandmother's cottage was bathed in a golden light and the long shadows of hollyhocks, growing either side of the path, stretched out in front of them, as if pointing Rachel and Adam towards the door.

Rachel stepped up confidently to rap the knocker, its brass gleaming as if it had just been cleaned.

"It's that same shape," Adam said.

"What shape?"

"Like that thing on the station windows and on the war memorial. What d'you think it is?"

"Your guess is as good as mine," Rachel said, about to knock.

Before the knocker touched wood, the door swung open, revealing Celia Root behind it in an electric wheelchair.

The old lady flung her arms out wide. "My *poor* darlings … I've been so *worried*…"

Rachel and Adam fell into the hallway and into their grandmother's open arms, all three promptly bursting into tears.

5

The kettle whistled on the Aga and Granny Root's wheelchair hummed across the tiled kitchen floor as she moved to take it off. For the hour or more since their arrival, Rachel and Adam had been recounting the strange events of their journey to their horrified grandmother.

For a woman in her late seventies, Celia Root was remarkably well preserved, and though the wheelchair gave the impression of frailty, it was only that. Though heavy, her make-up was immaculately applied and her silvery-blonde hair looked as though it was set on a daily basis.

"You poor things," she said. "What must you think of us?"

"Shouldn't we call the cops or something?" Adam said.

The old woman smiled indulgently. "There hasn't been a station here for years, darling. We have a local constable who pops in every few weeks, but he has two other villages to deal with. There's really not much goes on around here."

"We were probably just unlucky," Rachel said.

"That's right," Granny Root said. "I'll have a word with the commodore up at Waverley Hall. He's the local magistrate, tends to sort these things out…"

Rachel and Adam looked at each other. What on earth was a commodore?

"Anyway, you've got the worst behind you now." She smiled and squeezed Rachel's hand. "Now you can relax, and start to enjoy yourselves."

Sitting at the long kitchen table, Adam tapped out a number for the umpteenth time on his mobile phone and, after a long pause, thumped it down again.

"Nothing. Is there anywhere around here you can get a signal, Gran?"

"I don't really understand these mobiles, dear. You could try the telephone again."

Rachel's earlier attempt at calling home on the land-line had met with nothing but static and a series of electronic bleeps. The third time she'd dialled, a recorded voice had told her something she didn't understand in French, and New York had never felt further away.

"The weather's been a bit unpredictable, dear," her grandmother said, "and it sometimes affects the line. We had a power cut just last week, on Tuesday … or was it Wednesday?"

Rachel smiled affectionately, while Adam wondered what kind of Third World backwater they'd ended up in, where phones didn't work and power failed in the rain.

Granny Root put a large plate of warm scones on the table

in front of Adam. "Help yourself, darling."

Adam grabbed two scones and put them on his plate, slathering them with butter and jam, and shoving the first one into his mouth almost whole. His grandmother's eyes widened slightly, then softened into a smile.

"You poor darling, you're half starved."

While Rachel buttered her own scone with considerably less urgency than her brother, Granny Root brought a teapot to the table and looked at Adam. "Milk and sugar?"

Adam, mouth half open and full of scone, looked at his grandmother and mumbled.

"Not with your mouth full, dear. What has your mother been teaching you?"

Adam wiped the remaining jam and crumbs from the corner of his mouth with a knuckle. "Oh ... sorry, Gran. Can I get a soda?"

Celia Root appeared not to understand, or not to hear. "Sweet with plenty of milk after the shock you've had." She opened a drawer in the long table and took out a knitted cosy, which she fitted snugly over the teapot.

Rachel giggled. "Gran, why are you putting a hat on the teapot?"

Celia looked at Rachel blankly, then back at the teapot and laughed out loud as if she had momentarily grasped the absurdity of the tea cosy from Rachel's point of view. Seeing her eyes glittering, Rachel caught a glimpse of the handsome woman her grandmother must have been forty years before; the one Rachel had seen in those black and white photographs.

The old woman put her hand on the back of Rachel's, and looked her in the eye. "You are so like your mother," she said.

Rachel blushed, enjoying the compliment, basking in the warmth of her grandmother's approval.

Granny Root turned and smiled at her grandson. "Whereas Adam, I think, takes more after his father."

Adam, who was feeling nervous and vulnerable, as though he were making a bad impression, did not take this comparison very well. "Right," he snapped back, "except I haven't walked out on my family, have I?"

Rachel dived in. "C'mon Adam, that wasn't what Gran meant. It wasn't all Dad's fault, anyway. Let it go."

"I may have some orange juice in the pantry," Granny Root said loudly, desperately trying to change the subject.

"So Mom *made* him get a girlfriend?" asked Adam, his voice thick with sarcasm.

"Adam, you're being a pain."

"And who do I get *that* from, Rachel?"

Celia Root backed her wheelchair away from the table, moved over to the other side of the room and busied herself with an old radio on the windowsill. Outside, the golden light had turned to bronze and the sky had gone a dull blue-grey. The air was still heavy though, and Rachel felt short of breath. She held her hands up in surrender, trying to placate her brother. "Adam, Dad wasn't happy."

"Great. So now, none of us is." Adam stared intently at the pattern of flowers bordering his plate and rolled the remaining crumbs of scone around with his forefinger.

Granny Root could stand no more. "Children, please. You're very tired." She raised a hand to silence them and, with the other, turned up the volume of the radio. "Please … the wireless. I never miss this…"

A rich voice like that of a Shakespearean actor began to intone words that sounded like gobbledegook to Rachel and Adam.

"…issued by the Met Office on behalf of the Maritime and Coastguard Agency at one seven three oh on Friday, thirteenth of August. There are warnings of gales in Viking, North Utsire, South Utsire, Forties, Cromarty, Forth, Tyne, Dogger…"

Rachel and Adam looked at their grandmother, confused.

"It's the shipping forecast," she said. "Sounds like there's a storm coming."

6

In the village, the landlord hurriedly took down the umbrellas from the deserted benches outside The Star. The raindrops grew heavier, sticking the shirt to his back and bouncing off the long, waxed bonnet of the burgundy-coloured Bentley parked outside. The landlord made for the entrance, stepping daintily to avoid slipping on the wet cobbles in front of the pub, and slammed the heavy wooden door behind him.

Another thunderclap. Then the sky opened and the rain came down in torrents, lashing against the windows of The Star and washing away the dust of a long, hot afternoon.

From his vantage point high in the old oak, the boy watched the landlord go inside. Then nimbly, unhindered by the damp branches and dense foliage, he climbed his way down, limb by limb, to the foot of the tree.

He stopped for a moment in the shelter of the tree to watch the sign of the shooting star swinging wildly in the storm. Then he turned and padded across the wet green towards the inn.

*   *   *

"Same again, commodore?"

Commodore Gerald Wing pushed a large cutglass tumbler across the bar and stacked three pound coins neatly next to it. Without waiting for an answer, Tom Hatcham, the landlord, took the glass, and put it up to the optic of the whisky bottle behind the bar. A rumble of thunder overhead rattled the ancient windows.

"Nice for the ducks." Hatcham pushed the large whisky back across the bar and scooped up the coins. The enormous grey dog that lay at Commodore Wing's feet let out a heavy sigh, as if to acknowledge Hatcham's banal comment.

At a table, four villagers played dominos in silence. In the corner, Gary and Lee Bacon sipped illegal pints of lager and lime and poured coins into The Star's slot machine. The landlord and the commodore were happy enough to turn a blind eye. It was generally thought better to have youths like the Bacons where they could be watched, rather than have them running free, causing all sorts of trouble.

As if triggered by another clap of thunder that sounded outside, the heavy door of The Star flew suddenly open and a huge gust of wind sent beer mats and bits of paper flying. All eyes turned to see a slight, feral-looking boy framed in the doorway. He wore a dark hooded sweatshirt and tracksuit bottoms. As he pulled back his hood, water dripped from his long black hair, running into wide green eyes that flashed, vivid against an olive complexion. He stood, soaked to the skin, and he stared into the bar with an unblinking intensity.

Tom Hatcham threw a glance at Commodore Wing. The commodore nodded back. Hatcham stepped from behind the bar and strode to the door, squaring up to the boy, who did not move a muscle.

"Go. Away." Hatcham put his face close to the boy's, blinking away the splashes of rain that flew into his eyes through the open door. The boy did not flinch, nor give any sign he had heard Hatcham's words. Seeing that he was having no effect, the landlord took the handle of the heavy door and shut it in the visitor's face.

"Nicely done, Tom," one of the domino players said, breaking the silence.

Another nodded. "Enough undesirables for one day."

At the fruit machine Gary Bacon sniggered into his lager.

Hatcham watched for a moment as the boy's distorted dark shape – still visible through the frosted glass in the pub door – drifted slowly away, and then, in the blink of an eye, seemed to disappear.

As if obeying the commanding tone of Celia Root, the sky was growing darker by the second and, from their bedroom, the twins listened to the thunder getting louder, closer, shaking the walls of the cottage round them.

Rachel got up and walked across to the window. Sheet lightning fluttered in the distance against the sky and, below her in the garden, the foxgloves danced as they caught the heavy drops of rain on their petals. Once again, Rachel heard the low hum of bees buzzing. She watched as the flowers appeared to come to life and smiled as, one by one, an army of insects emerged from the trumpets of the foxgloves, their back legs heavy with pollen, and flew, snaking off against the dark sky to their hive.

"It's not even eight o'clock, and it's black as night out there," Rachel said. "Adam…"

She got no more than a groan from her brother, who was flat out on one of the twin beds, half asleep already.

Thunder erupted above her head and she winced at the sound of it, smelling the electricity all around and feeling the hairs stand up along her arms. A few seconds later, lightning broke across the moorland beyond the garden, and in its bright snapshot she saw a familiar circular shape, and something moving around in it.

She moved close to the window, pressed her face to the glass, and waited.

It was as though the next flash lasted five or ten seconds, as this time she saw the shape clearly. It was the same shape she and Adam had seen everywhere that day: a symbol of three intersecting crescents forming a continuous, pointed clover leaf, bounded by a large circle. But this time it was huge and cut out from the chalk on the land itself; white against the scrubby grey of the moor.

The air was filled with the hiss of static, and the rain

drumming on the thatch, and the low drone of bees rumbling on beneath them.

Another flash, and another, like bulbs exploding.

Rachel called to her brother again but did not look away from the window.

It was as though she was looking down on the chalk carving through a tunnel of light. The circle must have been a half a mile away, perhaps more, but she could clearly make out the figure that marched around inside. She narrowed her eyes, desperate to see more, and stared, unblinking, until she was sure about exactly what she was seeing.

There was a boy inside the chalk circle.

From the size of the moving figure, Rachel was able to estimate that the circle was maybe sixty feet across. She watched the boy trudge round and round, head down through the rain, tracing out the intersecting lines, pacing faster and faster, almost automatically.

As though he were moving in spite of himself.

"Adam, you need to come and see this."

There was no reply from the bed and Rachel continued to watch, almost as if she knew what was coming next, as the boy turned, walked deliberately to the centre of the circle and looked up.

She knew that he was looking at her. That somehow he could see her in her tiny window. She could hear the thump of her own heart taking its place in the complex rhythm of the rain and the bees, and she watched through the blackness as the boy raised an arm and pointed up at her.

Suddenly, the window cracked, loud as a gunshot, and a jagged line crept down the glass from top to bottom.

Rachel stepped back. Wanting to scream, wanting to run. Unable to tear her eyes away from the boy.

Staring out at him through the thickening curtain of rain.

Breathless…

7

Through the mist, the outlines of two figures appear like ghosts. One shape is male, one female. They walk towards each other, their paths crossing, then diverging, walking away as if pacing out a slow, elaborate folk dance. Then, as one, they turn again and stand face to face. They move automatically and, as the mist disperses and the figures become solid beings, it becomes clear that they are tracing out a pattern, cut out of the soil at their feet.

The woman is wearing a flowing, embroidered gown. Her hair is long and braided, concealing her face as she swings her head from side to side, as if in a trance. The man wears something highly polished, armour perhaps, that catches the pale yellow sunlight and glows through the mist. His face is hidden by the nose section of the pointed helmet he wears, and, embossed on the breastplate of his armour is the same, three-bladed symbol that they pace out below their feet.

The man moves towards the woman, slowly, deliberately.

Their hands reach out for each other and they touch...

* * *

Rachel blinked away the vision and found herself sitting on the edge of the bed, a yellow shaft of sunlight streaming between the curtains and on to the misaligned, pink roses of the wallpaper opposite.

Her brother was still fast asleep, a twist of dark hair only just visible on the pillow, sticking out from under thick blankets. Rachel stood up and went to the window, where a stray bee from the garden below walked lazily up and down the length of the window frame, looking for an exit that didn't exist. Rachel lifted up the latch and pushed open the window. The bee let out an angry-sounding buzz, before finding the cool air and tumbling out into the wet garden below.

Rachel knelt down, stuck her head out of the window and breathed in the clear, morning air. Beyond, she could see the chalk circle, exactly as the night before, but now brighter and more defined, the grass surrounding it greener in the rising sun. Rachel considered her dream. Where it had come from was clear enough. But what did it mean?

Who were the two strange figures? A knight and a maiden…?

Rachel's thoughts were interrupted by her grandmother's shrill voice from the bottom of the stairs.

"Rachel! Adam…"

Rachel pulled herself back into the room, catching the back of her head on the window frame. She yelped in pain, waking her brother.

Adam groaned and pulled the blankets over his head.

Rachel rubbed her head and called back weakly, "Coming, Gran…"

Adam had been particularly reluctant to get out of bed, still claiming jet lag and a sore nose from the day before. It was understandable, but, despite her own tiredness and a slight bump on the back of her head, Rachel felt strangely energized. Excited, even.

Granny Root seemed a little more at ease, too. It was a lovely morning and the old lady heartily encouraged them to eat a mountain of toast and several bowls of lumpy porridge. Maybe the whole storm thing had affected everyone's mood the day before, Rachel thought. Atmospheric pressure, or something.

Half an hour later, Rachel and Adam stood at the end of the garden behind the house, looking across the moor at the chalk circle.

"I can't believe it's that old."

Adam's interest in the place had suddenly perked up over breakfast, when their grandmother explained to them about the chalk circle. The three-bladed shape within the outer circle gave the village its name: Triskellion. There were many theories as to its significance, but most agreed that it was a Celtic symbol, formed by three, intersecting circles, and was anything up to three thousand years old.

"Nothing's three thousand years old." Adam shook his

head in disbelief as he and Rachel waded across the dewy grass, looking at the carved shape in the distance. A high breeze sent the shadows of clouds racing across the moor and over the Triskellion itself, making the landscape appear to move; fluid somehow, more alive.

The circle, when they finally got there, was far less impressive than it had been from a distance. For five minutes Adam traced out the chalky grooves while Rachel looked in vain for the footprints of the boy she had seen the night before.

"I mean, it's so, like ... big," Adam said.

Rachel looked back towards the village. "Maybe so you can see it from a long way away."

"That's just it though," Adam said. "How did they know what they were cutting out without seeing it from above?"

Rachel looked down on the curve of chalk at her feet, and conceded that her brother, with his customary, pedantic logic, had a very good point.

The vast open space of the moor was a novelty for Rachel and Adam, accustomed as they were to the skyscraper-hemmed streets of their native city. In the same way that looking up at tall buildings can make some people dizzy, the wide space and expanse of sky suddenly began to make Rachel feel unsteady on her feet. Unsteady, until Adam shoved her playfully, and ran. Rachel recovered herself and laughed, chasing her brother over the spongy moss of the moor, which gave extra spring to her footsteps.

They ran and ran and then stopped, out of breath; as they panted, they saw the village far behind them. After their experiences the day before, they were happy enough to head away from the village, and continued on towards the regimented line of pine trees that bounded the eastern border of the moor.

A green sign at the edge of the forest declared that this was Waverley Woods, part of the Waverley Hall estate, though there was nothing to suggest that it was either private or out of bounds. Rachel and Adam peered into the forest, which was dense with the fingers of tall pines. To one side lay a huge stack of logs where the fast-growing trees had been cut for timber. A straight, narrow track had been beaten between the rows of trees and Rachel and Adam stepped into the wood, drawn in by the resinous scent of the pine needles that covered the forest floor, and a welcoming chorus of birdsong.

"I love that smell." Rachel breathed deeply, scrunching a handful of the green needles in her fist. The air was instantly cooler in the shade of the forest. Sunshine swam through the branches, but under the trees it was as dark as twilight. Adam marched ahead down the track, swishing at the pine needles on the ground with a long stick.

They came to a large, circular clearing, where more trees had been recently felled and the woods seemed suddenly to stop. On the other side of the clearing the foliage was more established: older and slower-growing. Lush, green ferns sprouted at the foot of gnarled, thick trees, with leafy branches that reached out to the clear blue sky above.

"That's more like it," Adam shouted back at his sister, leaping across the clearing. "Something I can climb."

"Be careful," Rachel called after him, realizing as she did so that her words would have no effect. Adam disappeared into the old part of the wood and Rachel followed.

Here, the wood was even darker than it had been beneath the pines, and cooler. It was almost chilly. Rachel walked between the irregular trees for a few minutes, following a rough path between the ferns, straining to look upward for signs of her brother. She guessed that he was hiding from her, as usual.

Suddenly, the birdsong stopped as though at some prearranged signal, and the wood fell very quiet.

Rachel felt alone.

"Adam…?" She cupped a hand to her mouth. Nothing. "Aad-aam?"

Rachel tentatively moved on a few steps. She could smell smoke. The caw of a bird high above her made the hairs on her neck prickle. "Adam, this is stupid." Rachel heard the crack of a branch and a small, thick stick landed a few centimetres behind her, narrowly missing her head as it whistled past.

Rachel looked up and saw her brother high above her, perched on a branch, pressing his finger urgently to his lips. He steadied himself and gesticulated at her with his other hand to come up and join him. Rachel looked up at the tree, then round its base for a foothold. She wasn't much of a climber; that was Adam's department. Rachel was about to admit defeat, when a rope, knotted at regular intervals, was lowered down in front of her eyes by her brother. Rachel grasped it firmly and began to climb.

Several metres up, Adam's firm hand grabbed Rachel's arm and pulled her up to the thick branch on which he was balancing. Still urging Rachel not to speak, Adam spoke in a hoarse whisper, "Check this out…" He pointed to where the rope joined the trunk at the junction of the next branch. Another knot of ropes was lashed to the trunk and snaked away between the leaves, as did two further ropes, like the rigging of a sailing ship. The lower formed a kind of tightrope and the two higher ones were handrails. Pushing aside some branches and flat, green leaves, Rachel could see that Adam had discovered an aerial rope bridge between the trees. A complex network of ropes ran from tree to tree, with their final destination concealed, as they disappeared into thick, green foliage.

"But why do we have to—" Rachel's question was cut short by the flat of her brother's hand over her mouth.

"There's something going on over there," Adam hissed, nodding in the direction of the rope bridge. "Come on."

The ropes swayed and bounced as they took up Rachel and Adam's weight, but once they had their balance and had set up a rhythmic step, the bridge felt more rigid. Adam pushed on through dense leaves, which swished back into Rachel's face. Unable to spare an arm to protect herself, Rachel looked down at the ground far below and suddenly felt sick, as if she would fall. She shut her eyes tight, moving on in tiny steps until the whipping of the leaves stopped. She felt Adam's hand steady her, and, opening her eyes, found herself in an open area within the trees, suspended above the ground and beneath the tree canopy.

Rachel gasped, allowing herself to look quickly round. It was like a wooded cathedral; a vast open space created by the highest trees, which formed a roof over the top. Smoke hung in the still air. Below the green canopy, smaller trees, some skeletal and dead-looking, formed an internal structure, joined together by rope bridges such as the one they stood on, with galleries, walkways, ladders and crow's nests made from scrappy planks and branches.

Adam hauled Rachel up on to the wooden platform he had reached at the end of the rope, and Rachel was glad to have her feet on something more solid, even such rickety planks. Rachel followed Adam up a couple of wooden steps nailed to the tree trunk into a tiny tree house. There was barely room inside for both of them. It can only be a lookout, she thought. For hunting, or maybe as a hide for birdwatching.

Adam pointed to a small slit in the side of the hut.

Rachel pressed her face to the peephole and realized, with sudden, sickening certainty that they shouldn't be here.

8

From her vantage point, Rachel could make out a kind of encampment below. Several logs formed rough benches round a fire. On the other side of the fire was a camper van that didn't look as if it had moved for several years. It was painted green, covered in leaves and jungle netting, and where there had once been a VW badge there was now a spray-painted symbol.

A Triskellion.

In the centre of the encampment, at what seemed to be the focal point of the whole clearing, a tree had been turned upside down; its thick trunk sunk into the earth, the roots exposed to the open air like a pair of vast, cupped hands. Rachel thought how weird it looked, wrenched from the ground, uprooted, exposing the parts that shouldn't be seen. Stranger still, round the edge of the encampment stood figures so well camouflaged that they might almost have been mistaken for foliage.

When they began to move, Rachel saw that there were

fifteen or twenty people below her, dressed in rags, furs and leaves, their faces blackened with earth. One or two of them had branches or antlers attached to their heads, like mythical forest creatures. Adam pushed his face close to hers to get a look at the scene and Rachel could tell from his rapid breathing that he was every bit as petrified as she was.

On the ground, the headlights of the camper van blazed into life, spotlighting the upturned tree, as the door on the side of the van slid open. A tall man, wearing a worn, floor-length leather coat and knee boots stepped out and stood facing the upturned tree. His face was blackened, like the others, but his eyes stood out: a piercing blue. He stepped forward and leant against the tree with one hand as if deriving strength from it, muttering under his breath.

After a moment, he turned to face the camouflaged men that were gathered round the fire, and studied them, unsmiling. His long hair and beard looked wet, as if he had recently showered. He nodded at one of the forest people who, with two others, opened the back of a battered, white truck that was concealed in the bushes.

From the back of the truck the men wrestled two figures. Their heads were covered in sackcloth bags, but Rachel recognized one of them from his washed-out denims and T-shirt.

"It's those guys who beat you up yesterday," she whispered.

Adam hissed. "I know…"

The youths writhed and struggled, but the bear-like forest

men were too strong for them and dragged them to the upturned tree, tying them by their wrists to the outstretched roots, so that their chests were pressed against the rough bark. They bucked and craned their necks backwards, straining and twisting, trying to shake off the hoods and see their captors. After a few moments their grunts and protests faded to whimpers and finally stopped and the area inside the woods fell silent.

The man in the leather coat approached the limp, panting figures, and began to speak; his resonant voice audible even from Rachel and Adam's hiding place.

"Gary and Lee Bacon. You have broken the Code of the Green Men, and it is they who make the law in Triskellion." The man paced up and down, coming closer to the hooded head of one of the youths. "The Green Men decide who stays and who goes," he spat. "Not snotty-nosed chavs who attack anything they don't understand. You will live and die by the Code of the Green Men. Have you anything to say before sentence is carried out?"

One of the Bacon boys whimpered from beneath his hood. The sound of his undiluted terror turned Rachel's stomach to water. The man spoke again.

"Which of you punched the incomer?"

"Gary done it," came the muffled yelp from inside the hood.

"Loyal, too," said the man with the beard, trudging back to the camper van. "Do them both." He nodded to another of the forest men – a huge figure, his face black with charcoal, and what looked like a fox pelt mounted with a deer's skull strapped to his head.

The man walked towards the prisoners. The other figures tensed and drew closer, while, anticipating what was about to happen, the Bacon boys whimpered and moaned beneath their hoods.

Up in the tree, Rachel felt her lip tremble, and hid her eyes as Adam's fingers dug into her arms, unable to tear his gaze away from the terrible ritual unfolding below.

The man stepped up close to one of the captives. He grasped the neck of the boy's T-shirt and tore until the pale flesh of his back was exposed. He walked round the stump and ripped at the shirt of the second boy. When he had finished, the man stood back, allowing two of his fellow Green Men to step forward. Each clutched a long, flexible stick, and, on the nod of the man in the leather coat, they began to beat the Bacon boys.

Rachel and Adam clung to each other, huddled together in a ball as the screams of Gary and Lee Bacon tore through the silence of the woods. The thrashing seemed to continue for an age, with each cry of agony making Rachel and Adam flinch as if they were being beaten themselves. Finally it stopped and Adam ventured an eye back up to the peephole. Through the slit in the lookout, he could see the bodies of the two boys hanging limply from the roots. The single back he could see clearly was raised with angry, red welts.

Then, another leaf-covered figure moved forward towards the punishment tree. His face was blackened like the others, but on his head he wore a battered, black top hat. Ivy trailed round the brim, and, from the crown, sharpened twigs stuck out like spines. As he turned to face the nearer boy, Adam could see that he wore a long leather apron. He lifted something heavy from his side.

In his hand was a chainsaw. The man pulled on the starting cord...

Adam had seen enough. Using the noise of the chainsaw as cover, he grabbed Rachel and hurtled out of the tree house, dropping down on to the lower branch.

Rachel found that her vertigo had disappeared as she bounced back along the rope bridge. She followed her brother, stumbling in her haste, ignoring the sting of the branches flicking back into her face and catching in her hair. Propelled by adrenaline, they arrived back at the original knotted rope in seconds, throwing themselves back down on to the forest floor and tearing off together towards the line of trees.

Some fifty or sixty metres away, its crackle deadened by the thick woodland, the chainsaw continued to splutter and buzz...

In the clearing, the man with the chainsaw had cut through the ropes that were holding up the prisoners. The Bacons sat on the earth, nursing their wounds while other Green Men began to disperse back into the forest and into the tree houses above. The door of the camper van slid open again, and the bearded man in the leather coat walked over and pulled off the hood from each boy's head.

The Bacon brothers stared up at the man's blackened face, trembling like frightened dogs. The man took a wallet from a pocket inside his long leather coat and peeled off two fifty-pound notes. He tossed them down at the boys grovelling below him.

"Buy yourselves some shirts," he said calmly, without malice. "Now get out of my sight."

The man walked slowly back to the camper van, while the two boys snatched up the money and scurried off into the undergrowth like small, scared animals freed from a gin trap.

9

Rachel and Adam stood, panting, at the edge of the chalk circle.

Instinctively, the circle had seemed the place to head for. It was out in the open, where they could be seen by anyone who cared to look, but where no one would be able to corner or trap them. Still catching their breath, they took a step forward together into the circle itself and both felt perceptibly safer within its circumference.

Rachel turned and looked back across the moor towards the woods. Nobody had followed them. Hopefully nobody had seen them, because surely if they had been witness to some terrible murder, then they themselves would be in great danger.

"D'you think they … you know, with the chainsaw?" Adam appealed to his sister, thinking exactly the same as she was.

Rachel shook her head. "Nah. No way." But she said it as much to reassure herself as Adam.

They turned back towards the centre of the circle and

saw, beetling towards them from the direction of the village, a black-coated figure, waving a stick of some sort in front of him. From a distance it looked as if he were sweeping the moor, keeping it tidy.

"Hello-oo," the man called out in a honking, nasal voice. Before Rachel or Adam could answer, they heard a high squeal through the headphones he was wearing and realized that the stick was in fact a metal detector. He dropped quickly to his knees, producing a small trowel from a pocket and began burrowing in the earth. He looked like a giant mole in his big overcoat, spraying earth out from either side.

Within seconds, the man found what he was looking for and held up something covered in earth between his fingers. Adam drew closer to see what it was. The man brushed away the loose soil and held up a dull metal coin.

"What is it?" Adam asked.

"A halfpenny piece." The man handed the coin to the boy. "George the Third."

"George who?" Adam asked.

"King George the Third…" the man enunciated deliberately.

Adam turned the coin over in his fingers. On one side was a man wearing a laurel wreath. On the other, a picture of a woman carrying a trident and the word "BRITANNIA".

"So how old would this be?" Adam looked up from the coin at the man's craggy face. Rachel could tell from his tone that her brother was seriously interested.

The man rubbed at the coin with a blackened thumb revealing the date. "1807," he said. "Two years after the Battle of Trafalgar."

Adam looked closely again at the coin. If the age of the stone circle had sparked his curiosity, Rachel could see that this had got him completely hooked.

"So is this, like, worth a lot of money?" Adam rubbed the halfpenny between his fingers and the metal began to shine through.

"Not much. Few quid. Ten, maybe. People have been burying coins in this spot since coins was invented."

"Why did they bury them?" Rachel asked, wishing to appear interested herself.

"For good luck. People always knew the Triskellion was good luck, so they'd bury money here by the circle in the hope some of it would come their way."

"So have you found others?" Rachel continued politely.

"Plenty recently. Seems like the earth is spitting quite a few of them back out just now."

"You mean there are more like this? And older?" Adam was sounding keener by the minute. The idea that the last person to have touched this coin had earned it two hundred years before made his head spin.

"Much older. You want to see some?" The man's face split into a fearsome grin and he nodded at Adam. Adam nodded back.

The man thrust out a grubby hand. "Jacob Honeyman.

Beekeeper. How do you do?"

Adam shook the man's hand. "I'm Adam. We're staying up at Root Cottage with our grand—"

"Roots?" Honeyman barked. "You're *Roots*?"

"We're Newmans, actually," Rachel said. "Root is our mother's maiden name."

Honeyman slowly looked from Rachel to Adam, and then grinned, treating them to a fine view of his gums and irregular teeth. "Once a Root, always a Root," he said. The grin vanished from his face as quickly as it had appeared, then he turned abruptly and began marching away.

"Come on then, off we go…"

Before Rachel could make excuses about returning for lunch, her brother was off, following closely behind Jacob Honeyman, whose black coat flapped behind him as he marched away across the moor.

"There's a few really old ones in here," Honeyman said, placing a couple of flat wooden trays on the battered wooden table.

They had followed the strange man back across the moor to his house. At least, "house" was what he called it. To Rachel and Adam it looked more like a corrugated tin hut with tacked-on additions and windows that had belonged originally to several other buildings.

Honeyman lifted the cover, revealing that the trays were divided into small compartments, each containing a coin and a tiny label, handwritten in a microscopic, spidery script.

"Can I?" Adam reached out to the box and Honeyman nodded his permission. Adam picked up a small, irregular nugget of brown metal, which, on close inspection, was stamped with a dog-like animal on one side, and a star on the other.

"An Ecgbehrt penny. About AD 802, 810, something like that." Honeyman gave a self-satisfied smile, delighted at being able to air his knowledge. Adam picked up another. This one was larger and stamped with a monster or dragon. "Burgred," Honeyman said with certainty, naming another Saxon king. "Somewhere around about 852."

Rachel picked another coin out from the tray. It was silvery and more sophisticated than the Saxon ones they had been looking at. Honeyman took it from her.

"Roman," he said. "Probably one of the first struck in Britain. This one's a few years BC." He held the coin up between his thumb and forefinger, raised it to the light. The head of a Roman emperor was clearly visible, garlanded with laurel leaves. Honeyman turned the coin in his fingers. On the other side was a familiar shape.

"It's the Tri-… whatever-you-call-it," Adam said.

Honeyman nodded. "Triskellion," he said. "That's right."

Rachel and Adam stared, astonished: people had been reproducing this image for over two thousand years.

"Surely these things belong in a museum?" Rachel said. She couldn't believe that Jacob Honeyman possessed such a personal treasure trove.

"Thing is, what you lot don't understand, this whole country is many thousands of years old. People have dropped
coins everywhere, museums are full of 'em. So many they
can't even catalogue the flippin' things. They wouldn't give
these room space. The important thing about these coins is
that they're here. Buried by the circle."

"So why is this Triskellion so important?"

Honeyman chuckled at Adam's question. "Do you really
want to know?"

Adam did.

With the help of diagrams and sheets photocopied from
library books, Honeyman explained, as Granny Root had,
that the origin of the shape was Celtic and that it was formed
by three circles that intersected each other. He told them
that the circles represented the trinity of female goddesses –
the virgin, the mother and the old woman – worshipped by
pagans, long before the time of Christianity or any other
major religion. "And the circle that binds the three-bladed
shape of the Triskellion," Honeyman said, "represents the
circle of life itself."

By now, Rachel was as interested as Adam. Honeyman
was prone to long, rambling explanations, and his anecdotes
were often accompanied by an alarming twitch, prolonged
periods of scratching or an explosive cough. But the ancient
history, the romance of the circle and the fact that it was
somehow female, fired her imagination. Honeyman estimated that the circle had been cut out maybe a thousand

years before Christ, which would make it late Bronze Age. He told them that small artefacts in gold and silver discovered near by supported this, and that people had probably been leaving "gifts" at the circle since it began.

"Why would they bury their best stuff, though?" Adam wanted to know.

"To placate the gods mostly ... and to ensure a good harvest of crops. And I suppose it's worked, 'cos all the crops flourish round Triskellion. We never have a bad year. Mind you, some say it might have been a burial place ... or that it might have been a spot for human sacrifices." Jacob treated them to his grin once more, warming to his theme as he drew a yellow finger across his neck in a grisly way.

Rachel and Adam exchanged nervous glances. The beating of the Bacon brothers was all too fresh in their memory for them to be in the least bit fascinated by the idea of human sacrifice.

"I could tell you where to see some of the artefacts if you like," Honeyman said. "But how about some lunch first?"

Adam was about to leap at the offer, but then Rachel noticed the large vat of brownish liquid that was bubbling on top of the sooty wood-burning stove, and the pair of rabbits that hung from a hook above the dirty sink.

"We're not very hungry," she said.

10

It smelled musty inside the church: damp and dark and rich. *Earthy.*

Adam pulled a face, as though recoiling from a carton of milk gone bad. "What did the bee man say was in here?" He tried his best to replicate Jacob Honeyman's low croak. "'Treasures beyond belief'?"

"Yeah, but you have to remember he's crazy," Rachel said.

"He's nice, though." Adam stepped further inside. "And funny…"

Adam's first instinct about Honeyman had been right, Rachel thought. Despite a slightly off-putting appearance, the beekeeper had seemed trustworthy and unthreatening. There had been a warmth about him, and his hut, though messy and ramshackle, had felt welcoming and secure.

The previous afternoon, having had his offer of lunch turned down, Honeyman had taken the twins to the small-holding behind his house and shown them the rows of beehives he kept. He had put his hand deep into a hive and brought it out covered with bees. The bees had buzzed and writhed round his wrist like a living gauntlet. He had lifted the hand to his stubbly face, where a column of bees had peeled off from the rest and crawled over his lips, nose and eyelids. Rachel and Adam had stared, their mouths gaping in astonishment, as the bees moved all over the strange man without stinging him. Honeyman had grinned, delighted at their astonishment. He was, he announced proudly, the fifteenth generation of apiarist, or beekeeper, on this very site.

Honeyman had sent them off with a jar of cloudy, brownish honey, a large chunk of honeycomb suspended in the golden liquid. He had also given Adam the coin he had dug up that morning.

"For good luck," he'd said.

It was a hot and sticky Sunday afternoon and the cool inside the church was welcome. Bright sunshine streamed through the stained glass window at the far end of the small church and the twins had to shield their eyes from the dazzling beams of coloured light.

Rachel was not surprised to see the Triskellion symbol, picked out in rich red, blue and gold. Beneath the circular section of the window, Rachel could make out two figures: a knight in armour and a maiden, each one in a separate pane, a shooting star brightening the night sky behind them.

"Hey, Rach. Look at this…"

Rachel clambered between the rows of rickety wooden pews, and found Adam in a small chapel off to one side.

"This is co-ool," Adam whispered.

Rachel looked over her brother's shoulder. She felt a small chill run through her as she saw, in an alcove, the stone effigy of a knight. The figure lay flat, as though asleep, head resting on a carved pillow. It was sculpted from a cream-coloured stone, worn smooth in some places, chipped in others and obviously very old. The feet were long and narrow and on its head the figure wore a pointed helmet. The body was all but concealed by a long shield, on which was carved the Triskellion symbol.

"Guess it must be King Arthur, or Sir Lancelot or some-one," Adam hazarded.

Rachel was transfixed by the figure. She held her breath, her head throbbing as she tried to make sense of what she was seeing, of what she had already seen on the stained glass window. This was the same knight and the same maiden she had seen in her vision. But how could that be possible? She had never even heard of this church before, yet this morning she had been dreaming about exactly these two figures.

Jet lag? No, Rachel thought, not this time. This vision had been something else...

"May I help you?"

The sharp, precise tone made Rachel and Adam start. They had not heard the door open behind them. They turned to see a spindly man dressed in a long black cassock and dog collar, his alarmingly thin appearance perfectly matching his reedy voice.

"I see you've found our crusader…"

Adam stared, transfixed by the man's large Adam's apple, which bobbed up and down as he spoke.

"Crusader?" asked Rachel, genuinely interested. She recognized the vicar as the man who had sailed past them on his bike the day before. She looked down at the leaflet she'd picked up at the entrance: *The Church of St. Augustine, Triskellion. C. 1073. Vicar: The Rev. J. Stone, BA.*

"Yes," said Reverend Stone. "We think this is the tomb of our very own crusader, most likely Sir Richard de Waverley."

"Is it old? I mean, like … *how* old?" Even as he asked, Adam remembered that nothing in this village seemed younger than a few hundred years, including his grandmother.

"Around eight hundred years," the vicar said.

"So is his, um, skeleton and stuff actually in there?"

Rachel was embarrassed by her brother's need for graphic information. "Adam."

Reverend Stone held up his hand. "It's quite all right. I admire a questioning mind, and we're all fascinated by the gory details. Sadly though, on this occasion, there are none. Sir Richard's remains were probably buried where he fell, somewhere out in the Middle East." He pointed down at the carving. "We call this our crusader tomb, but it's really just a memorial, I'm afraid."

Adam looked disappointed. "Mr Honeyman told us there were some artefacts to see?"

"Artefacts? Oh yes, there certainly are. Follow me." The

reverend turned and hurried away, fumbling with a large bunch of keys; marching across the tiles and brasses worn smooth by centuries of worshippers.

Rachel and Adam watched as he opened the door to a small, whitewashed room at the side of the church. Faded maps on the wall outlined the parish boundary, and at the far end of the room were two glass-topped, mahogany display cases.

Reverend Stone ushered Rachel forward to look. In the first case were a variety of small relics.

"These are mostly Saxon. A couple of the rings are gold, but otherwise the pins and all the other bits and bobs are bronze." Reverend Stone extended a twig-like finger, pointing to the second display case. "But *this* is our pièce de résistance. This is why everything is kept under lock and key."

Rachel and Adam pressed their faces close to the glass. Laid out by itself on a piece of green felt was what looked, at first glance, like a curved, golden blade. Rachel stared at the crescent of metal. It was instantly familiar to her and yet not a shape she immediately recognized.

Reverend Stone grinned, thin-lipped and joyless. "Do you see what it is?"

Rachel looked at Adam. He didn't know. She looked back at the blade and it suddenly dawned on her that it was a part of something else. That if three such blades were placed tip to tip, they would form a shape she was coming to know very well.

"It's part of a Triskellion," she whispered. Now she was full of questions herself. "What's it made of?"

"Well, there's some gold certainly, but also one or two other elements we're not certain about."

"Hasn't a scientist tried to find out?"

"We wouldn't really be too keen on that. They'd take it away and lock it in a vault somewhere and we'd lose a piece of our history."

"Are there any other parts?"

Reverend Stone spread his arms wide. "Ah, well there's the mystery. Nobody knows what happened to the other two blades." He glanced at his watch. "Now I don't mean to hurry you, but…" He guided them back into the body of the church and locked the door behind him.

Rachel looked up at the stained glass window that dominated the altar. Questions continued to flood her mind. "What about the figures in the window?"

Reverend Stone rolled his eyes. He was beginning to look more than a little impatient; almost irritated.

"Who are they?"

"Well … I like to think that it's an image of Sir Richard de Waverley, off to the crusades, wishing his wife goodbye." Reverend Stone looked as if he was about to wish Rachel and Adam the same. But Adam had a question of his own.

"What's the inscription mean?" Adam was crouching down, pointing to the series of symbols engraved along the base of the tomb.

"I think you need several degrees in ancient languages to even make a start on those. Some people think it's an epitaph or a prayer. Or perhaps even a warning of some sort…"

"What do you think?" Rachel asked.

"I don't know," replied Reverend Stone, undoing the buttons on the front of his cassock. "But I *do* know I have a cricket match to umpire in five minutes." From a hook near the entrance he took a white umpire's coat and struggled into it, leaning against the heavy wooden door and stepping out into the sunshine.

Adam and Rachel followed. The blast of hot air was like opening an oven.

As he climbed on to his bicycle, the vicar turned back to the twins. "Maybe you'd like to come and watch?" He nodded towards his church. "You think some of the stuff in there is strange and inexplicable, wait until you've seen cricket…"

Rachel and Adam exchanged a look, before walking away from the church in the same direction as the vicar.

From the churchyard, the boy with black hair and wide green eyes watched them go. He whistled a simple tune, smiling and leaning back against a gravestone that rose up like fifty or so others, through the overgrown grass.

Blackened and crooked. The names of the dead long since worn away.

11

"He was *what* before *what*?" Adam asked.

The old man smiled, indulgently. "Lbw. Leg before wicket, young man. The ball pitched on off stump and moved back inside, you see?"

Adam nodded, none the wiser, then joined everyone else in clapping enthusiastically, as the batsman who had been dismissed walked off the field, and stamped up the rickety wooden steps towards the small pavilion.

"Well played," shouted several people in the crowd. The batsman touched the peak of his cap and smiled.

Adam raised his hand to shield his eyes from the sun and stared across the expanse of green until he caught sight of Rachel, who had wandered away to the far side of the pitch. He waved until she noticed him and began to wander back round the boundary.

It seemed as though most of the village had turned out to watch the match. There were people on every spare inch of grass round the edge of the pitch; enjoying picnics on tartan blankets while children played with plastic bats and balls; dozing in striped deckchairs or perched on shooting sticks.

The sky was duck-egg blue, and only the gentlest of breezes shook the tall oaks and hornbeams that encircled the pitch; shivering in the leaves like the sound of distant applause.

Hearing a murmur of excitement from the people around him, Adam looked up in time to see the ball being fielded by a familiar-looking figure on the boundary and thrown back hard; fizzing into the player behind the stumps, who swept off the bails and clapped.

"Good work, Lee…"

Lee Bacon. One of the boys who had attacked Adam by the war memorial, and had paid so dearly for it in the woods. Adam breathed an enormous sigh of relief. At least they were still in one piece…

"This is bizarre, isn't it?"

"Huh?" Adam looked up. He hadn't seen Rachel arrive next to him. She was beaming.

"Apparently, the bowler's got a square leg."

"And a hell of a googly," Adam said. "Whatever that is."

Rachel giggled. "And I thought baseball was complicated."

Adam turned away, distracted by the distant sound of a ball being hit. By the growing excitement, and then the alarm of the people around him.

"Catch it!"

"Watch it!"

"Look out…!"

Adam glanced up and saw the dark, speeding blur that could only be an extremely hard cricket ball hurtling down towards him. He heard Rachel scream, then others, and turned away the second before a hand reached out and caught the ball centimetres in front of his face.

There was a gasp from the crowd, then applause.

"Bravo!"

"Did you see that catch?"

"You should be out there playing," somebody said.

Adam opened his eyes to see Rachel staring at a boy in a hooded sweatshirt. He was somewhere around their own age. The boy's clothes were as dark as his hair and Adam thought he must have been boiling hot, but he seemed cool enough, moving the ball in his hands for a few seconds before throwing it back to a nearby fielder.

"Nice catch," Rachel said.

The boy smiled and pushed his long hair back from his face.

"I'm Rachel."

The boy nodded, as though hearing something he already knew.

Rachel pointed towards Adam. "This is my brother…"

Adam stepped forward and stuck out a hand. "Adam."

The boy took Adam's hand, though he seemed unsure exactly what he was supposed to do with it. "My name's Gabriel," he said.

The three children stood around a little awkwardly for a few seconds, until the crowd broke into ripples of gentle applause once again and the players began to leave the pitch.

"That's tea," someone said.

Granny Root buzzed around the room, skilfully manoeuvring her wheelchair between the tables, chatting with all and sundry, and dispensing tea from an enormous pot, which stood balanced on a tray in her lap.

The small pavilion was heaving; three long trestle tables accommodated the twenty-two men in white, as well as the umpires, scorers and assorted friends of the cricket club. There was a lively hubbub as players exchanged war stories, re-enacting heroic catches or memorable shots, while hungrily scoffing sandwiches and slurping tea.

Rachel, Adam and Gabriel stood in one corner of the room near the small bar. Rachel tried to make conversation with their new friend, but the boy wasn't saying much. He seemed far more interested in eating, and was still reaching for food long after Rachel and Adam had eaten their fill.

"I don't know where you put it all," Adam said. It was a reasonable comment considering how slight and stick-thin the boy was. Adam couldn't help wondering how long it had been since Gabriel had eaten a decent meal. The boy just stared back at him, half smiling, and continued to eat.

After about twenty minutes, the players began to drift away from the tables, preparing to continue with the match.

Rachel, Adam and Gabriel were about to head back outside themselves when an elderly man with slicked back white hair got up from his table and walked purposefully towards them. The walk was laboured and without saying anything to one another, both Rachel and Adam came to the conclusion that he wore a false leg.

The man stopped about a metre in front of the children and stood, casually tossing a cricket ball into the air.

"I'm Commodore Gerald Wing," he said. "You must be Celia Root's grandchildren."

Rachel and Adam nodded, and Rachel managed a nervous hello. The man seemed friendly enough, but despite the smile there was something about him that made them both extremely nervous. Adam thought he was like the crusty old headmaster he'd seen in an old English movie one rainy afternoon.

"And as for you…" Commodore Wing's steely gaze settled on Gabriel. Gabriel stared right back, still chewing. "That was one *hell* of a catch, young man."

Gabriel nodded, the strange half-smile on his face once again.

"One hell of a catch." The commodore threw the cricket ball a little higher, his eyes never leaving the boy's, then as soon as he'd caught it, he launched it hard and fast towards Gabriel, grunting with the effort of the throw.

Rachel gasped, and watched as Gabriel reached out and the ball smacked into his palm. He looked at it, turning it in his hand as if he were unsure what it was or where it had come from, before lobbing it lazily back to the commodore.

Rachel looked across at Adam. They realized suddenly that the entire room had fallen silent and that all eyes were upon them.

"Amazing reflexes." The commodore was red-faced, something tense around his eyes, but his voice was calm and measured. "Absolutely amazing," he said, before turning quickly away on his good leg.

It was as though someone had turned a radio on, with the conversation in the pavilion suddenly resuming as though nothing had happened. The children watched the commodore move back towards his table, one or two of the other players murmuring to him as he walked past them.

"Nutjob," Adam muttered.

Rachel hissed. "Adam!"

"Not as nuts as one or two others, mind you," Adam said. He moved towards the door, in search of a toilet. "But still weird…"

Adam was still drying his hands on a wad of paper towel when he walked out of the door behind the pavilion and all but collided with the Bacon brothers.

Gary and Lee stared at Adam, and the taller one smiled. It was anything but friendly.

"Excuse me," Adam said.

Gary and Lee were both carrying cricket bats, and it didn't

look as though they were there to practise their shots. Adam could feel his heart jumping against his chest. "Why, what have you done?" Gary Bacon chuckled at his feeble joke, and his brother joined in.

Adam stepped left, and then right, but could find no way past the two, bigger teenagers. "I don't want to miss the match," he said.

Lee hoisted his bat up on to his shoulder. "You won't miss anything. Game can't start until we're out there."

Gary raised his own bat and slowly swung it, as though despatching an invisible ball to the boundary. "We're opening the batting, see."

"Look, you'd better move out of my way," Adam said, suddenly. He was as surprised as anyone that his words sounded so aggressive; at the anger he could feel rising up quickly inside him.

"Or what?" Lee said.

Adam had always been the same. Got the hot temper from his dad's side of the family, that was what his mom had said. Rachel had been on the receiving end of that temper more than most, but then Adam reckoned that she usually started the trouble by saying the wrong thing.

Rachel and Adam. Big mouth, bad temper.

"Yeah." Gary took a step towards him. "Or *what*?"

Not that Adam's mouth wasn't plenty big enough…

"Or … or the pair of you might find yourselves tied to a tree again."

The colour drained in an instant from the faces of the two Bacon brothers. They looked at one another and then back at Adam. This time, there was no smile, not even a sarcastic one. There was something very dark in Gary's voice when he spoke.

"How d'you know about that?"

Now there was as much fear as there was anger; the air was crackling with it, and Adam wasn't the only one who was scared. He knew that he'd said the wrong thing. Gary and Lee were suddenly looking extremely worried and now there was no way of telling how they would react.

"We saw you, yesterday," Adam said. His mouth was dry and he had to suck up spit before he could finish. "We watched them in the woods, punishing you."

Something like a growl came from low in the throat of one of the brothers and Adam felt tears springing to the corners of his eyes. He knew that his words had hit home.

He also knew that a cornered animal was one that was liable to attack.

Lee cleared his throat. "You saw something you shouldn't have."

"That was a mistake," Gary said.

"Bad mistake…"

As they talked at him, their voices getting louder, tumbling across each other, Adam felt the anger and the fear bubbling up together. He felt his fists clench at his side, his jaw aching as he ground his teeth together, holding his breath…

"Should have hit you harder that first time."

Gary tipped his head back, then snapped it forward, spitting into Adam's face. "*Much* harder."

"Maybe it's *your* turn to get punished…"

And Adam ran at them, springing forward with his head down, barging his way between the brothers who shouted and swore in frustration as they grabbed at him and missed. Adam kept running, wiping the gobbet of spit from his face, furiously rubbing his wet and sticky palm across his T-shirt as he ran back round to the front of the pavilion.

And ran, and ran…

12

"We can't just disappear…"

Rachel was still pleading with Adam as they stepped on to the train but her argument continued to fall on deaf ears as it had all the way from the cricket pitch. Adam had not said a word as they had raced back to Root Cottage; as they had grabbed their rucksacks from the bedroom; as Rachel had scribbled a hasty note in worn-out ballpoint.

Don't worry. We'll call you…

The sliding door of the empty carriage hissed shut and Rachel noticed, with pleasure, that the compartment was new and smelled clean and plastic. An electric sign scrolled the list of destinations across the West Country and, much as Rachel had her doubts about leaving, the newness of the train made her feel optimistic. It would whisk them quickly and efficiently across the country.

It would take them back to the real world.

The engine whirred into life and the train pulled slowly

out of Triskellion station. As the hanging baskets of pink geraniums floated past, Adam allowed himself a tight smile and glanced at his sister.

Rachel smiled back sympathetically, but unable to conceal a little regret. Although the past couple of days had been unsettling and, on more than one occasion, downright scary, Rachel had begun to feel oddly at home in the village where her mother was born.

"Gran's going to be really mad..." Rachel said.

Adam shrugged. "I don't care. I'm out of here. This place is messing with my head. It's like you're not noticing any of this weird stuff any more."

"Maybe it just *seems* weird to us," Rachel said. "Like the cricket, or whatever, because we're not from around here. Have you thought that *we* might be the ones who are weird?"

Adam didn't look convinced. "I want to go home. And don't worry about Gran. She didn't seem to want us around anyway."

"Come on, that's not fair."

Adam leant back, gazed out of the window. "I'm not sure anyone wanted us around."

Celia Root cleared away the tea things in the pavilion, stacking plates in the basket on the front of her wheelchair, trundling across to the serving hatch, where the other village women took them from her to wash.

"Has anyone seen Rachel and Adam?" she asked no one in

particular. No one in particular gave her any answer beyond the shake of a head, so she wheeled herself back to remove the tablecloths from the trestles. When she had finished, she took a powder compact from her handbag and checked her make-up in the small mirror.

Outside on the veranda, Tom Hatcham, padded-up and waiting to bat, lumbered over to Commodore Wing, who stood on the steps, looking out over the pitch, his eyes narrowed against the sun.

"They've gone," Hatcham said.

Commodore Wing gave Hatcham no sign that he either knew or cared what the landlord was talking about. He shouted out a brief "Shot!" as Lee Bacon hit a four across the boundary, the red ball speeding into the rope that marked the edge of the pitch, bouncing up and thudding into the flaking, wooden steps beneath the commodore's feet.

As the train gathered speed, Rachel looked out at the green blur of trees that sped past the window, and let out a deep breath that she realized she had been holding for the best part of a minute. She could see Adam's spirits visibly lifting as the train headed away from the village. He flopped back in his seat, his feet up on the chair opposite, and his smile that little bit broader than it had been for several days.

But no sooner had the train reached full speed than it suddenly began to slow down again. The green blur outside the window refocused into trees and hedgerows. The brakes squealed against the hot rails and the train ground to a halt.

"Just the signals, I guess," Rachel said. She summoned a smile, but was unable to contain a glance back along the track herself, to shake off the feeling of having been followed. The engine ticked over, clicking and whirring, then slowly the carriage began to roll *backwards* along the track.

Adam glanced round nervously, then jumped up from his seat and paced over to the sliding door. The train continued to reverse for a few metres, then, its engine powering down, finally stopped altogether.

Adam stabbed at the buttons that would open and close the doors if activated by the driver.

Nothing.

Rachel realized that, unlike those on the old carriage in which they had arrived, these electric doors could not be opened from inside. "So much for a nice, new train," she said.

"I'm going up front. See what's happening." Adam pushed his way along the aisle and opened the door at the end of the carriage that joined it to the next one. Rachel did not fancy being alone in the otherwise empty carriage and quickly followed.

Three carriages down, Rachel and Adam found the guard's cabin, empty, but with a window open on to the side of the track. Adam stuck his head out and Rachel craned her neck to see through the small gap that remained. A man in a blue uniform, holding a dayglo orange flag, was walking away from them along the curve of the carriages, moving slowly towards the front of the train, which was obscured from them by the bend.

"Hey," Adam called, but the man didn't seem to hear. Adam turned back to his sister. "I'm not staying in here. I want to know what's up." He stretched his arm out of the window and reached down to where a handle on the outside released the guard's door. It swung open against the side of the train with a clang. Adam jumped down the metre or so from the train on to the coarse gravel of the track. Rachel hesitated a moment then, when Adam turned round, his arms open as if to catch her, she jumped too.

They walked alongside the train until the engine came into view, but instead of the signals they had expected, saw a vast oak tree lying across the rails. The driver had climbed down from the engine and was talking to the guard with the orange flag. As Rachel and Adam approached, the men looked tiny against the tree, its thick, scaly trunk as high as their necks and the dense green foliage spreading well beyond the limits of the track. It looked like a dead dinosaur guarding the line. Keeping intruders away.

Ensuring that, for a good while at least, as far as this stretch of railway was concerned, nobody was coming or going anywhere.

*   *   *

Concealed within the branches of a similar, but still upright tree, Gabriel watched the two small figures crunch along the gravel. He watched as they joined the guard and driver, studying their body language, and, even from a distance, he could see the twins visibly slump as they absorbed the news that they were going nowhere.

That there was no way out of Triskellion.

Gabriel looked away, through the branches, focusing his wide, green eyes directly into the afternoon sun. He seemed to breathe in the light and, as he did so, the branches trembled, as if ruffled by an imaginary breeze.

"Roots were rotten," the guard said to Rachel and Adam, as he used a special key to open the carriage doors. "We should count ourselves lucky no one was hurt."

Resigned to the fact that their escape bid had failed, the twins stepped meekly back into the carriage. The door hissed shut behind them. The engine powered up and the train began to reverse back along the track towards Triskellion.

Minutes later, the pink geraniums of Triskellion station came back into view, like a rewound film, and this time, unlike the first occasion they had pulled into the station, there was someone waiting to meet them.

As the carriage pulled in and came to a stop, Rachel saw the distinctive figure of Gabriel standing in front of her window. Despite her disappointment, Rachel felt her face flush. She tapped Adam, whose own face had not left his hands during the journey back, and he looked up.

part two:

the woods

13

C orn stretches out in front as far as the eye can see: tall, thick and golden, almost reaching eye level. The sun is vast in the sky, producing a light so strong and white that it bleaches the colour from the landscape. Whispering, coarse and dry, the corn falls aside, creating a path. It parts, as if pushed by unseen hands. Then it stops; falling flat, stalk upon stalk, in a domino effect, round a crater filled with black water.

The water is thick, still and oily, and something stirs deep down, snaking towards the surface like a fat eel, its skin now and then catching the light with a dark flash. Bigger now, and lighter, changing shape as it nears the air. Bubbles rise and burst, greasy as the sleek head breaks the surface, wet black hair stuck to the face. A neck and shoulders emerge, muscled and fully formed, yet also newborn. Rivulets of dark water run over the fresh body as it emerges from the pond, gliding through strands of weed and slime. Gasping for air.

The boy shakes his head, hair flying in slow motion. Beads of water captured, static, in the blinding light.

He stops and stands, staring at the sun. His eyes, green—

Rachel sat bolt upright in bed, the faded roses on the wallpaper moving sharply into focus. A wave of embarrassment washed over her as she turned and looked at Adam. He was also sitting up in bed, and Rachel knew instantly that he had had the same dream.

"That was *seriously* strange," Adam said. He jumped out of bed and rushed to the window, as if to reassure himself that the dream had not materialized outside the bedroom. "What did it mean?"

Rachel felt as though she knew *exactly* what the dream had meant, but it was not a feeling that she could put into words. "Dunno," she said to her brother. "Nothing probably. We've just been going through a lot of strange new stuff … and you know how sometimes we, like … you know…"

Adam did know.

Since they could remember, the two of them had woken some mornings with a shared vision from the night before. But this one stirred something new within Rachel, something a little scary, but also exciting. Something that gave her a warm feeling in the pit of her stomach.

It was a warm sensation that Rachel continued to feel throughout the morning and one which helped her calmly resign herself to staying in the village. Adam, on the other hand, had been unsettled by the dream in a completely different way, and renewed his efforts to escape.

The phone was still not working.

"It's not unusual, dear," Gran had said. "It's only been two days. Things can take a little longer to sort themselves out here."

Adam had slammed down the receiver in frustration, earning himself a steely reprimand from his grandmother. He knew there was little point asking if she had a computer, or if the village had an internet café. At Rachel's suggestion, he had taken himself off into a corner and attempted to communicate with his mother using more primitive tools: a pen and paper.

Adam grumbled over every sentence. At home, he fired off emails all day long, but this was the first letter he'd written to anyone in a long time.

After a lunch that was little more than some sardines from a tin, a few slices of bread and the almost tasteless, lemony drink that Granny Root diluted from a bottle, Rachel sat down to read a book. It was an old, dog-eared paperback she had found on the shelf in the sitting room. Her eye had been caught by the title: *Chalk Circles of Great Britain*. She found it hard to concentrate on the old-fashioned prose as Adam laboured and sighed over his letter, and Granny Root settled in the big chair for her afternoon nap and began to snore quietly.

The atmosphere in the room was stuffy and oppressive, but the sun was too hot for comfort outside. Rachel read the first line of the chapter again, then looked up as Adam mouthed the words to her, "I'm starving."

Rachel nodded her agreement, then attempted to read the first line for the tenth time.

A *"tink"* on the windowpane broke her concentration yet again. Then another as a pebble struck the glass. And another, the stone thrown so hard that Rachel was afraid it would crack the pane. Adam looked round, and he and Rachel jumped up to see where the stones were coming from.

Rachel adjusted her eyes to the bright sunlight outside and saw Gabriel, standing, framed by the archway of roses that led to the bottom of the garden. He was eating from a party-sized bag of crisps, and, seeing Rachel at the window, he waved and gestured for her to join him. Rachel looked at her grandmother sleeping, nodded to Adam to follow, and went outside.

Gabriel was now sitting on the grass, stuffing large handfuls of crisps into his mouth.

"Wow, chips," Adam said longingly, sitting on the grass. "We're starving. We had, like, baby fish in a can of oil for lunch."

Rachel scrunched her nose in agreement with Adam's description, and when Gabriel proffered the bag of crisps, they both accepted it greedily.

"I want to go up to the circle," Gabriel said. He had talked to them about it on the way back from the station two days before. He had said he knew things about it. "If you want to get a proper understanding of it, you need to come up there with me."

Rachel and Adam were keen. They liked the air of mystery Gabriel projected. He was … cool. They had asked him where he lived and he had told them that his parents were kind of travellers, who went off on long trips, leaving him free to do his own thing. Adam thought this was even cooler.

"That sounds fantastic," he had said.

Rachel had agreed; had said how lucky Gabriel was. But she had also thought how lucky he was to have parents who were still together.

Then Gabriel had told them about the circle…

"Sure, we'll come," Rachel said.

"Let's go," Adam said, rising to his feet.

Gabriel held up his hand. "Wait, I have a few things to do first. Errands and stuff, you know. Why don't you come on your bikes? I'll meet you there in an hour."

Rachel looked at her watch. Three o'clock now. "OK. See you there at four?"

"It's a date," Gabriel said. He spoke without emphasis, but Rachel felt herself redden all the same. Gabriel rose to his feet and tossed the bag of crisps to Adam, walking slowly away down the length of the garden and out through a gap in the hedge.

Adam turned to his sister, his look telling her that *he* thought that *she* quite liked Gabriel. "Wooooo," he said, making kissy noises with his lips.

Rachel laughed bashfully, then jumped on her brother, punching his upper arm with what he discovered, somewhat painfully, was considerable strength for a girl.

The twins couldn't settle, so, half an hour later, having told a dozing Granny Root that they were off on a bike ride, they set out on the lane.

They decided to take the long way round: down the lane, up past the edge of the woods and then out along the narrow road that ran through the middle of the moor towards the chalk circle. They could have walked it cross-country in ten minutes from Root Cottage, but the afternoon was beginning to cool, and the breeze as they freewheeled down the lane was welcome. They sped down past the pub then round the bend, stopping at a red postbox where Adam deposited his letter home. Then on, alongside the red-brick wall that marked the outer boundary of the Waverley Hall estate.

As the ordered limits of the wall gave way to the narrower lane, Rachel felt suddenly nauseous. Sick, and scared in the same terrible second, as though she were passing through something rank, and dangerous. As though it were passing through her.

Even as she registered it, she heard the nearby grumble of a diesel engine grow swiftly into a roar, and a mud-spattered Land Rover careered into their path round a blind bend in the lane.

"Adam!" Rachel screeched to her brother, two bike lengths in front of her. Adam swerved to the right, but not quickly enough for the truck to avoid clipping his back wheel, sending Adam and his bike skidding across the gravel. In turning to avoid Adam, the Land Rover was now headed directly at Rachel, who threw herself from her bicycle and into the scrub at the side of the lane.

In that split second, screaming and rolling, tumbling headlong away from the impact, she could have sworn that the Land Rover was being driven by a huge, grey dog.

The next few moments unravelled in slow motion. Rachel picked herself out of the bushes, thorns scraping her legs and catching at her clothes, until she sat, dazed, by the side of the road.

She looked over to where Adam was picking himself up at the roadside. He was brushing himself down, a hole scraped through the knee of his jeans by the rough surface of the road. Rachel felt instant relief; her brother was alive, and she had no more than surface cuts and bruises. She was shocked out of her relief by the angry, booming voice of the man getting out of the Land Rover.

"What the bloody…?"

Rachel looked up to see the imposing figure of Commodore Wing climbing stiffly down from the driver's seat and limping fast towards her, the huge figure of a grey Irish wolfhound loping along behind him.

"Oh, it's you." The commodore's temper instantly subsided. He smiled grimly, holding out a large, dry hand and helping Rachel to her feet. The giant dog sniffed Rachel, then licked her scratched arm.

"Sorry," the commodore said. "Bit of a shock. I'm not used to meeting anyone on this road. Couldn't see very well. Sunlight through the trees. Almost blinded me." He held his other hand out to Adam. "Nothing broken? Hope not. I really am most awfully sorry. My fault entirely."

Rachel found it hard to say anything. The man's sudden charm was every bit as alarming as his anger had been just a moment or two before. Adam looked pained, dabbing the blood from his knee with a tissue, but still managing a croaky, "No problem."

"Good," barked Commodore Wing. "The cycles have taken a bit of a prang, I'm afraid. Chuck 'em on the Land Rover and we'll get them fixed up."

Adam helped the commodore wrestle the bikes on to the back of the Land Rover while the dog, who the commodore called Merlin, continued to sniff somewhat suspiciously at Rachel. The bikes loaded, Rachel was about to turn and walk back down the lane, but the commodore stopped her in her tracks.

"Where are you off to, young lady? You're not walking anywhere after a close shave like that. Hop aboard, I'll take you and your brother up to the hall."

"What?"

"Get the quack to give you the once over. Least I can do."

Rachel and Adam both looked dumbfounded and the commodore registered their blank stares. "Sorry, the doctor. Get the doctor to check you. Shock and so on. In you get."

Rachel and Adam felt reluctant to go, but the man was so commanding, so clearly used to having people do as he said, that they fell in with his orders and climbed into the back seat of the Land Rover without a word. Merlin jumped into the front, followed by Commodore Wing, who slammed the door and fired the diesel engine back into life. Gears crunched and they roared off down the lane as if nothing had happened.

Rachel looked at her watch, then back over her shoulder towards the moor and the chalk circle. Five to four. They'd miss Gabriel.

She'd miss Gabriel.

As the dust churned up by the Land Rover's knobbly tyres began to settle on the road, Gabriel stepped out from his hiding place behind the wall. He smiled, delighted that things were falling into place so nicely.

He watched and waited for the vehicle to turn the bend at the bottom of the hill, then began to walk down the lane after it.

14

The Land Rover crunched up the long gravel drive towards the biggest house Rachel and Adam had ever seen. Sheep grazed on the grounds at either side of the road and Waverley Hall loomed impressively beyond. Adam would have called it a castle, but it didn't have battlements as such, just columns and balustrades and carved animals over the main entrance, all made from a yellowish stone. Drawing closer, Rachel could see the big, wine-coloured vintage car they had seen in the village, parked outside the front of the house. As the statues over the door became clearer, she could see a winged unicorn and a dragon. They glowered down from either side of a carved tree, its twisted roots and branches entwining themselves around the mythical beasts. On the trunk of the tree was a large shield engraved with the symbol of the Triskellion.

Despite the change from rage to effortless charm, the commodore's warmth had quickly dissolved. What little conversation there was in the Land Rover had been strained to say the least. Rachel had attempted a few polite questions, which had been answered with coughs, snorts and one or two clipped words.

"Have you lived here long?" Rachel had asked.

"Family's been here eight hundred years or so."

"Since Sir Richard de Waverley?" Rachel had said, keen to show off her recently acquired local knowledge.

"Who?" Commodore Wing had snapped back.

"Sir Richard de Waverley. The crusader. In the church?"

"Oh yes … of course," the commodore had said.

The rest of the journey had continued in silence.

As they climbed down from the Land Rover, a small man with very brown, hairy forearms and wearing a cap scuttled over to the car and opened the door. He was a little too slow for the commodore, who was already halfway out.

"Take those bicycles round to the stables and fix 'em up, will you, Fred?" The small man stared at the children. "Good man," the commodore said, before limping off up the steps to the house with the dog following closely behind. The small man nodded vigorously and scurried round to lift the bikes off the back of the vehicle. He grunted with the effort and pulled faces at Rachel and Adam, who watched him with some amusement.

"Are you coming in?" the commodore shouted from the front door. Once again powerless to resist, the twins followed him up the steps.

The cavernous hall inside the main entrance smelled of

wax polish, wood smoke and something else which neither Rachel nor Adam could quite place.

Maybe it was just age.

Two wide, wooden staircases flanked the hall at either side and in the middle sat a huge, stone fireplace where a few logs still smouldered from the night before. Above the fireplace hung a portrait of a man Rachel guessed must have been an ancient Wing. He was wearing a wig and a tricorn hat. Waverley Hall stood in the background while in the far distance, the carved chalk circle of the Triskellion was painted on the dark surface of the moor.

On the surrounding walls hung shields, broadswords, helmets, spears and the assorted horns and antlers of long dead animals. The commodore clumped across the stone floor and through a doorway by the side of the fireplace. Rachel and Adam followed him along a panelled corridor and into a sunlit room with French windows that looked out over a well tended lawn, then beyond across acres of parkland and down to a lake.

"Sit down," the commodore said. His tone was kindly, and he gestured at an assortment of armchairs and sofas that, to Rachel's eyes, looked frayed and beaten up. Rachel sat down in a cracked leathery chair that smelled strongly of dog, whereupon Merlin loped in from another room and, at her eye level, sniffed Rachel's face before laying its vast, bristly head in her lap.

Straining her head back to avoid the wet nose and massive

tongue of the wolfhound, Rachel noticed that there were large bits missing from the ornate ceiling. As her eyes darted around, she could see that the rest of the room, though comfortable for such a large space, was in similar condition. At her feet was a pinkish, threadbare carpet that must have once been woven with a floral pattern and the yellow striped paper on the walls was peeling at the corners.

The commodore had crossed to the phone, telling Rachel and Adam that he would ring for a doctor, but he seemed to be having no luck. "Damn thing's still on the blink," he said throwing down the receiver. "You seem OK though."

"We're fine," Rachel said.

He peered at them and looked as though he'd suddenly had a good idea. "Drink?" he said. He took a stopper from a cutglass bottle on a dusty tray in the corner and quickly poured three measures of golden liquid into glasses. Adam would have killed for a Coke, but resisted the urge to ask for one. The commodore pressed another bottle with a lever, and frothy water shot into the glasses, diluting the amber liquid. He passed a glass each to Rachel and Adam.

Rachel looked wide-eyed at her drink. "Is this ... whisky?"

"Er, yes," Commodore Wing said, as if noticing the fact for the first time. "What's up? Don't you drink the stuff?"

"Um, no ... at least I haven't tried it," Rachel said.

"Be good for the shock," the commodore said, taking a large gulp and swilling the whisky around like mouthwash.

Adam suddenly felt quite delighted that he was being

treated in such a grown-up way. He swirled the whisky round in the glass like a man of the world, holding it up to the light, thinking how nice it looked. Then, he tasted it. He took a large swig, just as the commodore had done. His first sensation was the taste of freshly dug earth, followed by the smell of old books. Something musty and old. Then the fire kicked in at the back of his throat and it was like the time he had tried to siphon petrol from a can in his dad's garage and had swallowed a mouthful. Adam could no longer contain the liquid as the fumes shot up inside his nose and he spluttered, spraying a shower of whisky and spittle over himself and across the commodore's carpet.

Rachel was mortified. Sensibly, she had only sniffed at her whisky deciding, wisely she now realized, against actually drinking it. "I am so sorry," she gushed at the commodore.

"Not to worry. Merlin'll lick it up. How old are you pair, by the way?"

"Fourteen," Adam rasped, still wiping his lips. "I'm really sorry."

"No, my fault." The commodore knocked back the rest of his whisky. "I don't really know what young people like, these days. Maybe we should find some tea instead. Come with me. The kitchen's miles away..."

Rachel and Adam trotted after Commodore Wing, who marched off briskly despite his limp, out of the scruffy room and down another long corridor.

"Bit of a guided tour," Commodore Wing said, betraying

no pleasure in giving Rachel and Adam such a treat. "Drawing room," he said, as they entered a room far smarter than the one they had been in. The elegant, upright chairs looked to Rachel as if they were covered in silk, and old paintings of landscapes hung on each wall. "That little watercolour of the moor is supposed to be a Turner," the commodore said, pointing at a little washy picture in the corner.

While Adam was dutifully showing an interest in what the commodore was pointing out, Rachel was drawn to the photographs on top of the piano in the corner of the room.

In a silver frame, a black and white photo showed the head and shoulders of a handsome young man. He looked like an old film star, with slicked-back dark hair and a uniform with a winged badge over the breast pocket. The roman nose and decisive jaw could only have belonged to the man who was in the room with them now. Next to it, another picture in a black frame showed a serious, good-looking young woman with a faraway stare, wearing a similar uniform. There was a colour photo of the commodore taken more recently, talking to a lady who looked like the queen. Rachel looked closer and saw that it *was* the queen.

There was one photo in a red leather frame that had apparently fallen over and lay face down. Rachel picked it up. The colour had faded and the photo looked as though it had been taken some time ago. It had been a sunny day, outside a grand building of some description, with the commodore standing ramrod straight, hands behind his back, in a checked suit with a waistcoat. Next to him stood an aristocratic-looking young man with long hair and a beard, and a somewhat superior look on his face. He was making a "peace" sign at the camera. On the young man's head was perched the kind of flat black hat that teachers wore in old pictures, and a cloak hung off his broad shoulders. Rachel thought it made him look like some kind of weird priest. She was captivated by the young man's arrogant face. It seemed familiar to her, and she was transfixed by the challenge in his piercing stare.

"Who is this?" Rachel asked, waving the picture at the commodore.

"What?" The commodore spun round. "Oh, that. That's my son, Hilary. Or, rather, was my son…"

Rachel felt as though she had put her foot in it. "Oh, I'm really sorry, is he…?"

"Oh no, he's not dead. Nothing like that. I just don't have much to do with him these days." The commodore glanced down at the photograph. "He changed rather a lot after that." The old man cleared his throat loudly and Rachel could have sworn that she saw his eyes moisten momentarily. Then he cleared his throat again.

"Tea," he barked, and marched out of the room.

Rachel and Adam followed him down another passage into a dusty room, with wall to wall bookshelves crammed with leather-backed books. More books were piled on the floor and a large brass telescope on a stand pointed out of the window. Glass cases held fragments of rock and fossil, and over a large mahogany desk covered in documents and maps, a striking oil portrait of the commodore in Air Force uniform kept watch over the room.

Adam was fascinated. Telescopes, maps, archaeological finds: this was the kind of room he *really* wanted a good look at. However, the commodore seemed to have no intention of letting him delve and continued on through the room, barking "study", as he closed the door behind them.

The kitchen was down a further set of stairs towards the back of the house: a dark, cavernous room lined with cream tiles and with copper pans hanging from the ceiling. "Tea," the commodore said again, as if he had run out of anything else to say. "It's Mrs Vine's afternoon off, I'm afraid, otherwise she'd make it." He wandered off into a big pantry, muttering about teabags.

"Shall I put the kettle on?" Rachel called. She felt like she should try to be helpful and didn't bother waiting for an answer. As water poured into the kettle from a spluttering tap over the sink, Rachel saw a wooden door that appeared to lead out into the back courtyard. She noticed that hanging from a rusty hook screwed deep into the wood was a large steel key.

Rachel put the kettle on the hob. She checked to see that Adam was looking elsewhere, and that the commodore was still busy in the pantry. Then, for reasons she did not

15

Rachel's head throbbed with guilt at what she had just done, as she and Adam wheeled their newly repaired bikes down the long driveway away from Waverley Hall. Her knees felt weak as, over and over again, she examined her own motivation for taking the key and, again and again, drew a blank.

Adam was puzzled by Rachel's mental turmoil, which he could almost feel himself, but had no clue as to its cause.

"Hey, there's Gabriel," Adam called out, breaking the mood momentarily. In the distance, half obscured by the railings at the main gate, Rachel could see the figure of Gabriel waiting for them near the entrance.

Rachel and Adam pushed their bikes past the huge iron gates of the hall and back out into the lane. Gabriel stood patiently on the other side of the road, as if not daring to step over the threshold of the estate.

It seemed as though he were not so much coming to meet them, as waiting for them to come to him.

Gabriel's face betrayed no emotion. He looked neither pleased to see them, nor particularly angry that they had missed their appointment at the circle.

"I'm sorry we didn't make it," Rachel said. "We had an accident."

"It's OK," Gabriel replied, turning and walking down the lane. Rachel and Adam followed.

"We were on our way up to the circle and we got knocked off our bikes…" Rachel said, trying to fill in the details. She wasn't sure whether Gabriel was angry with them or not.

"And the commodore guy took us back to Waverley Hall," Adam said, as if to endorse Rachel's story.

Gabriel stopped suddenly in the middle of the lane and turned to look at them. "Did you get the key?" he asked. Rachel's mouth opened wide as she gasped. A grin spread across Gabriel's face.

"What key?" Adam said, looking confused. Then he saw the look on Rachel's face. "What key, Rachel?"

Rachel delved deep in the pocket of her shorts and pulled out the large steel key she had taken half an hour earlier.

"You *stole* a key? From *him*?" Adam asked incredulously. He jerked his thumb back at the hall, imagining the heap of trouble that would be dumped on them should the commodore find out. "You must be…"

Rachel held up her hand to silence her brother, all the time fixing Gabriel with her eyes, remembering how she thought she had heard his voice through the train window.

How she had felt compelled to take the key from the door.

It was suddenly clear to her. "You're like us," she said.

Gabriel smiled his agreement.

"What do you mean, he's like us?" Adam demanded. "He's not American…"

"No, Adam," Rachel said calmly. "He's like you and me … you know how we can sometimes feel what the other one is thinking, influence each other's thoughts?"

"That's our secret," Adam said, looking betrayed.

"No," Rachel said. "He can do it too. Look at him. Can't you see?"

Adam turned to Gabriel, his features twisted into an expression of defiance that barely masked the hurt.

"I'm a friend," Adam heard Gabriel say, before he realized that Gabriel hadn't said anything at all. That he had spoken to Adam just using his mind.

Adam looked at Rachel and she nodded; she had heard it too.

Gabriel held out his hand to Adam. Looking straight into Gabriel's eyes, Adam took it, and, by shaking hands, accepted that the three of them shared a very special bond.

"Right," Gabriel said. "What are you two doing later on?"

Supper seemed to take for ever as Granny Root doled out endless spoonfuls of shepherd's pie, insisting that the twins detail the events of the afternoon. Adam splashed large dollops of the brown sauce from the bottle that had been put

out on the table on to his plate. The vinegary sauce seemed
to make the pie taste much better. Actually made it taste of
something.

Rachel patiently explained how Commodore Wing had
narrowly missed them. How – Fred, was it? – had fixed their
bikes. How the commodore had taken them to the hall in
case they needed a doctor.

"Were you looking where you were going?" their grandmother asked.

Celia Root had implied, by her response, that the near
collision had been their fault.

Adam immediately became defensive. "He was driving
way too fast. He didn't see us, then he shouted at us."

"I think he was shocked, Adam," Rachel said, defending
the commodore's instant reaction. By saying something pos-
itive, she had hoped to alleviate her own guilt for stealing the
key. It didn't work.

"Oh yes, dear," Granny Root agreed. "Gerry Wing's a
sweetie underneath it all. He's just very used to issuing com-
mands to people. He's been very good to me over the years.
Of course he's in a lot of pain with his leg…"

Of all the words that Rachel could think of to describe
Commodore Wing, "sweetie" was not one of them. And neither was "Gerry".

"So his leg … is it wooden?" Adam asked, his curiosity getting the better of him.

His grandmother laughed out loud. "Wooden? He's not a

pirate, darling. Of course not. I think it was metal when he first lost it. But now they make them very lifelike. Plastic, I think."

Now that the subject had been broached, Rachel wanted more. "So how did he lose it, Gran?"

Celia took a deep breath, and for a split second Rachel saw a look pass over her grandmother's face that could have been admiration, sympathy or something else.

"There was a terrible accident," she said. "His wife died."

Rachel suddenly saw the face of the handsome woman in the flyer's uniform. The *black* frame on top of the piano.

"It was terribly sad," Granny Root said thickly. She stared into the distance for a few moments before suddenly gathering the empty plates together, signalling the end of supper, and wheeling her chair away from them towards the sink.

Rachel threw a look at Adam, then got up to help.

They washed the dishes in silence and afterwards Granny Root trundled away to watch television. "It's *Treasure Hunters*," she called out from the sitting room. "I never miss it…"

Rachel and Adam politely joined their grandmother in front of the television. Rachel listened to the enthusiastic tones of the TV archaeologist as he tramped across a rainy British field: waving his arms about and explaining where the Romans had once been; looking out for ridges and dips in the landscape that gave him clues.

Adam seemed interested enough, listening intently as his

grandmother added her own commentary to the programme, but Rachel was unable to settle, or concentrate on the facts the presenter was outlining.

Butterflies of anticipation fluttered around her stomach as she stared at the screen. She knew, as soon as her grandmother went off to bed, that she would be looking for clues of her own.

16

Less than one hour later, Rachel and Adam were
standing in the near darkness, just inside the
entrance gates of Waverley Hall.

Granny Root had announced her usual, early bedtime
soon after *Treasure Hunters* had finished. Adam had helped
her through to the downstairs bedroom and the twins had
breathed a collective sigh of relief before grabbing torches
and slipping out by the back door.

They had not seen a single soul as they'd cut across from
the garden over the field, or as they'd stolen through long
pools of shadow past the pub where, as Gabriel had
promised them, the commodore's old red Bentley was still
parked outside.

Now, as they stood hidden from the road by the gatehouse,
there was nobody to be seen near the grounds of Waverley.
Least of all Gabriel, who had promised to meet them there.

Adam's teeth began to chatter, not because it was particularly cold, but because his nerves were beginning to get

hold of him. His hand deep in his pocket, he turned over the coin that Jacob Honeyman had given him. He took it out and flipped it; looked at it in the dying light.

Heads. A good sign, perhaps.

It was against Adam's better judgement that they were here at all, about to snoop around the cavernous house while nobody was home. Somehow, walking back that afternoon, Gabriel had convinced the twins that exploring the house was a good idea, that it would reveal some of the secrets of the village. Rachel had momentarily wondered why it was so important to find out more about the circle and the village, but Gabriel had impressed upon her his need to find something, a truth, a revelation that might change all their lives.

Rachel had been persuaded by Gabriel's calm and gentle manner and suddenly creeping around a spooky old manor-house in the dark had seemed like the best idea in the world. Adam had been more reluctant, wondering if Gabriel had somehow managed to hypnotize them both, but found himself agreeing to the plan all the same. Gabriel had flattered them; had told them that he could only do it with their help. After all Rachel had got him the key, hadn't she?

They were already in deep.

Rachel looked up at the cloudless night sky. The patterns of the main constellations twinkled clearly above her head. One star appeared to flare brighter than the rest, then faded to a speck of light. Rachel watched for a moment as the light died, and wondered whether Gabriel would turn up at all.

Just as the doubt was taking shape in her mind she turned her head to see Gabriel peering at her, his face close to her own, his green eyes almost luminous in the twilight.

"Whoa, you freaked me out," Adam whispered hoarsely at Gabriel. "Where did you come from?"

Gabriel pointed upward towards the roof of the gate-house. "Up there. Just wanted to make sure the coast was clear."

Rachel looked round and turned her face upward again towards the sky. It was as clear as it was ever going to be. She looked at Gabriel, who smiled reassuringly.

"Ready?" he asked.

Moments later they found themselves at the back of the hall, crossing a flagstoned yard to the back of the house by the kitchen steps. Adam shone his torch at the kitchen window while Rachel tried the door. It opened easily into the darkened kitchen and the three of them crept in.

"He probably hasn't missed the key at all," Adam whispered, as much to himself as the others. "No harm done."

"Do you know which way the room with the books and the telescope is?" Gabriel said, without bothering to lower his voice. Rachel and Adam flinched at the noise, wondering how Gabriel knew about the study.

"This way," Rachel said, pointing out of the kitchen with her torch to the back stairs.

The study door was closed and Gabriel stepped forward to

open it, pushing as the bottom caught against the carpet on the other side. He walked into the darkened room and Rachel and Adam followed him.

Gabriel snapped on a desk lamp, which suddenly cast deep shadows across the study, illuminating the stern features of the commodore, who stared down from the portrait on the wall. Rachel felt herself gulp. It was almost as if the man himself were watching them. Gabriel, however, had no such qualms. "It's just a picture," he said.

Adam stared at the picture. He didn't look so sure.

"Did he show you any ... maps or anything?"

Adam shook his head. Commodore Wing had been at pains to whisk them through this room, without letting them look at anything much.

Gabriel set about leafing through the documents that were strewn on the desk, unrolling a tube of yellowed parchment covered in small, scratchy handwriting.

"What are you looking for?" Rachel asked.

"Not sure till I find it. But I think you'd call it a survey map or something."

Rachel peered round the room, closely scrutinizing one or two framed prints on the wall that appeared to detail the landscape of the surrounding area. "Any of these?" she said.

Gabriel shook his head. "This one won't be on show," he said. He set about searching with renewed vigour: pulling books from the shelves, opening drawers and rifling through the contents. Rachel and Adam exchanged a look. This can't be right, they were both thinking. What if someone were to come back?

Gabriel turned to look at them, reading their thoughts and stopping his search momentarily.

"Stop worrying," he said. "The old man'll be gone long enough."

Commodore Wing nudged his empty tankard back across the bar and got stiffly to his feet. He nodded, grunting a curt, "G'night," to Tom Hatcham, who was busy drying glasses.

Hatcham looked at the clock above the bar. "Early night, commodore?"

"Busy day," Commodore Wing answered. "Had Celia Root's grandchildren over at the hall earlier. Bit of a run-in with their bicycles."

"Oh yes?" Hatcham raised his eyebrows, curious to know more.

"Nice kids actually. Girl's charming. Very bright, like her mother. Boy didn't seem too bad, either. Don't think we'll have any trouble from them."

Hatcham appeared to think about it as he watched the commodore limp over to the door, followed by the massive figure of the Irish wolfhound.

"Hope not," he muttered to himself.

Slamming the bolts on the door, Hatcham heard the roar as the Bentley's engine was fired into life and the low purr as the car moved off into the night.

* * *

"I think this might be what we're looking for," Gabriel said.

He was holding up a thick, folded document, tied with a piece of string, that he had retrieved from a large wooden chest on the floor. On the outside of the vellum, drawn in ink, was an ornate version of the Triskellion.

Rachel looked round the study. Gabriel had moved books, letters, pictures and chairs in his efforts to find the map. The portrait of the commodore seemed to look down on them with increased ferocity at the chaos in the study. Rachel hurriedly began to tidy up, straightening furniture and closing drawers as Gabriel carefully unfolded the map.

Adam stopped his own feeble attempts at tidying and looked over Gabriel's shoulder. The map looked very old and was covered in dotted, inky lines that made continuous intersecting, circular patterns in an irregular grid.

Like Triskellions within Triskellions.

"It's the village," Adam said. "This must have been made hundreds of years ago." All he could see of the village they knew was the moor with the chalk circle, the church and what looked like a small settlement of huts where Waverley Hall now stood.

Where *they* now stood…

"Rachel, check this out," Adam said, turning to his sister.

"It can wait till later," she replied briskly. "Look, help me to clean up, will you? We can't leave anything out of place."

Suddenly a door slammed near by. Inside the house.

Rachel and Adam froze for an instant, staring helplessly at each other. What should they do? Hide?

Run...?

Before either of them had a chance to decide on the best option, the door of the study crashed open and the commodore stood framed in the doorway. At his side, the huge wolfhound strained at the leash, growling and baring his fangs.

The commodore was pointing a shotgun.

He bellowed at them in a voice that would have struck terror into a parade ground of battle-hardened servicemen.

"What the bloody hell do you think you two are doing?"

In the split second before she burst into tears, Rachel registered the word "two". She was already starting to shake as she turned her head.

Gabriel had completely disappeared.

17

Celia Root seemed immune to her granddaughter's sobs, raising a hand to demand silence and refusing to look at her.

Rachel felt as if a veil had been lifted. As soon as the commodore had discovered them in his house, the scales had fallen from her eyes and she'd seen clearly how stupid she had been. She'd cried as the commodore had bundled Adam and herself into the Bentley and continued to weep all the way back to Root Cottage.

It was not just about being discovered breaking into Waverley Hall. Somehow, all the tensions and fears of the previous days, weeks – months even – seemed to be pouring out of her. Her face had quickly turned puffy with tears and red with undeniable guilt.

Adam said nothing, his head hung in shame, as Commodore Wing paced around the sitting room of Root Cottage.

"I can't believe it. Leave the damn house empty for a

couple of hours and this happens. I'm absolutely furious, Celia."

Rachel raised her head a little to see her frail grandmother. Wearing a floral dressing gown and supporting herself shakily against the back of a chair, Celia Root's eyes darted around the room, unable to settle upon anything, least of all the three other occupants of the room. Rachel sobbed harder as she saw the terrible shame carved deep across her grandmother's face.

"I don't know what to say, Gerald, I really don't," Celia Root spoke in a hoarse whisper, staring intently at the floor.

"And as for this cock and bull story about the boy leaving his music pod or whatever it is…" the commodore shouted, waving his arms about.

Rachel took a deep breath. "It's not true," she said.

Adam stared fiercely at her. "Rachel…"

"It's not true that we left something behind." She sucked in another breath, fighting the urge to sob again. "We were just … curious."

Granny Root and Commodore Wing looked at Rachel.

"Curious enough to break into someone's house and go through their private affairs?" Commodore Wing demanded.

Adam looked up, the fierce tone of the old man's voice bringing him to the verge of tears. It hadn't been his idea. He'd been against it. It was Gabriel's fault. Adam wasn't going to take the rap; he'd tell them about Gabriel. Rachel looked at her brother and guessed what he was about to do.

She gathered a little courage and decided that a small attack might be the best form of defence.

"No," Rachel said. "That was really, really stupid, and we're really sorry. But, you know, we've only been here a few days and already we've been beaten up and nearly run over. People have been kind of weird to us, when Mom said we'd be welcome here. Not exactly the friendliest place, is it? It's like everyone's hiding things from us. We just wonder what the big deal is, you know?" She tried to hold the commodore's gaze, but faltered after a few seconds, and sobbed again.

Adam raised his head a little, amazed at his sister's nerve. Commodore Wing looked at Celia Root, his eyes widening.

"Well, I'm sorry if we haven't hung out all the flags for your arrival, dear," the old woman said. "We tend not to make such a hoo-hah about things over here. I thought Kate ... I thought your *mummy* might have explained..."

Commodore Wing held up his hand. The fire seemed to have gone out of his rant and he almost looked sorry for Rachel. Her impassioned speech appeared to have moved him. "Well, you're lucky we haven't taken it any further," he said. "Nobody's hurt, I suppose. Perhaps that tumble this afternoon has shaken you up a bit. Good night's sleep should do the trick. I'm sure you won't do it again."

Granny Root was more amazed than anyone at the commodore's sympathetic tone. She'd seen him in a rage before and they didn't usually subside as quickly as this. She seized the moment.

"I think you should be very grateful that Commodore Wing has taken such a charitable view. It's really very reasonable of him, considering that you have behaved like common burglars. I cannot tell you how ashamed I am." She pressed a crumpled tissue to her eye for added emphasis. "Now, I suggest you apologize and get out of my sight." She thrust out a shaky arm and pointed a bent finger towards the staircase.

Rachel stepped forward. "I really am very sorry, commodore. It certainly won't happen again."

Commodore Wing nodded.

Adam did the same. "Sorry, sir…"

In turn, the twins leant down to kiss their grandmother's proffered cheek, inhaling the distinctive smell of powder and peppermints, before instinctively reaching for one another's hands and climbing slowly up the stairs to bed.

Celia Root looked across at Gerald Wing, who pursed his lips in thought. "I really can't apologize enough, Gerry," she said. "I think we could *both* do with a drink."

"I'll do it," he said, limping over to the corner table and reaching for a bottle.

"I can't thank you enough for taking a sympathetic view."

"Well, doesn't do to make too much of a drama out of it, eh?"

Celia Root took the glass that the commodore was offering. "No, quite. I do think that the awful business of Kate, of the divorce and so on… Well, it might explain their behaviour a bit. But I must still punish them somehow."

"Hmm," said the commodore, taking a gulp of his drink. "I think we should probably drop it. We wouldn't want them to think we *did* have something to hide." He drained his glass and looked directly at Celia Root. "Would we?"

To say that Rachel was surprised to see Gabriel sitting in the wicker chair in the corner of the bedroom would have been an understatement. Adam was too furious to wonder at it. Still smarting from their dressing down and their own humiliating apology, he was ready to vent his anger and batter Gabriel's head against the rose pattern on the wall behind him. The calm smile on Gabriel's face did nothing to dissuade Adam, and Rachel had to grab her brother firmly by the arm to restrain him.

"Where did you go? What are you doing here?" Rachel hissed, as angry as her brother, but less inclined to violence.

"Yes, sorry about that," Gabriel said calmly. "There would have been big trouble if he'd found *me* there."

"Oh, right," Adam spat back. "So finding us there was no trouble at all?"

Rachel hushed her brother. "Sssh. They might hear downstairs."

Gabriel sat up straighter in the chair. "Well, think about it. You got a mild telling off, but then didn't you see how he backed down? Whether you *think* you are or not, you're one of *them*. Both of you. You're protected, which is why

I need your help. Because I'm not."

Rachel had never felt less protected in her life. But she knew that Gabriel was right. The old man had backed down and become surprisingly forgiving. In thinking about it, Rachel completely forgot to ask how on earth Gabriel had come to be in their bedroom.

Gabriel smiled widely at the twins. From behind him on the chair he pulled out the thick, folded map he had found in the study at Waverley Hall and waved it at them. "Fancy a treasure hunt tomorrow?"

Rachel and Adam were not sure that they did.

"Come on," Gabriel said. "Just to see if this map still makes any sense."

"I guess we could," Rachel said.

Adam scoffed. "Right, if we're not totally grounded."

Rachel nodded. Her brother had a good point. "Anyhow, where would you start?"

Gabriel unfolded the map and laid it out on the floor in front of him. He pointed to a spot across the moor where a large bee had been drawn in black ink and carefully painted with yellow stripes.

Gabriel looked up at the twins. "Tell me about the man who looks after the bees," he said. "*He'll* know."

18

The sun sets over the moor, throwing the three figures into silhouette and casting long shadows that stretch across the chalk circle. Two of the figures hold hands as they stand in front of the third. The third is taller, black-faced and beaky in profile, hooded in a long cloak, like a huge bird of prey.

It is a ceremony.

The cloaked figure holds out a book in front of the couple, a man and a young girl. A beam of orange sunlight glints off the pointed helmet of the man as he unlinks hands. He produces a glowing, metallic Triskellion, which he places on the book.

The hooded man grasps the object in his right hand and holds it out to the girl, who links her fingers through the blades of the golden amulet. The man in the helmet does the same. The two are joined, with the blessing of the third who mutters an unintelligible incantation. The Triskellion glows and the three remove their hands, leaving the amulet hovering gently in *midair. It begins to spin slowly, then quicker, until it is no more than a blurring golden light that then rises, hovering momentarily over their heads before shooting off into the red sky.*

The hooded man kneels to kiss the ground at their feet, then raises himself.

The girl turns to look at the man.

She smiles, she looks radiant.

She looks like Rachel...

Try as she might, Rachel couldn't shake off the disturbing dream as she trudged across the spongy moor towards Honeyman's cottage the following morning. Disturbing, but also oddly thrilling, now that it was obvious that the girl in the dreams was her. Sure, the brain plays strange tricks, she told herself, but her brain must have placed her in the vision for a reason. Dreams always meant something, didn't they? It was weird, but also ... romantic.

Rachel stopped, realizing that, deep in thought, she had marched ahead of the others. She turned to see Gabriel, some distance behind, setting his own languid pace, as always. Adam ambled along beside him, sulkily. He had not wanted to meet Gabriel at all, but when they had found they hadn't been grounded, and were more or less ejected from the cottage after breakfast, he'd had little choice. There wasn't a lot else *to* do, after all. Gabriel had been there, waiting for them at the gate, smiling; as though there'd been no doubt in his mind that they would turn up.

As they marched across the moor, Rachel could hear that Gabriel was speaking softly to Adam, reassuring him, persuading him.

"It'll be fine, you'll see," he said. "You're not in trouble. You can't let a couple of old people tell you what to do. This is a great adventure. Your *life* is a great adventure."

Rachel listened to Gabriel's soft monotone, thinking how hypnotic his voice was. How his words seemed to wash gently over you, making you feel better, however bad things were. And by the time the boys caught up, Adam's mood *did* seem to have lifted.

When they arrived at the beekeeper's cottage, Gabriel stopped and winked at Rachel. She felt herself redden; felt beads of sweat breaking out between her shoulder blades.

Jacob Honeyman broke into a broad smile as he threw open the door to his shack and saw the twins standing under the corrugated tin porch. As Rachel and Adam stood slightly apart to reveal Gabriel standing behind them, the colour drained from the beekeeper's face.

"This is Gabriel," Rachel said.

Honeyman's jaw hung slackly as he continued staring at the boy, unable to speak a word. Rachel coughed and the beekeeper seemed to rally a little. "Hullo," he said. "I thought you'd come one day."

Rachel looked at her brother and screwed up her brow in silent question, but Honeyman's exact meaning was lost in one of his sudden explosions of coughs and twitches and a furious bout of scratching.

"You'd better come in," he said.

Jacob Honeyman sat watching Gabriel's every move in dumb amazement, while the boy unfolded the map on the table. As Gabriel flattened the vellum out, Honeyman stood up and looked over the drawn landscape, his finger hovering over the various landmarks – the chalk circle, the ancient church – then tracing out patterns with his finger where the map was covered with the intersecting lines.

"Where did you get this from?" Honeyman whispered in awe. "I didn't know this existed."

"They've been looking after it for us at the big house," Gabriel said.

Rachel looked over at her brother, the question obvious in her bemused expression.

Honeyman drew his finger back towards where the bee was marked on the map. "This is where we are … this is where my ancestors were … what seven hundred years ago when this was drawn."

"This is where all our ancestors were," Gabriel said.

"All our ancestors?" Adam asked.

"All our ancestors," Gabriel repeated. "The beekeepers have been here for many centuries, and your family … your grandmother's family, the Roots, have been here as long as the Wings."

Suddenly it became clear to Adam: the knowledge that he

and Rachel did belong here; the confidence that this place was as much theirs as anyone else's. That this strange little village was as much a part of their make-up as New York was. Maybe more so, seeing as their family would have been here long before any Europeans lived in America. A large part of what made the twins who they were, of their own genes, originated on this very spot.

As if picking up on Adam's thought, Gabriel continued, "My family too … even though we've travelled about. This was the first place they settled. This was where they started families." He waved his hand over the map, and as he did so, a stray bee flew in from Honeyman's kitchen and landed squarely on top of the bee that had been drawn in the right-hand corner.

"What are the chances of that happening?" Adam laughed, then stopped abruptly when he saw that the other three had fallen silent. They watched the bee intently as it was joined by another. Then another, and another. In total, thirty or forty bees flew in from the kitchen or through the open window and landed on the map.

They watched, holding their breaths, as the bees, far from crawling randomly over the map, began to marshal themselves into formation behind the first, largest bee, their tails buzzing from side to side.

"It's a waggle dance," Honeyman whispered.

"A what dance?" Rachel asked, not taking her eyes from the bees. They were now forming a ragged, vibrating line.

"A waggle dance. They use it to pass each other information – about where nectar is, or anything else they need to find. They use it to navigate, too. The speed and the angle of waggle relates to the distance and direction of the prize." Honeyman pointed. "The big one, *there* … he's the forager. He knows where the stuff is and conveys the information to the others."

They continued to watch in amazement as the bees, like a miniature tribe dancing a sacred ritual, crawled across the map, following the dotted lines that were traced faintly on the surface. They buzzed between the chalk circle, the church and a point in the woods marked by the drawing of a tree with a twisted trunk. After three or four circuits, a shape began to emerge, and the three points on the map were gradually linked together by a continuous pattern of bees.

"Whoa," Adam sighed. "Some trick."

"I don't think it's a trick," Rachel said. "I think they're mapping something out for us. Like they're trying to tell us…" She looked across at Gabriel, who was nodding gently. "Tell us what?"

"Well, they're marking three points between the church, the circle and the woods … and you can see the pattern they're making." Gabriel looked from Adam to Rachel. "Can't you figure it out?"

Rachel and Adam remained silent. Stumped.

Suddenly in an explosion of coughs and twitches, Honeyman jumped to his feet, breaking the silence. "It's telling us where the missing bits of the Triskellion are," he said. "The golden Triskellion." He was panting with excitement, pacing around the room and clutching nervously at the collar of his grubby jacket. "We know one's in the church … this is telling us where the other parts are. I've spent thirty odd years reading, researching, digging and metal detecting … and in the end the bees done it."

"Well, the bees did it with the map," Gabriel added. "And we wouldn't have the map without Rachel and Adam. And Rachel and Adam might not have been quite so enthusiastic if you hadn't sparked their interest. So let's just call it teamwork, shall we?"

"But why is finding these bits so important?" Rachel asked. "I still don't get it."

Honeyman huffed impatiently. "If we put this artefact back together, it will be one of the … no, *the* most important pre-Saxon artefact in the country." Honeyman folded his arms with finality, then thought again. "The most important artefact in the world." Honeyman nodded thoughtfully, grinning and jabbing his finger towards Gabriel. "And he's the one who can get it. I know he is."

"I like to think of it as restoring the family jewels," Gabriel said. "Well, the family jewels of the village at any rate."

"I still don't get it," Adam said.

Gabriel put a hand on Adam's arm, looked at each of them in turn before he spoke. "What do you think? Shall we go and find them?"

19

Hilary Wing opened the front door to his lodge. It was a small, red-brick building buried deep in Waverley Woods that had been used as shelter for the large Victorian shooting parties that once gathered on the estate. Hilary Wing looked none too pleased to see that he had a visitor, and fixed him with the full glare of his cold, blue eyes.

"Morning, Hilary," Tom Hatcham said, adopting the deferential tone he used to speak to Hilary and his father. It was difficult to tell whether he meant it or not.

"What is it, Tom?" Hilary Wing pulled the door closed behind him. He rarely let people into the lodge and walked several steps away from the building to speak to the publican.

"I just heard that the hall's been broken into."

"What?" Hilary snapped.

"Well, yes, I just seen Mrs Vine in the village and she said that the commodore, your father, had told Fred to change the locks, and—"

"Spit it out, Tom. I *know* he's my father and I don't want the bloody village gossip. Tell me what happened. Is anything missing?"

"Too early to tell, but it was them kids. The American ones … and the funny one. Mrs Vine seen the three of them walking up the drive." Hatcham flicked a nervous glance towards Hilary. He knew he wouldn't be pleased.

"The funny one? The weird gipsy kid? I thought you'd frightened him off days ago. You're not doing the job I pay you for."

"I did frighten him off, me and three others after we caught him on the church roof. Gave him a thick ear, so to speak. But it's like he's funny in the head or something; it's all water off a duck's back to him. Kid's not frightened of anything we say or do."

Hilary Wing stroked his beard, staring at the trees. "We'll see who's not frightened. And I think we know how to administer a short, sharp shock to our American visitors."

Hatcham nodded. "Sooner the better, if you ask me. They're snooping round the church and everywhere. Developed a keen interest in archaeology if you know what I mean. Old Bee-features has set 'em off."

"Digging about? I'll soon put them off that. The strange kid, though, might require more drastic measures. See if you can find out what's missing from the hall, will you? I'd ask the old boy myself, but, you know…"

Hatcham knew that Hilary no more wanted to talk to his

father than his father wanted to talk to him. He watched as Hilary turned away and went back into the lodge, shutting the door behind him without a goodbye or a backward glance.

The following lunchtime, having armed themselves with rucksacks, trowels, a compass and various tools, the twins gathered once again at Honeyman's shack. Gabriel was already waiting for them outside.

Honeyman had added to the work done by the bees, and there were sketches and calculations scribbled on pieces of paper scattered all over the floor. On the map itself there were bits of cotton tied to pins and lines had been drawn on tracing paper laid over the original document.

Honeyman pointed to a spot right in the middle of Waverley Woods. "You want to start looking about here," he said, stabbing a finger at a clump of three trees that had been illustrated on the map.

"I hope it's nowhere near that encampment we saw," Adam said, shuddering at the memory of the beating they had witnessed.

"No, no," Jacob said. He waved his finger over another part of the map. "All the crusties and hippies gather over the other side, near the new pine growth."

"Crusties?" Rachel asked, unfamiliar with the word.

"We call them crusties, I suppose, because they live outdoors a lot. Camping, living in tree houses and what have you, so they don't wash much."

Rachel looked at the circle of grime around Jacob Honeyman's frayed shirt collar. The comments about personal hygiene were a little rich coming from him.

"Do they actually live in the woods?" Adam asked.

"Some do, but mostly they move around, going to music festivals and celebrating the solstice. Mind you, they protest about new roads being built across old land, so they're not all bad."

"What was the second thing you said?" Rachel asked.

"Solstice? There's one in the winter and one in the summer. It's when the sun is either furthest from or nearest to the earth."

"Like the longest and shortest days of the year?" Adam asked.

"Exactly," said Jacob. "The longest and shortest days, which were worshipped by the ancient druids as the beginning and end of the seasons. A lot of our monuments, like Stonehenge and even our own chalk circle, were put there to line up with the sun at the solstices."

"So what exactly do these crusty guys do?" Adam asked.

"They do whatever Hilary Wing tells them."

"*Hilary Wing?*"

"D'you know him?"

"Well, I've seen a picture," Rachel said.

"Well, he's their leader and he fancies himself as a bit of a shaman or high priest or whatever, and he winds them up to believe that they're all descendants of the druids and that they should worship the sun and suchlike. They uphold the old traditions of woodcraft and witchcraft, and all that nonsense. So, at the solstice, he rounds them all up and they worship round the Triskellion as the sun goes down. Then they dance about like nutters and get drunk as farts mostly."

Honeyman grinned and rolled his eyes, but Adam and Rachel remembered the man with the blackened face in the woods. The power that he had had over his fellow wooddwellers. Now they knew that the charismatic man was Hilary Wing himself.

"So you don't believe in any of that stuff?" Adam asked.

"I believe in archaeology," Jacob said decisively. "I believe in what I can see, what I can dig up, evidence of what's actually been here." Honeyman put his hand firmly on Gabriel's shoulder. "And I believe in what I can touch, what I can hold in my hand."

Gabriel, who had been sitting in silence since they'd arrived at the shack, looked up at Honeyman and smiled.

"Keep believing," he said.

At the edge of the woods, Gabriel held up Jacob's newly drawn map and attempted to plot where they stood. Rachel looked over his shoulder and laughed.

"You're holding it upside down," she said, pushing him in a friendly way and snatching the map. "Look, I think we're about here." She pointed to a spot where field and wood came together.

"Navigation was never my strong point," Gabriel said.

Adam was studying the compass. "So if we walk through the woods in a straight line from here, towards the east…"

"I think we should spread out and walk in three straight lines," Gabriel said. "That way, we have three times the chances of finding the tree with the twisted trunk, if that's where we're supposed to start digging. We can meet up in the centre of the woods later on."

"No way." Adam jumped in quickly, then regretted his haste. "I mean, these woods are really big, we'll just get lost."

"I agree with Adam," Rachel said. "We almost got lost before."

"Fine," Gabriel said. "You two go together from here, I'll start two hundred paces round the outer path to the south and I'll meet you in the middle."

"How will we know when we're there?" Rachel wound a lock of hair round her index finger, betraying her nerves.

"If Jacob's right, it'll be obvious. We'll just know." Gabriel gave a small wave and set off. Rachel looked at Adam, who shrugged, and together they took their first tentative steps into the crackling undergrowth of the woods.

Jacob Honeyman had two reasons for not joining Rachel, Adam and Gabriel on the first leg of their dig. Firstly, he saw this initial outing as more of a reconnaissance mission, un-likely to uncover anything straight away. He would join the kids later on with trowel and metal detector once they'd established a few more clues.

Secondly, since the phones had come back on for the first time in days, he had some catching up to do. He had research of his own to be getting on with.

He waited what seemed like an age for the old, grimy PC to boot up. There was a long series of buzzes, clicks and boings, and, once the mail window had launched, he began to compose his latest mail.

Dear Mr Chris Dalton,

Many apologies for my delay in contacting you again, but the telephones have been down here for a while. Modern technology, eh?!

Neither do I want to entrust such an important correspondence to the hands of the Royal Mail, as post is always going missing here and you never know who might be reading it.

In short, things have moved on down here since we last spoke. There have been some very interesting new developments since the abundance of coins I told you about. I have made another important discovery and there is a new lead in the search for the missing pieces of the Bronze Age amulet that sparked your interest in the first place (my email of September last).

I would explain more, but I think things

are best kept until we meet, don't you?
Thank God you're the sort of person who
really understands how important all this
is. I feel like I know you already, and I
know you'll do right by us.

How are your efforts to get permission to
dig going? Good, I hope. Once you get all
the legal stuff sorted, I'm sure some of
the stick-in-the-muds down here will realize
that it's not what's on the surface that
counts (which is really just dirt and chalk)
but what lies beneath...

All the best,

J. Honeyman

Jacob entered the address in the box at the top of the mail window: chrisdalton@treasurehunterTV.com.

He pressed "send" then waited, rocking back and forth in his chair, watching the development of the progress bar then marvelling as his email shot out into the ether.

He wandered through to the kitchen and pulled out a celebratory can of beer from the fridge.

He had good reason to be excited, and hopeful.

But he'd lived in this village all his life, so he knew that he also had very good reason to be afraid.

20

Adam held the compass in a shaft of sunlight that cut through the dense tree canopy overhead. As the needle swung and settled, he pointed out a track that headed east. Though it was clearly a path, it was one that had not been trodden regularly for some time, with ferns and spiky brambles tangled across it, and it snaked away into darkness where the forest grew denser.

Rachel and Adam hesitated a moment as they considered their options. The wood was unnaturally quiet, save for the faint humming of bees somewhere over their heads and the noise of other insects rattling and clicking in the undergrowth. By now they had reached that part of the wood rarely penetrated by sunlight, and the damp forest floor smelled rotting and musty.

"Creepy, isn't it?" Rachel said. "Why does Gabriel always insist on doing everything differently?"

"Wish your Gabriel was here to protect you, do you?"

Rachel punched her brother in the arm. "He's not *my* Gabriel."

Adam winced and rubbed his arm. Rachel always punched hard and he knew there would be a bruise later. "Anyway, I'm glad he's not here. He always gets us into trouble."

"Like we can't do that for ourselves?" Rachel's sarcasm was wasted on her brother, who was already pointing the compass at the two other available paths.

"That one's definitely north ... and that one's south-east." He thought about it. "It's got to be *that* one." Adam nodded again at the tangled path ahead. "We'll need some sticks."

Moments later, Rachel and Adam were swishing long branches across their path, battering back the foliage in front of them. The ferns fell back easily, allowing them to move forward, but the prickly brambles were more tenacious, snapping back at them, scratching their hands and pricking their legs through their jeans. After several attempts, they found that the best way of making progress was by one of them beating down an area, then allowing the other to step over it while holding back the brambles with the stick. Progress was slow and, in the damp air of the wood, they were quickly tired and sweaty and it wasn't long before they had to take a break.

They found a small clearing beneath a large chestnut tree. Rachel looked at Adam's reddened face, his hair plastered to his forehead as he examined the scratches on his hands and attempted to pull a thorn from the flesh of his thumb.

"It doesn't hurt while you're actually doing it," he said. "But as soon as you stop everything stings."

Rachel nodded her agreement. She was keenly aware of the stinging prickles on her legs, hot and sticky beneath her jeans. She guessed that her face was every bit as red as Adam's and the sweat was clammy on her neck. She felt as if hundreds of the tiny insects disturbed by their progress were crawling all over her. As the idea took hold in Rachel's mind, she felt compelled to scratch urgently at her head, her scalp tingling. She pushed her fingers hard through her thick hair, feeling the instant relief as her short fingernails scraped the skin underneath, finding small bits of twig and bramble trapped in the tangles.

"Got it," Adam said, extracting the small barb from his thumb.

Rachel looked across to her brother, and saw something dark swoop towards her head. She screamed in surprise as the bird hit her and yelled at Adam.

"What is it?" Her hands flew instinctively to her head, and she felt something sharp stabbing at her fingers, as whatever had swept out of the sky clung to the matted curls of her hair.

"It's a crow," Adam shouted. "Keep still…"

But the more the bird tried to disentangle itself, the more Rachel shook her head in panic, and the more the crow's talons got caught up.

Adam opened his mouth to speak again, but froze as Rachel's shrill squeals of panic turned into a single, piercing howl of pain which ripped through the still of the forest.

Adam was screaming himself as he ran to help his sister, seeing the trickle of bright red blood running down her forehead into her eyes. He raised his hand towards the bird, which had now embedded its claws in Rachel's scalp. Rachel screamed again and tried desperately to blink away the blood from her eyes. Adam reached out towards the crow, which made an angry cawing sound at him and, as he made to pull it away, drove its large, black beak into the web of skin between his thumb and first finger.

Now Adam's howls of pain joined those of his sister as he clasped his bleeding hand. He dug quickly into his rucksack, pulling out one of the trowels they had brought to dig and raising it over Rachel's head.

"No, Adam!" Rachel screamed, her face streaked with blood and tears. "You'll kill me. Go and get help. Gabriel can't be far away."

Adam stood helpless, not knowing what to do.

"*Please*, get Gabriel…"

Adam, pained and panicked, repeated Rachel's cry. He shouted Gabriel's name at the top of his voice, before tearing off into the forest in the hope of finding someone who would know what to do.

"Gabriel!"

Adam pushed on through the forest, leaping over fallen logs and jumping clumps of tangled bramble. Behind him,

Rachel's voice grew gradually fainter, until he couldn't hear it at all, and his own voice had quickly become hoarse as he repeatedly shouted Gabriel's name.

He stopped momentarily, attempting to regain his breath, and realized suddenly that he had lost any sense of the direction in which he was headed. He wiped a grimy hand across his sweaty face and looked to his left and right. He wheeled round and looked back in the direction from which he had come. But the trees had closed behind him and he could not be sure from where he *had* come.

The wood was still and silent.

He called Rachel's name, terrified that not only had he failed to get his sister any help, but that now he had lost her as well. He should have stayed with her, he thought. Should have made another attempt at helping her. But he had panicked...

"Rachel! Gabriel!"

He could feel his sister's fear and pain every bit as much as he was feeling his own. He couldn't bear it for another second. He knew he had to do something and do it fast. He picked a direction at random and launched himself into the thick wood once again. He had to find Gabriel, or someone who could help him.

Quickly finding another, more established path, forking off to his left, Adam renewed his efforts. He ran as fast as the foliage would allow, until, on the far side of a line of thinning trees, he could make out a small, red-brick lodge.

There was a trickle of smoke coming from its chimney.

Adam cleared the trees and ran, his lungs bursting, up the muddy path to the lodge. He all but fell on the door, thumping it with his fist then rapping hard on the dull, brass Triskellion-shaped knocker…

Only a few hundred metres behind Adam – sight and sound obscured by dense woodland – Rachel lay sobbing, her head cradled in Gabriel's lap.

Gabriel tenderly wiped the blood, dirt and tears from her face with a tissue and ran his long fingers through the damp hanks of Rachel's hair.

"These birds are territorial," he said. "Maybe there are young near by. It just got tangled up…"

And as he worked, gently shushing her while the sobs died away, the pain seemed to ease from Rachel's wounds, and the cuts and scratches themselves seemed to fade beneath his hands.

Beside them, on the ground, its head twisted backwards, lay the broken corpse of a large crow.

21

The door of the lodge swung open and Adam found himself staring into a pair of piercing, pale blue eyes. With a sickening jolt of recognition he realized that they belonged to Hilary Wing. After what he had seen done to the Bacon boys, Adam almost turned and ran, but he was immediately disarmed by the man's friendly tone.

"Hi," Wing said. He was wearing the same long leather coat that Adam had seen from his hiding place in the trees. His eyes twinkled and his face folded into a warm smile.

"I need help," Adam shouted. "We got lost and…"

Hilary Wing watched Adam splutter, the smile still playing across his features. "Yes? You got lost?"

"And my sister got attacked by a bird." As soon as he'd blurted it out, Adam instantly regretted it. He knew how absurd, how unlikely, it must have sounded.

"Really?" Wing didn't look as though he thought it was remotely unlikely.

"We need to help her."

"Of course we do," Wing said. "Come in for a minute. I'll get some stuff together and we'll go look for her." He stepped back from the threshold and ushered Adam in.

Adam stepped in without a second thought. This man was clearly scary if you got on the wrong side of him, but he was being friendly enough now. Besides, Rachel was in trouble and it wasn't as if Adam had anywhere else to turn.

The door opened into a sitting room dominated by a wood-burning stove in front of which sat a big, battered leather sofa. The walls of the room were covered with rough wooden planks, like the inside of a log cabin. Smoky oil lamps lit up the antlers and animal skins that were mounted on the walls while a tatty stuffed fox stood on a long sideboard, teeth bared, a small rabbit trapped beneath its paw. From a shelf above, a stuffed owl looked down on a row of small animal skulls that were lined up on the mantelpiece, all covered in molten wax from the large candelabra perched over them.

"I won't be a moment," Wing said. "You're Celia Root's grandson, aren't you?"

"Do you know her?"

Something passed across Wing's face. "I do ... well, my father does at any rate. They've known each other a very long time." Whatever had changed his mood was gone as quickly as it had come and the smile returned. "I'm Hilary Wing, by the way."

Adam knew exactly who he was, of course, but grasped

the hand that was offered none the less. It felt as though Wing had broken his fingers when he shook it, and Adam wiggled them back to life as Wing fixed him with a stare that made Adam feel as if he was being asked to explain himself. Even though he thought that Hilary Wing was probably the last person he should talk to, he found himself gushing, eager to please.

"We got lost, me and Rachel. We were looking for the Triskellion thing…"

Wing laughed, low and easy. "I think you'll find it's that big chalk circle up on the moor. Not too difficult to find, really."

"No. A bit of the *gold* one, like the one in the church. There's a map…" Adam checked himself, remembering where the map had come from, and realizing how stupid he was to be babbling on like this.

Wing stopped what he was doing and looked at Adam. The smile was dying at the corners of his mouth. "A map?"

"Just this thing a friend of ours drew on tracing paper," Adam said, thinking on his feet. He moved back towards the door. "Listen, I think we should get back to my sister now."

Wing nodded, and disappeared through a yellow curtain printed with red elephants that hung in a doorway at the far side of the room. Adam waited, pacing anxiously around the room; feeling the seconds tick away and knowing that they needed to get out into the forest to help Rachel.

"Please can we hurry up?" he shouted. There was no answer from the next room.

He stared round at the stuffed animals, noticing the stubs of rolled-up cigarettes and unwashed glasses stained with red wine left carelessly about the place. He nervously drummed his fingers on the sideboard, aimlessly drawing a Triskellion in the dust on its dirty surface.

"What are you doing?"

Adam turned to see Wing standing behind him. He was carrying a shotgun.

"What's that for?"

"I use it to hunt," Wing said. "All sorts of wildlife around here." He broke the barrel and squinted down the tubes. "Now be a good chap and get me some cartridges, would you? There should be a bag hanging on the back of that door." He swung the barrel, gesturing towards a door in the corner.

Adam went over and with trembling fingers unbolted, then opened the door, while Wing polished the stock of the gun with a cloth. Just inside hung a green, military-style bag full of red, brass-capped cartridges. The door opened directly on to a brick staircase that descended steeply down into darkness and Adam balanced carefully as he tried to unhook the bag.

"Do you need all of these?" Adam asked. He tried to unhitch the bag which was caught around a coat hook.

"No," Wing said, and a second later the door crashed towards Adam with the force of a hard kick and slammed shut.

Plunged suddenly into darkness, Adam toppled momentarily, grabbing at the canvas strap of the bag for support, but losing his grip. He fell backwards down the brick stairs, hitting himself on the limewashed wall, before landing in a heap on the mud floor at the foot of the stairs.

Adam felt a sharp pain in his back and opened his eyes in the pitch black.

Nothing, save the stars that burst and faded before his eyes. He registered the sour tang of mildew in his nostrils and heard the bolt at the top of the stairs slide decisively shut.

22

Adam attempted to move…

Lying on the damp, earth floor, he felt a sharp pain in his ribs, where he must have hit something on the way down the stone stairs. Feeling was gradually returning to his legs, which were angled above him on the steps. He blinked, attempting to see through the darkness as his eyes adjusted. But he could still see nothing, nor hear anything but the rush of blood in his own ears.

He dragged himself into a sitting position and rubbed at his sore ribs, then staggered to his feet, wincing as he put weight on the ankle he had twisted as he fell. Supporting himself against the cold brick wall, Adam felt around for a light switch, but found none. He put one hand in front of the other, trying to find a corner: something to locate him, to allow him to build a mental picture of the room in which he was imprisoned.

As his hands edged along the wall, he began to realize that the room was round in shape, like a brick vault. Then his fingers slipped into a hole, or alcove of some sort. Holding on to the edge with one hand, Adam waved the other into the deep, dark cavity, making contact with something wooden … and hollow.

Adam drew his hand away sharply. What was it? A box? A box of *what*?

He continued round the wall and found another alcove, then another, equally spaced round the wall and all with wooden boxes inside. Adam dared not probe further to find out how big or long these boxes were, but putting his hand into the fourth alcove, he discovered a box that had no lid.

Adam steeled himself and tentatively put his fingers inside the box. He felt something, and recoiled, then, after taking a deep breath, put his hand inside again. Sticks? No … smoother, he thought.

Bones.

Adam pulled his hand away, his mind racing as he visualized himself surrounded by coffins piled high with rotting bodies. Was this some kind of mausoleum? Or did Hilary Wing regularly slaughter people and bury them down here?

He stepped back from the wall, his heart beating so hard that he could feel it banging against his ribs. He stood, stock-still, in the centre of the room with his eyes tightly shut and his arms clutched across his chest, hands balled into fists. As he tried to calm himself, Adam took deep, slow lungfuls of the peppery underground air, regulating his breathing until he felt a little calmer. Telling himself that they were just boxes, and that if they *were* bones inside, they were probably just the remains of animals. Taxidermy was clearly one of Hilary Wing's hobbies, after all.

One of his hobbies.

Adam didn't want to think about what some of the others might be.

Without thinking, he reached into his pocket and found the coin that Honeyman had given him. As he turned it over and over between thumb and finger, he began to banish the horrific images that his mind had conjured up and, slowly, another image began to form. With his eyes shut, Adam began to see a picture of the room around him as if it were fully lit, but in monochrome; as if it were night vision on a video camera.

He saw it clearly: bricked and circular, with alcoves that contained wooden boxes. He saw the stairs, twelve of them, leading back up into the lodge and he saw the earth floor at his feet. Reaching out, he found that the position of the alcoves and the steps related *exactly* to those in his mind's eye.

It was amazing.

Somehow – perhaps it had been the stress of the trauma, or the deep breathing and concentration – Adam could see in the dark with his eyes shut.

Amazing … and scary.

As he looked round, the black and white shapes in the cellar began to take on colours: the bricks, a dark brown mass, bluish round the edges where they were cooler; the niches in the wall glowing green, as if their relative heat or moisture level gave them a colour, like a thermal image.

Adam marvelled at his new-found vision for a moment. He waved his head around, eyes tightly shut, astonished at the variations in colour that the cellar projected, until he came to rest on what appeared to be a glowing orange disc on the wall ahead of him.

There was a blank section of wall in between the alcoves, where the pattern of bricks changed. There was an arch clearly visible, and the orange light glowed and shimmered like a full moon at its centre.

Adam took two steps forward and held his hand to the wall, touching the centre of the disc. It was warmer than the surrounding bricks. Suddenly he could feel an energy spreading into his hands and up his arms; could feel a strength pouring into them. He pushed at the circle and felt the brickwork shift under his hands. He leant his full bodyweight against it and shoved until, with a dull clunking sound, an area of wall gave way under the arched section of brickwork, and fell to the ground.

Adam stepped back from the cloud of dust and disintegrating mortar; tried to refocus his internal vision. The orange disc of light was still there, but was now hovering above a hole in the bricks almost as big as he was.

Adam thought for a moment. Tried to be rational.

There was no way he was going to escape by going back up the stairs into the lodge. The thick wooden door was heavily bolted, and he certainly didn't want to risk walking into anywhere where Hilary Wing was waving a gun about. He did not want to think too hard about what Hilary Wing might have in store for him, but he knew that if he stayed where he was, he would be a sitting duck.

And now there was a hole in the wall; a hole that looked suspiciously like the opening to a tunnel…

Adam pushed his head through the area of orange light and into the blackness. There was certainly a cavity there, but as he probed further with his arm, he could feel earth crumbling in front of him.

It smelt warm, damp and fertile.

Adam scratched at the soft earth with his hands. It fell away, creating a bigger hole still. As he felt the peaty soil crumble beneath his busy fingers, he pondered a moment and then stepped over the remaining bricks into the earth cavity and began to work faster.

Began to tunnel.

Gabriel supported Rachel with an arm round her waist and Rachel steadied herself against his shoulders. As they stumbled through the thick undergrowth, Rachel ran her fingers through her hair, feeling for scratches and checking her fingertips for traces of blood.

"There's nothing there," she said. "Not a scab or a scratch." She turned her head to look Gabriel in the eye. "What did you do?"

Gabriel smiled and waved his hands. "Magic fingers," he said. "C'mon, we should get you home."

"What about Adam?" Rachel asked. But before Gabriel could speak, her question was answered by the roar of a shotgun dangerously close by. Shotgun pellets peppered a tree overhead and a flock of small birds that had been hidden deep in the branches took flight, swooping and zigzagging around their heads in a frenzy.

Gabriel's green eyes darted around, searching for the gun.

"Who's shooting at us?" Rachel asked.

Gabriel nodded towards the dark figure thirty metres away, working its way towards them through the spindly trees. "Quick, follow me…"

Rachel grabbed at the hand that was offered and, as she took it, it were as though Gabriel had disappeared. It wasn't the first time this had happened; he had been there one minute and gone the next since the first time they had met.

But this time, Rachel disappeared with him.

Jacob Honeyman opened the door to his shack and gulped when he saw who had come to visit.

"What have you been saying, Honeyman?" asked the first man, pushing him in the chest, forcing him back into the cottage.

"Been blabbing, Jacob?"

"No … *please*."

"Giving away our secrets?" The second man punched

Honeyman hard in the face, knocking him to the floor.

The beekeeper moaned and continued to plead as the first man shut the door behind him; screamed as the first kick found its target.

23

Deep underground, Adam heard a gunshot. Or at least he felt the vibrations of a gunshot ripple through the earth around him. Somehow he was able to sense the orchestra of tiny squeaks and hisses made by the thousands of insects that surrounded him, ultra-sensitive to any minute change in their environment.

Adam could guess who was doing the shooting, and the possibility that Hilary Wing might be targeting his sister made him dig with greater determination.

As the earth fell away easily in front of him, Adam felt sure that someone had dug through here many years before. Cavities opened up in front of him, supported by gnarled roots and rotting, wooden props. He felt suddenly at one with the bugs and worms as he tunnelled his way through the peat, his body twisting and turning, pulling himself along through the earth on his elbows. His eyes were still shut tight against the falling dirt, but he continued in his mind's eye towards the orange orb of light that continued to glow ahead of him, his hands working away at the soft soil like a giant mole.

In the forest above, Rachel and Gabriel stepped gingerly through huge fans of damp fern, ducking under swags of bindweed, keeping their heads down.

Rachel told herself that Gabriel had not *literally* disappeared. That would have been ridiculous. But he did seem to have a knack of making himself invisible when he needed to: of somehow diverting the eye so that he did not attract attention. He was good at blending into the background. It was a skill that he would need to put to good use now. It was obvious that whoever was doing the shooting had a keen eye, and probably knew the woods like the back of his hand. Just when Rachel was starting to think that they had shaken him off, another gunshot rang out, a little too close for comfort.

Rachel and Gabriel ducked low into the ferns.

"He's still after us," Rachel whispered hoarsely.

Gabriel smiled. "I think he's just guessing. Or maybe he's just shooting birds."

Rachel shivered at the thought. She pulled out the crumpled map from her pocket and looked at it, no longer sure which direction she was facing. "Which way now?"

Gabriel did not glance at the map. Made a firm gesture ahead with his hand. "This way."

Rachel was starting to think that for someone who had earlier claimed to have no sense of navigation, Gabriel seemed to have a pretty good idea of where he was headed.

She didn't have time to think about it for very long.

Another shot rang out, even closer this time.

Gabriel grabbed Rachel's hand. "Let's go..."

Adam's fingernails, already split and ragged, dug into something solid. Wet chunks of rotten log came away beneath his fingers, but the bulk of the wooden prop lay jammed across his path. He scraped away at the soil packed tightly around him on either side, but the earth was firm and unyielding. The log must have been a tunnel prop that had collapsed into the narrow shaft, blocking the way.

The golden glow still hovered directly ahead, but now following it seemed impossible. Adam let out a deep sigh and lay still for a moment, suddenly feeling completely exhausted. With his eyes shut, he tried looking back, but he had dug so far that he could no longer sense the entrance to his tunnel. Shifting his weight from side to side and pushing his shoulder to the wall, he quickly realized that the space was too tight for him to turn round.

There was no going back.

Adam opened his eyes momentarily. Blinked away the damp particles of soil from his eyelids.

Nothing.

This deep into the earth it was pitch black. Light had never penetrated this narrow tunnel. As Adam shut his eyes again, trying to keep the golden glow alive in his mind's eye, he suddenly realized that this was what it must be like to be buried alive.

"Adam's in trouble," Rachel said.

Safe for the time being in the high branches of an oak tree, Rachel had suddenly been reminded of her brother. It had felt like a punch in the stomach.

Gabriel said nothing. He sat next to her, lying back on the high branch, casually, as if it were only a metre from the ground.

"I can feel it," Rachel said. "I know when he's OK ... I always have this feeling that he's right here beside me, but..."

Rachel could not find the words to describe the sickly, hollow sensation that was spreading through her gut. The sense of an energy fading, of part of her drifting away, slipping from between her fingers. Rachel chewed at her bottom lip and looked round among the leafy branches as if they might give her a clue to Adam's whereabouts.

"You don't think...?" A sudden panic had inflected her urgent whisper; the question she couldn't quite bring herself to ask.

Gabriel considered for a moment, shutting his eyes as if deep in thought. Then he sat up, fixing Rachel with his green eyes. "No. I don't think he's dead."

"Thank God."

"But you're right about one thing. Your brother's in trouble. Something's not going according to plan."

Rachel wasn't aware that there was a plan, other than their stupid idea about hunting for some old bit of tin in these creepy woods. She looked to Gabriel; waited for his next bright idea. Gabriel said nothing, then, after a moment, simply pointed towards the ground and began to climb down.

Adam's breaths were getting shallower.

There was just enough air getting through to the tunnel, but now he had stopped, Adam had become aware that he was not getting quite enough oxygen, and his mind was beginning to drift.

The golden light still shimmered in front of his eyes, but was becoming pale and merged with other images. He felt quite relaxed, and as his breaths became shorter, he felt as if he were slowly drowning in the moist, warm underground air.

Slowly, from the flood of golden light, rose an image of his mother, smiling, leaning over him, stroking his hair like she had when he was ill as a child. It was very comforting and gradually Adam became resigned to the thought that he might never see her again. Maybe that's why she was appearing to him now, to comfort him, to say goodbye. To say all sorts of things…

Adam realized that he was about to pass out.

24

Rachel jumped down on to the soft undergrowth at the base of the oak and promptly burst into tears. She was tired and frightened. She had suddenly felt something that took the wind out of her and tore through her with a terrible stab of grief.

"He's losing consciousness," she said. "I know it. He's been shot or something, Gabriel... I can feel it *here*." She clutched her hand to her chest and, for the first time since they had met, Gabriel looked confused. "Where is he?" she yelled. "*You* seem to know everything. *You* sent us off." Rachel jabbed her finger accusingly at him.

Gabriel stared at the ground, then looked up at Rachel. "I don't know where he is." A look of what might have been guilt passed over his face. "Something's gone wrong."

"Well, do something, will you?"

"Like what?"

"*Anything.*" Rachel clasped her stomach and doubled up as if in terrible pain. "You're the one with all the spooky powers."

"No, I'm not," Gabriel said. "Not the only one."

"What?"

"That's why you're feeling his pain. That's why you can hear me without me talking. I need *your* help." Gabriel held out his arms and pulled Rachel close to him. "And two heads are better than one."

Gabriel took Rachel's head between his palms and pulled her face to his, pressing their foreheads together and shutting his eyes. Still moaning, still in pain, Rachel complied.

And let him into her mind.

"We have to find this tree," Gabriel said. "You've got to concentrate. Picture the tree, picture it in as much detail as you can. I don't know what it's called, but it's like it has five or six trunks, all wound together to make one big trunk. Really wide…"

An image began to form in Rachel's mind. Roots pushed from the ground, morphing into twisted trunks, growing together, bonding into one large organism a metre or so across. The trunks began to sprout branches in her mind, then leaves. Dark green, not like an oak or an ash, but evergreen and finger-like; spreading out over the trunk and away, wider and wider…

"It's got evergreen leaves," Rachel said, "and the bark is kind of reddish and stripy." Even as she spoke, she realized she didn't need to; that Gabriel was getting exactly the same picture. He held her head a little tighter between his palms. The picture in Rachel's mind grew and became more intricate:

the leaf canopy spreading as if they were watching speeded-up film of the tree's growth.

"The leaves are poisonous." Rachel spoke inside her head. "And it was planted many years ago to protect against something evil."

Rachel had no idea where these ideas were coming from, but the sense was loud and clear. Other foliage began to sprout and grow, until the tree, which had been standing alone, was surrounded by other, smaller trees and a carpet of dense vegetation. As the picture became busier, Rachel felt herself rising above it, floating up through the branches until she was above the tree. Going higher, clouds raced by in a blur across a bright blue sky and, looking down, she could see the rest of the forest sprouting around the tree at incredible speed.

"It's amazing, I can see *everything*," Rachel said. Rachel thought...

Near by, she watched as a small red-brick cottage rose from the ground in the blink of an eye. Rachel felt herself move, felt herself flying over the woods and, swooping a little lower, she could see two small figures among the trees below. Dipping lower still, within touching distance of the treetops, she realized that she was watching herself and Gabriel who were standing only a short distance away from the tree.

Given the position that she could see herself and Gabriel standing in, she worked out that the tree was about fifty yards to their right, and around the same distance again from the red-brick building.

"Come back now, Rachel, come back down to the ground."

Gabriel's voice echoed in Rachel's head and she felt herself return to her body. She slipped easily into her own flesh once again, having watched the life cycle of a tree, planted almost three thousand years earlier, pass by in just a few seconds.

Rachel and Gabriel opened their eyes simultaneously.

"It's over there…" they both said at the same time, and pointed off to the right.

Adam drifted in and out of consciousness.

He thought he had been dreaming. As well as his mother, he had seen images of his childhood: happy days in Cape Cod playing on the beach; watching humpback whales up in Provincetown. Being pushed through Central Park in a buggy by his dad. A warm feeling. Then suddenly, an image of Rachel, anguished and tear-stained, had driven away all others and he had come back to reality with a start.

His sister's agony gnawed at Adam's gut like hunger pains, and suddenly his senses felt keener. The orange glow was still just about there, but had faded now. An instinct for survival that had seemed to have left him, began to surge again through his body like a current. He moved his arms and legs until he felt the pins and needles begin to dissolve from his limbs. Perhaps the rest had done him good, he thought.

Wearily, Adam rolled himself over on to his stomach and began to claw away at the earth either side of the fallen prop, and as he did, a large chunk of flint emerged from the soil.

Rachel stepped over the last of the brambles and nettles that they had trampled down. Her arms were covered in stings and her jeans and T-shirt were stained with the juice of the blackberries that they had beaten out of the way. She looked as if she was covered with hundreds of small, bloody wounds.

Rachel and Gabriel emerged into the clearing, looked up and gasped. Towering over them was the biggest tree that Rachel had ever seen. It was the tree from her vision, certainly, but even bigger in scale than she had imagined; a gigantic tree some ten metres round. They stepped up to where the roots emerged from the ground like sturdy stilts, holding up the whole structure. Where they joined the trunk they formed hollows and great fissures, providing underground homes for all sorts of creatures.

The sun was beginning to go down, bathing the red trunk in golden light.

"So what do we do now?" Rachel said, running her fingers down the crevices in the bark.

"At some point we need to try digging," Gabriel said. "But we need to find Adam first. I think we're quite close."

Rachel didn't know how Gabriel could be so sure, but her

anxiety over Adam began to fade a little. There was hope, she thought.

"There's *always* hope," Gabriel said.

Gabriel pressed his palm against the tree and shut his eyes tight. After a few seconds he opened them again.

"Do what I'm doing, and try to focus your thoughts on Adam. Concentrate really hard. We'll find him…"

Rachel put her hand against the rough bark and squeezed her eyes closed. She thought about a happier time, a time before they'd ever come to Triskellion, and brought to mind a vivid picture of her brother's smiling face.

Adam spat out a mouthful of earth and damp splinters. The sharp edge of the flint wore easily away at the edges of the rotten wood. Miraculously, he was still breathing, despite the effort involved in hacking away at the fallen prop. Just when things had seemed completely hopeless, he had felt a rush of new energy move through him, like a second wind. The feeling filled him with hope and, as he whittled down the rotten wood in front of his closed eyes, the orange disc of light that had guided him this far throbbed with a bright, strong glow.

Adam drew back his fist in the narrow space. He imagined it as a steel piston crashing through damp cardboard, and smashed away what remained of the rotten prop with a single punch. The earth on the other side was soft and yielding and Adam scooped it away in handfuls, at the same time trying to clear debris from his nose, mouth and ears. The further he had got into the tunnel, the thinner the air had become, and Adam knew that he had to make one, final, desperate attempt at freedom.

He moved his hands faster and faster and, as Adam scooped and pushed handfuls of soil behind him, he became aware that his tunnel was taking a slight upward turn.

He became aware of the ground above him.

Rachel clung on to the rough bark with both hands. The image of Adam was strong in her mind and she was sure she could feel the whole tree tremble beneath her fingertips.

"Can you feel that?" she called to Gabriel, trying to maintain her concentration.

A metre away from her Gabriel nodded. "Something's happening," he said. "Don't stop. Whatever you do, don't stop…"

Adam felt the earth shudder a little as soil began to fall away from him under its own force. He guessed that just as he might have been getting somewhere, the removal of the prop had started some sort of avalanche, and he was now certain that he was going to be buried alive.

The earth seemed to be moving and rolling beneath his stomach; moving him along on a slow wave as it filled his mouth and nose and ears. Adam stopped digging for a moment, frozen with panic, and felt himself being pushed, squeezed upward through the earth like toothpaste from a tube. Smashing through the wooden prop had clearly triggered something; something that was doing its best to expel him from beneath the ground.

"It feels like an earthquake," Rachel said, her fingers held tightly in the ribs of the bark. She raised her voice over the deafening roar inside her head. "What's going on?"

"I don't know," Gabriel shouted. "But I think we're about to find out…"

Adam's face was being pressed into the soft soil. He felt his whole body being crushed, then released, by the ground around him, massaging him forward and upward until, with his eyes still shut, he sensed light.

Pinpricks at first, then bigger splotches of pale light that shone like stars.

Thick tendrils reached into the ground either side of him. They seemed to move like tentacles, dragging him along, pushing his head into a cavernous opening surrounded by roots. He pulled himself along, guided by the length of a root and strained his head upward into the opening, as if emerging from quicksand.

Shaking and blinking and spitting out earth, Adam gasped at the moist air and opened his eyes. He was no more than head and shoulders above ground and it was still quite dark.

But he could see again.

Illuminated by shafts of golden sunlight that shone

through fissures between the roots, Adam appeared to be in
a shallow cavern beneath a tree – maybe a fox's earth or
home to a family of badgers. Twisted roots formed a canopy
directly over his head and, dragging an arm from the soil, he
pulled himself up a little further, while the earth continued
to spew him out.

The space was tight and there was only room for Adam to
continue crawling, panting for air, towards the golden glow
coming from what looked like a wasps' nest; a huge, fleshy
fungus the size of a space hopper that hung down from the
bole of the tree over his head. As Adam tried to work out
what the object was, he realized that the earth was still pulsing behind him, pushing him upward against the roots, trying
to force him out. He kept crawling, scrabbling towards the
source of the light, towards the nest or whatever it was, and
found himself being pressed up against it.

It felt more like a large, deflating balloon or airbag than a
nest. A bladder of some kind, filled with liquid.

The earth kept rising behind him and pushed Adam
harder and harder against the bulbous, waxy skin. He tried to
keep it away with his hands, but the membrane stretched
and they disappeared into the pulpy mass. The earth was
closing in behind him, pressing hard against his back, pushing his face into the soft, musty-smelling sac, suffocating
him.

And as the earth gave a final surge forward, the bladder
burst. What seemed like gallons of milky liquid poured over

Adam, filling his eyes and nose and mouth with sticky, dis-
gusting-smelling goo. Adam tore his hands free and thrashed
around blindly, reaching out, once again, to save his life…

The trembling seemed to have stopped. Rachel waited a few
seconds to be sure and then called out to Gabriel. "Look,
there's something coming out of the tree!"

Gabriel jumped down and ran to the large hollow at the
base of the tree's roots. Just as Rachel had said, something
was emerging from a hole beneath the tree.

Rachel looked closer, screwing up her face in distaste.
"What is it?" Nothing would have surprised her now and, at
a first glance, she thought that the clammy, white thing waving from the soil might be some kind of giant, bloodless
maggot.

"It's a hand," Gabriel said. "Help me…"

Gabriel grabbed the slippery hand and with Rachel's help
started to dig away at the soil round the hollow. Moments
later they pulled Adam from the earth into the last rays of
orange light. He was soaked, filthy and stinking; his head
shrouded in the tatters of the burst membrane and every
inch of him covered in soil.

Adam fell to his knees, exhausted. He rubbed away the
earth from his eyes, then howled triumphantly as he lifted up
his hand.

Rachel and Gabriel gasped.

It was dirty, and dripping with a thick, creamy liquid, but

there was no mistaking it as the late afternoon light passed across Adam's face and arms and mud-encrusted hands. As it played across the golden blade of the Triskellion that was clutched between his trembling fingers.

part three:
the tomb

25

*Y*ellow light from the tallow candles flickers round the circular walls of the hut, dancing across the wooden beams and making the hanging furs seem alive.

The man stands in the doorway, holding back a heavy curtain, a helmet under his arm. His angular face is anxious, his green eyes adjusting to the gloom of the smoky dwelling. He puts his helmet on a bench; his focus fixing on the wooden pallet where the maiden lies, drained and exhausted. Her eyes are shut, but she tosses, turns and mutters, caught in a troubled sleep. Her chestnut curls are damp and stuck to her face.

The man steps further into the room, barely seeing the old woman who emerges from the deep shadows. She is holding something. A baby. No. Two babies, wrapped in cloth – bandaged almost, like tiny mummies.

The old woman holds the infants out to the man, who takes them in his arms and looks down at their tiny faces: eyes the same colour as his own, twinkling, alive. Alive and perfect.

The man looks over at the sleeping girl and smiles, tears rolling down his smooth cheeks...

Adam looked at his sister, asleep in the bed opposite. Her hair was spread across the pillow and her eyelids moved as the eyes darted beneath them. The skin on her face twitched as though she were in pain and her lips mouthed random words.

He shook her shoulder, but she was fast asleep.

He watched as she muttered and thrashed about, and knew that she was having the same dream that had just woken him. A dream of twins; a dream of the distant past. A dream in which an ancient version of Rachel appeared to be married to Gabriel...

The Star was uncharacteristically busy for a Monday night. The television crew, though unpopular with many of the villagers, was undoubtedly good for Tom Hatcham's business. Not only were the presenter and his producer staying in the rooms upstairs, but so were the cameraman, soundman and half a dozen other people. Hatcham had no idea what they all did, but they all had an apparently insatiable appetite for pub food and beer, and compared to most of The Star's customers they didn't seem to care how much it all cost.

"Probably got expense accounts," a customer muttered from his vantage point on a bar stool.

"They get paid more than what I do, and that's the truth

of it," said another. He punctuated his point by draining what was left of a glass of beer, nearly three quarters of a pint, before banging his glass down ready for another. Hatcham served him automatically as the kitchen door swung open and a flustered barmaid brought out what seemed like the hundredth plate of breadcrumbed scampi that evening. She looked to Hatcham for guidance.

"Over by the window." Hatcham nodded towards his largest table, in the corner, where the genial host of television's *Treasure Hunters*, held court in a loud voice.

"So Noel says, 'Why don't you do the show yourself, if it's such a good idea?' And you know what? That's exactly what I damn well did. The rest, as they say, is history … or archaeology!"

All but one of the people at the table with Chris Dalton collapsed into convivial laughter, while Laura Sullivan, his all-round producer, researcher and right-hand woman rolled her eyes. She had heard the story many times before. It was true, up to a point; Dalton had certainly popularized TV archaeology. But each time the tale was retold, it showed him in an increasingly flattering light. The show's popularity had made Chris Dalton very rich, but it didn't make him any easier to work with.

He picked up a large chip from the plate that had just been put in front of him, dipped it in mayonnaise and bit into it. "Bloody chips are cold," he said to no one in particular. He looked at Laura as if she ought to be doing something about it.

"I think they're a bit hassled," Laura said. "I guess they're not usually this busy."

"I'm not surprised."

"Try not to complain, Chris, will you? We don't want to upset anyone here. Charm offensive, remember?"

Dalton was perfectly capable of creating a major stink over a few cold chips, but he knew Laura was right. It was a sensitive business going into these villages and digging up their past. Some of them welcomed the publicity and the temporary brush with fame, but others saw it as an unwelcome intrusion that had nothing to do with preserving the past and everything to do with making money.

It was clear to Laura that this village was the latter kind. The parish bigwigs had done all that they could to stop the TV show filming in Triskellion, and the local MP had done everything in his power to prevent the dig on the moor. However, the county council had overridden the villagers' objections. They had argued that *Treasure Hunters* was a popular TV show and that bringing it to Triskellion would be a huge boost for tourism in the area and a much needed source of income for local businesses.

When the barmaid arrived at the table and asked if everything was all right, Dalton turned on his most dazzling show-business smile. "Absolutely superb," he said. "My compliments to the chef." When she shyly asked if he would mind signing an autograph, he happily scribbled on a napkin for her.

"Is that Kelly with a 'Y', or with an 'IE'?"

Dinner over, the table began to break away. The camera-man got up to play darts with the sound engineer, while Amanda, the production assistant, yawned loudly and said something about turning in early as she was pregnant.

Laura leant over to Dalton. She had made sure that all the paperwork was in place to make the dig legal, but something else was bothering her.

"Chris?"

"Yis, me old cobber?" Dalton said. He never missed an opportunity to mimic Laura's Australian accent with a very bad version of his own.

"I have one big worry about this. OK, we've got permission to dig, fine. But there's absolutely no evidence that there is anything under the chalk circle. It's really not typical of Bronze Age burial barrows."

Dalton shrugged. "But this bee guy, Honeybum or what-ever he's called, is absolutely convinced. How many letters and emails has he sent me? How many parcels of bloody fossils?"

"Sure, there's *some* stuff there," Laura said patiently. "It's an ancient site. But if we go crashing around in our size nines, dig it up and find nothing *major*, it's us with lots of egg on our faces."

"Laura…"

"It'll set us back for anything else we want to do."

"Laura, Laura, Laura…"

Laura took a deep breath. She knew she was about to be patronized.

Dalton sighed. "Laura, love. How much have you learned about telly since you've been with me, eh? You are a *fantastic* producer. You're organized, you're thorough…"

"I did actually study archaeology *properly* for seven years before I joined this circus, you know?" Laura gave him a good hard look, making sure, as she always did, that her credentials as a serious archaeologist were noted. Despite two years working with her, Dalton had a habit of forgetting that she knew her stuff.

"I know, I know," Dalton said. "You are a *top* archaeologist." There was a twinkle in his eye suddenly. It was one he'd turned on for the cameras a hundred times over two series of *Treasure Hunters*. "And you're not a bad-looking one either, when we see you on screen…"

"Oh, shut up."

Laura hated it when Dalton did this. It annoyed her, knowing that he would *never* have employed her, would never have put her on screen, had she looked like the back of a bus. As it was, she knew she looked better than *that*. At twenty-seven, she was tall and willowy: honey-skinned, with a mass of curly red hair. But she was so much more than that. She was tough: she had trudged through the outback alone for days on end. She was smart: she had taken all the major prizes at the University of Western Australia for her work on Aboriginal dreaming sites, and her thesis on Bronze

Age societies had been published to critical praise.

And now Chris Dalton was doing his "little lady" act on her.

Dalton could see he was annoying Laura, and quickly changed his tone. "Listen, here's the deal. We've got fabulous countryside to film, a picture-postcard village, a church with a crusader tomb and an amazing artefact. We've got a local nutter in a patched-up coat who has a knack of finding stupid amounts of coins with a cheap metal detector. Get him down on tape spouting his theories about burial sites, corn circles or whatever, I'll do a re-enactment as a Bronze Age druid burying my wages for luck ... *bingo*, we've already got TV gold."

Laura looked across the table at Dalton's shiny, enthusiastic face. He was right. It was hardly rigorous archaeology, but it was already sounding like a very watchable TV show.

"*And...*" Dalton continued, "when we dig under the circle, we'll do it live. Build the tension. We'll have the whole country watching. Then, if we *do* find something, we've hit paydirt, publicity, global fame. We're talking a bagful of BAFTAs here."

Laura laughed at Dalton's confidence. "And if we find nothing?"

"All the above." He smiled when Laura looked confused. "We expose Honeybum as a crank who's wasted our time and we still end up looking like the caring professionals we are. We can't lose, whichever way things turn out." Dalton winked at Laura, balancing his hands in the air to describe his perfectly thought out win/win scenario.

Laura drank the last of her fizzy water. "OK, Chris. You've sold me, but I'm not going to victimize anybody if it doesn't work out. It's a show, but I don't think it's right to string up the poor guy who put us in touch with all this. If there is nothing there, it's our risk, OK?"

"Whatever you say."

Laura stood up. "I'm going for a bit of fresh air. I might stroll up to the circle, see what sort of vibe I get from it."

Dalton stood up and put on his leather jacket. "I'll come with you. These streets are not very well lit."

The look on Laura's face told him in an instant that he was not especially welcome. He made an elaborate yawning gesture and looked at his watch. "Actually, I think I'll turn in," he said. "Got a few calls to make anyway and we've got a busy day tomorrow."

Laura nodded and strode away towards the door of the pub.

"Don't talk to any strange men," Dalton called after her, jokily. He gave a general wave to the bar, and another to his crew playing darts, before slapping a wad of notes down in front of Tom Hatcham. "Thank you, landlord! Charming hostelry. Excellent victuals. Good night, good sir."

Dalton nodded to the stern military-looking man, who sat by the bar sipping brandy. He leant down to pat the head of the giant wolfhound at the man's feet, then went up to his room.

"Seems like a decent enough bloke," Hatcham said, sweeping up the pile of cash from the bar.

"I thought he was an idiot," Commodore Wing growled. "Nice-looking girl, though."

Hatcham grinned at the commodore's evaluation of Laura, and was about to add one of his own, but was pulled up short by the old man's steely glare.

"Just make sure we don't get any more of this kind of interest, Tom. We've lost the fight on the archaeology, but I don't want them snooping around anywhere else. They'll dig up all sorts of stuff that doesn't need digging up. Clear?"

"Don't worry; Honeyman's had a very serious warning. I don't think he'll be saying too much more to anyone about the village."

Wing slammed a palm down on the bar. "I don't just mean Honeyman," he said. "I don't want *anyone* talking to them. Understand?"

26

From the comfort of her bed, Rachel watched a bee slowly circle the ceiling light in the bedroom, its wings working barely enough to keep it in the air. Did they hibernate, she wondered? There were certainly fewer of them hovering about the roses in front of the cottage, now the weather had cooled.

She would ask Jacob. He could tell her.

It had been a week since that terrible day in the forest, and though the morning sun still shone through the bedroom window, there was a hint of autumn chill in the air. This time of year always made Rachel think of study. She usually got butterflies in her stomach thinking about the start of a new school year, but now everything had changed. The American school term would start soon and this year she was looking forward to going back. Back to the regularity, and the security.

Back to the certainty.

The anguish Rachel had been through, and Adam's

near-death experience, had certainly dulled their taste for
adventure. Gabriel had suggested that they lie low for a while
and neither of them had needed much persuasion to do so.
They had spent more time alone at the cottage: reading, lying
about in the garden and letting the last few afternoons of the
summer drift lazily by. Rachel and Adam both agreed that
this was partly because they needed the rest and recupera-
tion from their ordeal. Neither needed to admit to the other
that it was also because they were terrified that Hilary Wing
was at large and after their blood.

They had not ventured into the village, nor gone anywhere
near the woods. And all the while, their amazing discovery
lay wrapped in cloth and hidden under a floorboard beneath
Adam's bed.

Their grandmother, who was just about speaking to them
again, had been horrified at the state they had returned in that
evening. But when they protested that they had been shot at
in the woods by Hilary Wing, she had shrugged it off. She had
told them not to be silly; had explained that Hilary was probably shooting at pigeons and quickly changed the subject.

One thing *she* had seemed pleased about, however, was
that Rachel and Adam had seemed far more content to be
around the cottage, and had seen less of "that strange friend"
of theirs.

It was Gabriel's suggestion that they didn't see each other
for a while. He said that he was going away, but was reluctant
to say where. Rachel and Adam had presumed that he was

catching up with his family, wherever they were.

Initially, Rachel had felt a bit rejected, and had missed Gabriel a great deal, but for the last few days she had found herself "talking" to him when she was alone in the garden or on short walks along the roads around the cottage. The messages she was receiving in her head were as fleeting and vague as Gabriel himself. They arrived like random text messages that popped up in her mind to reassure her that he was still around and to remind her about the secret she had promised to keep.

That all of them had to keep.

At first, Gabriel had urged them to tell absolutely no one about the second Triskellion blade, but Rachel had argued that they were duty-bound to let one other person in on the secret. He had helped them find it, after all.

Through swollen lips, Jacob Honeyman had let out a whoop of joy when Rachel and Adam told him that they had found the blade. He had blinked at them through blackened eyes and insisted that they did not tell him where they were hiding it. "What I don't know, I can't tell," he had said, holding his ribs as he stood up to see them out.

"What happened to you, Jacob?" Adam had asked him.

"Fell down the stairs," Jacob had replied, tut-tutting at his own clumsiness.

And as Rachel had walked away down the path from the shack, she had realized that the explanation Honeyman had given for his injuries was more than a little odd; was not even a good attempt at a lie.

The shack *had* no stairs…

Laura Sullivan had found the villagers even less forthcoming than she had anticipated. Along with Chris Dalton and their assistant, she had spent the morning around the village, chatting to passers-by, patting children on the head and getting to know a few of the shopkeepers. Those villagers who hadn't blanked their enquiries completely had offered little more than a fixed smile. Most "knew nothing" about the history of the village or "weren't interested" in being on TV.

Dalton had become increasingly frustrated. "Ninety-nine point nine per cent of the country are gagging to get their ugly fat mugs on the telly, and we choose the one place where they're all as publicity-shy as Lord flippin' Lucan. Great…"

Laura didn't know who Lord Lucan was, but assumed he must be a very shy person indeed. She had suggested to Dalton that perhaps he should go back to The Star for lunch, while she tried to track down the man who had brought them to Triskellion in the first place. Dalton had quickly agreed, and not just because he was exhausted and liked the look of the pub's steak and ale pie.

They needed to talk to Jacob Honeyman, and thus far the beekeeper had been conspicuous by his absence.

Honeyman peered at the woman through a crack in the door. When he was certain that she wasn't about to beat him up, he opened the door a few centimetres.

"What?" He gave the woman on his doorstep no invitation to enter his shack.

"Hi … Jacob, is it?"

"Maybe."

"I'm Laura Sullivan. *Treasure Hunters*. Remember? We spoke on the phone … you sent the mails… You met Chris, the presenter." Laura held out a hand, waited.

Honeyman's beady eye studied the hand through the doorframe then snaked out his own and shook the tips of Laura's fingers, before retracting his hand with reptile-like speed.

"I can't talk," he said. "I told you everything I know in the emails and the letters and what have you. That's it. Job done."

"But I thought you were going to do a piece to camera for us. Explain some of your ideas … about the burial site, who you think might be buried there, and why. Do you remember?" Laura spoke quietly and persuasively, but Honeyman still showed no sign of knowing who she was. His eyes darted around over her shoulder and she couldn't be sure that he was taking in anything she was saying.

"Like I said, I can't talk."

"Why not?" Laura asked.

"Things have changed, is why not."

"That's a shame…"

"What I said is true, but I can't talk no more." Honeyman

drew his forefinger across his mouth. "My lips is sealed."

Laura stared down at the toes of her muddy walking boots. This was proving difficult. Not only were the villagers refusing to speak to them, but now their main lead was withdrawing his support. The show was turning into a disaster.

"Jacob, please help us a little, here." She raised her voice, carried on even though Honeyman had already begun to shake his head. "Look, you were the one who got us started on this project. Without your local expertise, we're a bit stuck. I really need your help. If we mess this up, it's my neck on the line, too."

Honeyman looked at Laura through the door. She hadn't smarmed him like the presenter had when they'd met. She was plain speaking, and he liked that.

"Please," she said.

She seemed honest and he would have liked to help her. But the pain from his cracked rib reminded him that it would be unwise. Then he had an idea.

"Excuse me for being reticent," he said. "But I have my reasons, OK?" She nodded, and he leant a little closer to her, lowered his voice to a whisper. "It's true. Under that circle is the biggest archaeological discovery you'll make in your career, that *anyone* will ever make. I can't help you no more than that."

Laura said nothing.

"But I know two people who might…"

27

Rachel was surprised to open the door of Root Cottage to the tall, red-haired woman with a beautiful smile. The few people that did call at Root Cottage were either very old or delivering letters or occasionally collecting for repairs to the church roof.

The woman held out her hand. "You must be Rachel."

Rachel couldn't quite place the accent, but guessed that Laura wasn't English. "Hi," she said, shaking hands. She tried to keep the suspicion out of her voice; a suspicion that would not have been there two weeks earlier. "Yeah, I'm Rachel."

"My name's Laura Sullivan. I'm the producer of *Treasure Hunters*. The TV show? You may have seen it?"

"Yeah, my gran watches it, but she's out shopping. She'll be back in a couple of hours."

Laura shook her head. "Actually, it's you I wanted to speak to, if that's OK. Are you American?"

"Yeah, we live in New York," Rachel said. "But my mom was born here."

"Well, we're both outsiders then." Laura smiled. "I'm from Australia."

Rachel waited.

"Listen … Jacob Honeyman said you might be able to help me."

"Jacob?"

"Can I come in?"

Rachel stared at Laura Sullivan and felt the suspicion begin to subside. She looked over her shoulder and, knowing that her grandmother would be at the shops for some while yet, opened the door wide to let Laura in.

"Is your brother here?" Laura asked, as she stepped inside.

"Upstairs," Rachel said. "He's not feeling too good."

Adam had taken advantage of his grandmother's shopping trip and attempted to phone home. It had been about 7.30 a.m. New York time when he'd called and he'd been worried that his mother might not have been awake yet.

She was, and already in tears. Adam could hear it in her voice even as she picked up the phone, cleared her throat and said a tremulous, "Hello."

It tore at Adam's heart to hear his mother's voice and even more to hear the sobs that kicked in once she recognized his. He had been ready to unburden himself; to tell her how horrible their stay in Triskellion had been. How scary, how dangerous. He had been desperate to ask if they could come home early. But when he heard about how bad a time his mother was having with the divorce, the need to be brave

was suddenly more important than anything, and he told her
things in England were fine – that he and Rachel were having a great time.

He had passed the phone to Rachel, who had coaxed her
mother along with sympathetic words, assuring her that
everything would work out for the best. Adam had left her to
it, fighting back the tears and skulking off to their room, feeling worse than he had before he had made the call.

Rachel had watched him go, feeling less than certain that
things would work out at all...

"Great cottage, isn't it?" Laura said, sitting down in
Granny Root's favourite armchair. She took a good look
round. "We don't really have places like this at home."

"Neither do we," Rachel said. "We don't really have anything old."

"Same in Australia," Laura said. "None of the buildings
went up much more than a hundred years ago. But we have
the Aboriginal sites that are many thousands of years old, so
we're doing what we can to preserve them. It's funny really,
seeing as I'm here to dig things up."

"Yeah?" Rachel's curiosity was suddenly sharpened by the
notion that someone else was investigating Triskellion.
"What are you digging?"

"Well, we have permission to dig up at the chalk circle."
Rachel's eyes widened in disbelief. "Is that a problem for
you?"

"Dig up the circle?"

"Of course we'll put it all back exactly as it is. Look, I'm an archaeologist, first and foremost, and a TV producer second. I specialized in Bronze Age burial sites as part of my doctorate…"

"You're a doctor, too?" Rachel asked, impressed.

"Sure, but you can just call me Laura," Laura said, laughing. "There're a few interesting theories about this circle. Some people reckon it's a Bronze Age burial plot, maybe an important one, the tribal chief or something. It's not like others I've seen, that's for sure, so if it is a burial site, it would be the first of its kind. The area around has been throwing up heaps of stuff, coins and so on, which means at the very least it's a site of special significance, and obviously has been for a very long time—" Laura stopped, followed Rachel's gaze to the figure standing at the bottom of the stairs.

"This is my brother, Adam," Rachel said. "He's really into archaeology, too."

Adam stared at his sister; he was not looking too happy. "I heard you talking to someone…"

"Hi, Adam." Laura smiled at him. "Glad to hear you're a fan of archaeology. Clearly a man of taste."

Adam turned, then blushed. Managed a "hi" before dropping down heavily on to the sofa.

"So what do you guys know about the area?" Laura asked. "Jacob said you've done some impressive detective work, finding bits and pieces."

Rachel and Adam exchanged a look that spoke volumes,

urging one another not to give too much away. As Rachel spoke, she heard Gabriel's voice in the back of her mind, telling her to be calm, to go easy.

"Sure, we've read up on the local history since we've been here, you know, the tomb in the church, the circle ... not much else to do here, really. Adam has found a few bits ... just coins and that kind of thing."

"OK."

"Maybe we could help," Adam said suddenly.

"Hang on," Rachel said.

"Great." Laura sat forward in her chair. "You're just what I need. Two, talkative, media-friendly archaeology fans. You both have a bit of knowledge, you'd both look good on TV."

"On *TV*?" Rachel almost shrivelled with embarrassment at the thought of it. "Oh no, I couldn't go on TV."

"Course you could…"

Rachel shook her head. "No way."

Laura shrugged, more than a little disappointed.

"Sorry," Rachel said.

Laura turned to Adam. "How about you?" she said, smiling at him.

Adam reddened again. "Sure," he said. "Why not?"

28

Yellow tape marked an area fifteen metres or so away from the chalk circle, where four men had started digging, watched by another man in a leather jacket. The cameraman circled, camera on his shoulder, getting some general footage of their progress. Two days after their first meeting, Rachel and Adam stood with Laura Sullivan watching the preparations for the excavation.

"They're starting a long way from the circle," Rachel said.

"It's perfectly normal," Laura said. "We want to dig underneath without disturbing the surface of the circle itself. If it is Bronze Age, then whatever's underneath will be no more than two, three metres below, so we'll dig a shaft diagonally down to get to it." She made an angle with her hand to show the kind of direction in which they were digging.

"Makes sense, I guess," Rachel said.

Adam said nothing. The talk of digging, even the idea of being underground, made him shiver; his mind flashing back for an instant to a very dark place beneath the woods.

The man in the leather jacket walked away from the dig and across towards Rachel and Adam, rubbing his hands as if he had been doing some of the work.

"Ah, you must be our local experts. All the way from the US of A!" Dalton tried his hand at an American accent, oblivious to the look between Rachel and Adam. "Lovely Laura's told me all about you."

"Rachel, Adam ... this is Chris Dalton our presenter," Laura said.

"Presenter, executive producer and owner of the production company to be precise," Dalton said. He gave a small bow and an elaborate flourish of his hand as if he were an Elizabethan courtier, while Laura nodded to affirm that what he had said was true. "So, Laura, have you been through the questions with young Adam?"

Laura nodded. "We've talked through a few facts about the surrounding area, the estimated age of the circle and so on. And we'll show a few of the coins Adam has borrowed from Mr Honeyman to illustrate the point."

"Great," Dalton said. "That'll give us a few sound bites."

Adam looked puzzled.

"Chris means quotes," Laura said. "So, are you happy to go through some stuff with Chris and Amanda?"

Amanda, the production assistant, had just waddled over, dressed head to toe in wet weather gear and carrying her ever-present clipboard. She smiled pleasantly and waved at Adam.

Adam waved back. "Sure."

"I'm going back to the church," Laura said. "To do a bit more work." She turned to Rachel. "Do you want to come with me?"

In just two days, Rachel had come to feel that in Laura, she had found an adult she could really trust. Laura was everything she wished herself to be: intelligent, brave and honest. For the first time since she had come to Triskellion, she felt safe, she felt protected. And, having found a new friend, she was starting to think about Gabriel a good deal less.

She looked across at Adam and saw the same expression that had been plastered across his face for the last two days. She could tell he felt the same way about Laura that she did, though it was perhaps for different reasons. He stared at her when she talked, and blushed almost every time she spoke to him.

Despite their brief acquaintance, if Laura Sullivan had asked either of them to come with her, Rachel and Adam would have followed her anywhere.

In the church, Laura knelt down and took detailed digital photographs of the tomb and the faint inscription round its base.

"Any idea what it says?" Rachel asked. "The vicar thought it was something to do with a crusader called Sir Richard de Waverley."

Laura stood up. "Yes, I'd read that, too. But there's a couple of things that don't add up."

"Like what?"

"These are runes. You know what runes are?"

Rachel shook her head.

"They're an early kind of alphabet that came even before the Saxons, say about two or three BC, OK?" Rachel nodded. "So if this guy Waverley was a crusader, he wouldn't have been around until about nine hundred years later. See my problem?"

"So, what do the letters mean?" Rachel asked.

"Well, I'm not fluent in rune, but there are one or two symbols I recognize." She knelt down again and Rachel knelt next to her. "This one here…" She pointed to a symbol that looked like a jagged streak of lightning.

"This means *sowilo*, or the sun. It's a very ancient, powerful symbol. It was used as recently as the Second World War by the Nazis, as part of their insignia."

Rachel pulled a face. She knew all about *them*.

Laura traced her finger over the next readable rune.

"This is a very common rune, *raido*, meaning journey or ride. So we've got sun-ride, or sun-journey maybe. Could relate to the shooting star on the stained glass window, perhaps. Then there's a few missing, but here's the sun symbol again." Laura pointed out another lightning shape. "But this time, it's attached to the *mannaz* rune:

This one signifies 'man'. So we've got sun-man, man of the sun, whatever that might mean…"

"Sun-worshipper?" Rachel suggested.

"Could be," Laura said. "Back then people really did worship the sun. They didn't just lie about in it all day." She went back to the inscription. "Then it all gets a bit more mysterious." She traced her finger over an area where the runes had been worn or deliberately chipped away. "This quite often happens, because ancient people were superstitious, thought the runes themselves had magic properties. Sometimes they'd destroy inscriptions they thought contained bad messages or curses."

Rachel pointed to where the inscription became readable again. "What about these ones?"

"I'm not sure about most of them," said Laura. "But that one is *iwaz*, the ancient name of the yew tree, which was really important to the druids."

The name rang a bell with Rachel. "What's a yew tree like?"

"They're massive with huge, twisted trunks made from several parts grown together…"

"With kind of stripy red bark and evergreen leaves?"

"That's the one," Laura said. "They've always been significant landmarks, for sacred sites and so on."

Rachel remembered the huge tree from which Adam had emerged with the Triskellion blade. As though the blade had been safeguarded by the tree for hundreds, maybe thousands of years. Snippets of information came back to Rachel. "The leaves are poisonous, right?" she asked.

"That's right," Laura said. "They've always been powerful to the druids for that reason. They say that they used to get rid of unwanted babies by giving the pregnant mother yew berries."

"Gross," Rachel said, wincing. All the time, her head was spinning with flashes of information. With ideas and images that were beginning to knit themselves together little by little: the yew tree; the knight and the maiden; the baby twins; her mother; her grandmother; Gabriel…

Fragments of a dream. Pieces of a jigsaw.

"It's not all bad," Laura said without looking up. "They're still using yew bark in chemotherapy today to combat cancer. Which gives us a clue to this last symbol, *kauna*:

It means illness, so maybe illness refers to the poison of the berries … so we've got yew-illness, something like that."

The images swirled, screaming inside Rachel's head, making her feel sick and dizzy.

Laura looked up. "You OK, Rachel? You look pale."

"I'll be fine," Rachel said, steadying herself against the cool stone of the carved knight. She tried to refocus her mind. "So you think this tomb is much earlier?"

"Certainly the base of it is." She nodded towards the carving. "I think our friend here, that the village has always thought was a crusader, is probably someone much, much older."

"So, what about Sir Richard de Waverley?" Rachel asked, trying to put the pieces together.

Laura stood up and, like Rachel, instinctively patted the tomb. "If you ask me," Laura said, "Sir Richard de Waverley never existed."

"What?"

"Look, the Wing family has been at the centre of village life since records began, no question about it. They built Waverley Hall, the church, virtually all the village as we know it. I've done a heap of research on this and it looks to me like this Richard de Waverley character is something they made up."

"Why would they do that?" Rachel asked.

"Who knows? Maybe to gloss over some family scandal way back, or to divert attention from what this tomb really represents."

Rachel could feel the hair on her scalp prickling. She

blinked slowly and imagined herself standing on the edge of a precipice, looking down into the black mouth of a dreadful secret; about to tumble headlong into something from which there would be no return. "So who do you think it does represent?" she asked.

Laura took a step nearer the statue, reached out towards the crack that ran across the dead stone face. "That's what we're going to find out."

29

"**A**nd … action!" Chris Dalton dropped his hand in front of the camera, giving the sign for no one but himself to speak, and began to move.

"Peaceful village, England," he boomed. "The bleak splendour of the moors…" The cameraman, who was doing his best to keep pace, widened his shot and Dalton spread his arms expansively as if the whole area belonged to him. "We're here in one of the oldest settlements in the country to investigate the very thing that gave this village its name. The Triskellion. The huge chalk circle carved into the ground in a strange ancient pattern. Is it a place where druids worshipped the sun? Is it the burial place of an important Bronze Age family?" Dalton stopped, put on a mysterious voice and put his face close to the camera. "Or is it something else entirely? Is it perhaps some kind of prehistoric compass?" He cocked his head and smiled. "We're here to find out in this week's … *Treasure Hunters*." He froze for a few seconds and then relaxed. "And … cut!"

"Nice one, Chris," the cameraman said. "Do you want to go again?"

"No need," Dalton said. "I think I got it in one take, don't you, Amanda?"

The production assistant looked up from the clipboard and nodded enthusiastically. The take was fine, but there was little point arguing even when it wasn't.

"Let's move on." Dalton looked round. "Where's the kid?"

Amanda pointed.

They walked over to where Adam was standing by the Triskellion, Dalton calling out as they approached. "OK, Adam," he said, "we're going to film the questions we went through. Happy to have a go?"

Adam nodded. Having a TV camera pointed at him did not bother him unduly after some of the things he'd been through, and Adam had always relished his appearances in school plays, speaking in front of class and that kind of thing.

But then Chris instructed Amanda to bring the morris dancers over.

Adam looked over to where a couple of cars were parked near the *Treasure Hunters* van. Seven or eight men were beginning to assemble, dressed in leafy costumes, their faces painted green or in one or two cases black. They wore an assortment of top hats, furs and antlers on their heads. Adam's stomach flipped over.

He had seen men like this before.

Chris Dalton saw him looking at the men. "Morris

dancers, they call themselves," he said. "The Green Men."
He scoffed. "Green loonies if you ask me. We thought they'd
add a bit of local colour, dancing round the circle, jingling
their bells and shaking their sticks while we film." Dalton
directed Adam to stand in the middle of the circle. "It'll make
a great shot," he assured him.

The camera began rolling, and Dalton called "action"
again.

"I have with me here Adam Newman. Now, although
Adam lives in America, his mother's family have come from
Triskellion for centuries. Hi, Adam…"

"Hi," Adam said, trying to stop his voice from wavering.
From the corner of his eye, he could see the Green Men
assembling at the edge of the circle.

"I understand you are a keen amateur archaeologist," Dalton said. "Can you tell us what you know about the chalk
circle?"

"Er, well, we know that the symbol is probably Celtic and
was carved during the Bronze Age."

"Which makes it how old?" Dalton asked the question as
if he already knew the answer himself. Adam glanced around
nervously before he replied.

"About three thousand years," Adam said.

Dancers were now positioned at points round the circle,
their painted faces staring impassively towards Adam at the
centre. Each of them carried a thick, wooden stick, stripped
of its bark.

"Three. Thousand. Years." Dalton gave a whistle as if impressed. "And can you show us some of the things you've discovered here?"

Adam opened his palm, revealing a selection of coins, pins and brooches that Honeyman had lent him.

"Coins and other pieces that date back to Roman times, and beyond." Dalton began to walk away from Adam, the cameraman following him. "But here's the big question. Is there something far more valuable buried beneath our feet?"

As Dalton stepped out of the circle, leaving Adam stranded in the middle, he gave the morris dancers a nod to start.

A drumbeat struck up and, one by one, the dancers started a shuffle and a hop, tracing a pattern along the chalk lines of the Triskellion. They began to move faster and faster, crossing and skipping past each other where the lines intersected, clashing their sticks together with a noise that made Adam flinch. Bells attached to the legs of their costumes jangled as they danced and leapt to the beat of the drum. It appeared to Adam that, as they got faster, the circle of dancers was tightening in on him – so close that he could smell their sweat. It seemed as though they were skipping a little nearer to him each time they passed; smashing their sticks together closer and closer to Adam's head.

The circle of men concealed Adam from the camera and meant that he could no longer see anything beyond the tangled crush of the dancers themselves. It tightened still further until Adam was completely hemmed in by the scrum of Green Men, their sticks interlocking above head height, forming a canopy that completely closed him in.

Then the chanting started: quietly at first, sounding like a traditional song. Then it became louder, building in volume and intensity until Adam could make out what they were saying.

"We know what you stole from us … give it back, give it back. We know what you stole … give it back, give it back."

Adam felt giddy as the chanting grew and the circle spun wildly round him.

"We know what you stole…"

He looked round madly, his heart thumping as fast as the dancer's drum, searching for a way out and seeing none.

"Give it back, give it back…"

Adam's stomach lurched when he suddenly registered a pair of very pale blue eyes, and he watched helplessly as another man began to detach himself from the circle. He saw the man raise his arm, but his scream was lost beneath the drone and the drumbeat, as a willow pole crashed down on to his head.

As Adam came round, all he could hear were arguments. The loudest voice of all belonged to Chris Dalton.

"Of *course* we're not responsible. They should be insured against this kind of thing."

Then Adam heard another voice, a local one, apologizing,

and explaining that he had lost the grip on his stick. Dalton called him a bloody fool. Then Adam heard Amanda's voice. "He's coming round…"

Adam opened his eyes to see Amanda leaning over him, pressing a damp towel to his forehead.

"Adam? You had a bit of a bump on the head. Don't worry, I'm a qualified first-aider. You've got a nasty lump, but I think you'll be OK. We'll get you checked out. I've called a doctor."

Rachel appeared in Adam's field of vision, panting, as if she had been running. Laura was standing behind her, and, seeing her, Adam tried to be brave and got up on to one elbow.

"Don't move, Adam," Laura said. She laid a hand on his shoulder and squeezed. She looked concerned, but when she wheeled round to Amanda, the worry in her face turned quickly to anger. "What on earth happened here?"

Amanda led Laura off into a huddle, whispering and pointing at the pair of remaining morris dancers who were packing their things away. Laura glared at them, and at Dalton.

Rachel leant in close to her brother. "What happened, Adam?"

"We've been betrayed, that's what," Adam whispered. "Someone's told them we've found the blade."

"I don't understand. Who?"

"It's got to be Jacob."

"No," Rachel said. "Jacob wouldn't." She shook her head, kept shaking it, but at the same time she was wondering whether Jacob would. He had been the one who had invited the TV crew to the village, after all.

"Then it's your lovely Gabriel, isn't it?" Adam hissed. "He's the only other person on earth who knows."

Rachel said nothing. Gabriel had been quiet for days. There had been no messages since the television crew had arrived in the village.

She looked across the moor to where the cars were parked. A tall morris dancer in a long leather coat and top hat, his face completely blackened, was watching her. When he realized Rachel had seen him, he raised his hat to her, before climbing on to a big motorbike and roaring off.

Adam climbed slowly to his feet. "It's not really important who told them anyway," he said. "All that matters is that they're prepared to kill us to get it."

30

Dalton peered into the tunnel that had already taken his team a solid three days to dig. And now it was starting to rain.

"How much longer?" he shouted into the tunnel, shielding his hair from the drizzle with Amanda's clipboard.

Dalton was getting impatient. He didn't like going into the tunnel. It was wet and dark. And scary. The dig had only just got back on track, having nearly been aborted after the incident with Adam and the morris men. It had taken all Dalton's considerable charm to smooth things over following the accident. He'd sent a letter (actually written by Amanda) to Adam's grandmother, together with a cheque for two hundred pounds which Mrs Root had immediately donated to the appeal to restore the church roof.

Now there seemed to be some kind of delay. They were supposed to be transmitting the dig live on TV that night, on a special edition of *Treasure Hunters*. Dalton checked his watch. It was nearly six, and the first part of the show was due to go out at seven.

"Can we hurry this up?" Dalton shouted to no one in particular. "We're live in an hour."

Laura Sullivan, wearing a hard hat with a torch attached to the front like a coal miner, poked her head out of the tunnel. She was covered in mud.

"We've got to be patient, Chris, OK? I think we're at the entrance to a burial chamber. At least, there are bogoak props holding up something and barring our way." Laura wiped specks of dirt from her eyes. "I've sent some splinters off for carbon testing to get a date on them."

"Can't we just guess?" Dalton said. "I mean, they're going to be about a thousand years old, roughly. Let's just make an estimate and plough on." He peered down into the tunnel. "Can't we just chainsaw through them or something?"

Laura rolled her eyes. "Chris, this is important. We have to show every single consideration for a site of this age. We can't rush it. We'll put out the first part of the show at seven. Then see how we get on between then and eight when the update goes out."

"OK." Dalton puffed out his cheeks in frustration. "But I want results by the eight o'clock transmission. If we've got nothing to show, the punters will stop watching. We're looking for four million viewers for this show. Minimum."

Dalton stepped out of the tunnel entrance to see that a crowd was already gathering in the drizzle behind the tape that cordoned off the dig. Word had quickly gone round that the site was revealing coins, shields, swords and more arte-facts that suggested a burial mound, but now a rumour was growing that the archaeologists had found something else. Something big. Despite the villagers' reluctance to offer information, a certain morbid curiosity had drawn them to the circle, eager to see what of the village's history would be uncovered.

And of their own.

"Going live in … three, two, one…" Amanda looked at her stopwatch and gave Dalton the nod to start speaking.

"Good evening and welcome to a very special live edition of *Treasure Hunters*." Dalton stared straight into the camera and adopted his most dramatic voice. "Tonight we are com-ing to you live from the ancient village of Triskellion, where we hope we are on the verge of a very important discovery…"

He paused. The moment where he knew from long expe-rience that the show's title sequence would play in. The camera turned on to the crowd, revealing a cross-section of the village's inhabitants to the viewers at home.

Pale faces framed by waterproof hoods peered through the fine drizzle into the arc-lights that illuminated the tunnel: Reverend Stone, the Bacon brothers and many other of The Star's regulars.

Close to the tape, at the opening of the tunnel, stood Rachel and Adam, having been ushered into prime positions by Laura. Next to them, her wheelchair protected from the rain by a yellow cycling cape, was Granny Root, her lips pursed as she watched the action unfold. Alongside her, his face fixed in a frown beneath a black umbrella, stood Commodore Wing. It was not the company Rachel and Adam would have necessarily chosen to accompany them to the dig, but they took some comfort from it.

While they were with their grandmother and the commodore, they were safe from Hilary Wing.

Adam and Rachel stared up at the projection screen that had been erected close by, so that the villagers could watch events as they were broadcast live. After the *Treasure Hunters* titles, Adam watched the sequence that had been filmed a couple of days earlier, just before the "accident". He saw himself, several metres high on screen, without the large plaster that was now stuck to his head, and heard himself say, "We know that the symbol is probably Celtic and was carved during the Bronze Age."

An aerial shot showed the chalk circle from above, then Adam winced as horribly familiar music was heard; as the picture changed and he watched clips of the morris dancers, jigging round the circle, looking perfectly harmless.

The camera cut back to Dalton, live, who proceeded to build the tension, showing some of the swords and shields that had so far been dug up during the excavation.

"It's all very exciting," he said. "Very exciting…"

Then the camera moved inside the shaft where, by torchlight, Laura Sullivan and her fellow archaeologists worked away at the heavy oak beams that were blocking their way.

"We're making good headway, Chris," Laura said, her voice muffled and her muddy face close to the camera. "These beams, which seem to be protecting some kind of burial chamber are beginning to shift a little. We're replacing them with expanding steel scaffolding props as we go. Hopefully we'll have some good news for you when we come back at eight…"

"Thanks, Laura," Dalton said. He turned back to his camera. "So, make sure you join us back here at Triskellion at eight o'clock when we may be able to show you just what lies behind those mysterious oak beams. See you then." He grinned at the camera and gave a small salute.

"OK, Chris, they're off us," Amanda said.

Dalton pulled off the small microphone attached to his jacket. "Right, I'm busting for a Jimmy Riddle," he said. "I'll just find a bush."

Amanda nodded, not that she was the least bit interested in where her boss attended the call of nature, and Dalton walked off into the darkness behind the arc-lights, doing his best not to get his expensive hiking boots too dirty.

He found a gorse hedge, just beyond the location van, and had just started to unzip his jeans when he became aware of someone near by. He rapidly did up his trousers and turned to see a boy standing directly behind him. Staring.

Dalton sighed. He was used to being gawped at by

members of the public. Schoolchildren would regularly shout, "Found any treasure, Chris?" as he walked down the street, or tried to do his shopping.

But this kid was different; *looked* different. He just stood and stared, until Dalton felt as though the boy's wide green eyes were looking straight through him.

"What do you want?" Dalton asked. "An autograph?"

The boy said nothing and continued to stare at Dalton.

"Well?" Dalton said. He was starting to get a little annoyed.

Five seconds passed … ten … and then the boy held out his hand, palm up.

"Oh, I see," Dalton said. "'Spare some change for the poor country boy.' That it?"

The boy waited.

Dalton shook his head and tutted, rummaging in his pocket. "Same everywhere you go," he said. "Touch the rich bloke off the telly for a few quid. Well, here you go." He took his hand from his pocket and placed a pound coin on the boy's upturned palm. "Now, buzz off and let a man have a piss in peace, will you?"

A look of what might have almost been anger passed over the boy's face, and he continued to hold Dalton's gaze, his own not flickering.

"Well?" Dalton made a "shooing" motion with his hand, but the boy didn't move. He simply looked down at what had been placed in his palm. Then, as he did so, the pound coin burst spontaneously into flames, spluttering and glowing white like a firework.

Dalton staggered back. "Jesus…"

The boy looked up then, and smiled.

Dalton did his best to smile back. "Nice trick," he stammered, before turning, tripping over his feet as he hurried back towards the lights.

Gabriel watched him lurch away, then tossed the burning coin into the air. Followed its bright arc as it spun high across the distant bank of trees, like a shooting star.

It was becoming darker, and the rain was getting heavier. It hissed and steamed against the hot arc-lights surrounding the dig. Granny Root began to shiver.

"I'm frightfully cold, Gerry," she said, in a squeaky voice that made Adam snigger.

The commodore coughed, oblivious to the rain. "I'll wheel you back to The Star. We'll get a whisky or two and warm up there for an hour."

"That sounds perfect," Granny Root said. "I'm sure the children won't mind us old buffers leaving them on their own…"

Rachel and Adam said that they didn't, and the commodore pushed the wheelchair away towards the road.

Celia Root waited until she was sure they were out of earshot. "Do you think they will put two and two together, Gerry?" she asked in a frail voice.

"I'm not sure it matters any more. This is not just our secret any longer."

The old woman sighed and pulled the blanket a little tighter round her shoulders.

"This is *everyone's* past they're digging up back there, and nothing in Triskellion will ever be the same again."

In the darkness, Commodore Wing bent down and gently kissed Celia Root on the top of her head.

31

"**W**elcome back to this very special edition of *Treasure Hunters...*"

Chris Dalton spoke earnestly, leaning in close to the camera lens, his hair plastered down by the rain. It was unlike him to allow his hair to get wet, but he felt it made him look rather heroic, as if reporting from the front line.

"There has been an amazing development here at Triskellion," he said. "Just fifteen minutes ago, Doctor Laura Sullivan and our team of archaeologists made a major breakthrough. They have managed to remove some of the timber props that were barring the way, and have opened up what looks very much like a burial chamber. We're hoping to go over to Laura now and see just what's happening 'down under', as it were. Laura...?"

The camera cut off Dalton and an image of Laura Sullivan appeared on the plasma screen next to him, her features bleached out by the spotlight on her face.

"Hi, Chris," Laura said breathlessly. "Yes, this is really amazing. We're about three metres below the chalk circle and have opened up a cavity, which you can just about see behind me." Laura gestured over her shoulder and shone a strong torch into the gap they had made between the wooden props. Her two fellow archaeologists were removing another wooden support and the torchlight drifted on into the space beyond them. "And the most exciting part is that we can already see a sarcophagus or large coffin of some kind just a little way into the chamber. Looks almost like a tree trunk that's been hollowed out." The camera pushed past Laura, until, filling the screen and lit solely by the torch, the outline of a large wooden mass was visible.

Dalton talked to Laura on the screen. "So, how soon do you think it will be before we can see it properly?"

"Well, once the main beam came away, the other props were pretty easy to pull out. They fit together like a puzzle." Laura pointed the camera towards the end of one of the beams and traced her muddy finger along a notch that had been cut into it. "So, we're bringing them up to the surface to reconstruct them, which will be interesting in its own right. The wood's in amazing condition and seems to have been preserved by the marshy wetness of the moor and the acidity of the soil."

"That's incredible," Dalton said.

From his position near the plasma screen, Adam could see the beam. He had seen one very like it before. It was just like the prop that had been supporting the tunnel underneath Hilary Wing's cellar.

Could that tunnel have been made by the same person, or people, who had constructed this underground tomb?

"Then we're going to get some airbags under the sarcophagus to see if we can move it," Laura continued. "Hopefully in the next hour or so…"

"Great stuff, Laura," Dalton said. He turned back to the camera. "We'll be back with more exciting updates throughout the evening. So join us back here on *Treasure Hunters*, after the National Lottery and the news…"

He held a fixed smile at the camera while Amanda counted down the five seconds until he was off-air.

Probably the only person in Triskellion who was not watching *Treasure Hunters* stood in the nave of the darkened church. The stained glass window above him was barely illuminated by a cloud-covered moon.

He dragged the heavy oak lectern across the stone floor in front of the altar, then, summoning every ounce of strength, he heaved it beneath his arm and, using it as a battering ram, smashed open the door to the side room.

There, in the display case, where it had lain for a hundred years or more, the first golden blade glowed in the weak light from a dirty overhead bulb. He reached into his bag for a claw hammer, which he brought down sharply on the glass, shattering it into hundreds of shards which tinkled like tiny bells on the stone floor of the silent room.

Then, with a gloved hand, he lifted out the blade and studied it; breathless for a second, before wrapping it in a cloth and placing it in his bag.

In The Star, each member of the dominos team peered at their National Lottery ticket as they sat beneath the television screen mounted high above the bar.

"Not a blinking sausage so far," one said. The syndicate had won fifty pounds six months ago and all still lived in hope of the big win, although when Tom Hatcham had asked what they would do with £17 million, they claimed that it would not change their lives in any way.

The door swung open suddenly and Hilary Wing strode in, shaking the rain off a wide-brimmed hat and shoving it into his shoulder bag. The pub fell silent for a second, then everyone went back to their drinks or turned again to look at the TV.

Everyone except Commodore Wing and Celia Root, sitting by the fire and looking distinctly uncomfortable as Hilary strode over to the bar. Hilary gave his father a barely perceptible nod before turning to Hatcham and ordering a drink.

Rachel and Adam began to shiver.

The rain had stopped, but the damp had begun to penetrate their clothes. It felt as if it had got through to their bones, but wild horses could not have dragged them away from the scene that was unfolding in front of them.

Laura Sullivan's team had made astonishing progress.

As soon as they had raised the sarcophagus on airbags, it had almost seemed to roll *itself* back along the shaft they had dug, like an underground train, slowly emerging from a tunnel and arriving at the platform as it reached its destination. Rachel and Adam watched, open-mouthed, as the trunk-like shape was eased out of the entrance to the shaft, a team of four rolling it gently on the airbags, guided by Laura Sullivan.

Chris Dalton paced up and down in excitement, waving his arms about, directing the cameraman to get dramatic shots of the sarcophagus emerging so that they could broadcast it in the next update.

"That's great," Dalton barked. "Now, get down and do a low angle…"

The cameraman crouched low and tracked along the ground, groaning a little as he went. His head, as well as his back, was beginning to ache from all Chris Dalton's directions.

"Now tilt up to Laura," Dalton instructed. "Laura, take the hard hat off and wipe your brow for dramatic effect. That's great. Maybe you could toss your hair back…"

Laura, exhausted from five hours digging below ground, was in no mood to toss her hair about like a shampoo model. She continued to guide her team as they brought the sarcophagus to the surface. And for the moment, her hard hat remained on.

"Cut!" Dalton shouted. "Laura, what are you playing at? I'm trying to make this dramatic."

Laura had heard enough. She threw her hard hat on to the muddy ground and marched over to Chris Dalton.

"What am I *playing* at? I am playing at digging up probably the most significant Bronze Age burial this country has ever seen ... and I am not going to be told to ditz around like some bimbo by a guy who is frightened of getting his boots dirty or his hair wet. Get it?"

From their position just behind the tape near by, Rachel and Adam could hear every word of the exchange; could see the anger in Laura's body language.

"Go, Laura," Rachel whispered under her breath.

Dalton had begun to whine. "But, Laura, like I said, I'm just trying to make it dramatic."

"So, digging under a mysterious chalk circle, finding swords and shields and jewellery and arrowheads and then unearthing what appears to be a huge coffin made from a tree trunk thousands of years old isn't dramatic enough for you?" Laura spoke very close to Dalton's face.

Dalton paused a moment, considering his answer, wondering how far he dare push her, a wry smile growing across his face. "Well, actually, no. It isn't. It's not dramatic enough. It's fine for you anoraks, but I want something that's really going to blow away our audience." Then, realizing that the eyes of the near by crowd, and especially those of Rachel and

Adam were on him, he leant in close to Laura and whispered into her ear.

Watching the expression on Laura's face, Rachel was sure she was going to hit him. But Laura just nodded, deflated, then watched as Dalton strolled away.

Laura looked round, and seeing Rachel's look of concern, walked over to her. "Hey, how are you guys doing?" she asked.

"Oh, don't worry about us," Rachel said. "What about you?"

"Been better."

"I don't mean to be nosy," Adam said, "but what was he saying?"

"Adam." Rachel said. "It's none of your—"

"It's OK," Laura said. "I've got nothing to hide." She coughed and kicked at the mud beneath her feet, then looked up again at the twins. "He wants the coffin out and opened up next time we go live on air."

The twins exchanged a look.

"Opened up?" Adam repeated. He was horrified and fascinated at the same time.

"Can you do it?" asked Rachel.

The archaeologist's expression hardened; set itself back into the look of determination she had had when she was letting Dalton know exactly what she thought.

"Over my dead body," she said.

32

"There is absolutely *no way* we can open it up out here," Laura hissed. "It's raining, it's cold … even just the exposure to oxygen could destroy whatever's inside."

Chris Dalton stood with his arms folded. He was not looking at her, and appeared not to hear a word she was saying.

"We need to do it away from here, under lab conditions," she continued. "With everything properly monitored in the light of day. Please, Chris, this is really important."

"Listen to me," Dalton said, as if he had just begun to pay attention. "We have millions of viewers lined up for our ten thirty update. They're not going to sit and watch a lump of old wood for an hour, even if you jump up on top of it, take your clothes off and dance the cancan. We're going to get it open."

"You can't," Laura said.

"The head of programming thinks I can," Dalton said, dialling a number on his mobile and handing it to Laura.

"Maybe you should speak to him. He already has permission from the government heritage people."

"I don't believe you."

"Oh yes. At least *they* understand the draw of a good show. Capturing the public imagination, blah, blah, bringing tourists to the area, etcetera, etcetera…"

Laura knew she had lost the battle. She cancelled the call with her thumb and thrust the phone back into Chris's hand. "Well, you're on your own," she said.

Chris shrugged. "Your loss. You'd get all the glory. But have it your way. We're back on in twenty minutes, and *I'm* going to open it up. Live on air. Now *that*, for your information … is drama."

Dalton turned to the camera wearing his most earnest expression. The sort that doctors or newscasters held in reserve for really *important* news.

"Welcome back to Triskellion…"

Rachel and Adam stood huddled with Laura, inside the cordon now, but out of the camera's shot. Rachel sensed that Laura wanted them close by for support, because although the archaeologist could not bear to watch, neither could she detach herself from the unfolding scene.

The rest of the village had come back out of the pub and their houses for the ten thirty transmission, and a very large crowd was gathered behind the tape. Raised up on steel trestles and bathed in the phosphorescent light of the arc lamps, the wooden sarcophagus looked massive and primeval, like a huge animal awaiting slaughter.

The whole scene had the air of a public execution.

Rachel shivered. She was chilled to the bone, and without warning a small sob rose in her throat and she felt as if she might cry. She swallowed hard, trying to stifle the urge, and stealing a quick glance at Adam she could see that he, too, was welling up.

What was it about this scene that was so unbearably poignant for them, she wondered.

Chris Dalton was still talking, stretching out his introduction, building the excitement for his TV audience, although the atmosphere at the dig was already as tense as Rachel and Adam could bear. Film of the dig at various stages was being broadcast on the plasma screen next to them as Dalton described the progress that had been made. Rachel saw a picture of the chalk circle taken from a helicopter, then one of the beginning of the tunnel, then a shot of Dalton triumphantly holding up the corroded blade of an ancient sword.

An image of Laura came up on screen from somewhere deep underground. Laura squeezed Rachel's shoulder, reassuring her that she was by her side. Then, the sequence of the sarcophagus being eased from the tunnel came on to the screen and, once again, Rachel and Adam shuddered simultaneously at the eerie spectacle of the great wooden log being pulled from the ground.

The screen cut back to Dalton live. He spoke in a whisper, "And now the team have informed me that we are ready to open the sarcophagus."

Together, Rachel and Laura moaned softly.

"We're about to see what secrets it has been holding, deep under the earth of this village, for, who knows, maybe three thousand years or more. Let's go…"

Dalton beckoned the camera to follow him and he took the few muddy steps over to where Laura's colleagues were preparing to open the lid. The four archaeologists surrounding the log looked like surgeons; their hardhat-mounted torches shining down on the wet, black bark.

"We can just see a few signs carved into the log, here," Dalton said, running his finger over the surface. "If you bring the camera in close we can see what looks like part of the Triskellion symbol carved on the top…"

Watching the plasma screen, Rachel, Adam and Laura, so familiar with the symbol, could clearly make out two intersecting lines gouged deep into the bark. Rachel heard Laura take a sharp intake of breath and hold it, then realized that she herself had been holding her breath for some time.

"OK, people. The moment of truth. Let's go to work." Dalton whispered dramatically at his colleagues, as if he were about to lead them into battle.

The archaeologists began to work at a line that ran laterally along the log, obscured from vision by thousands of years of mud and rot. A pair of long levers was put in place at either end and they began to work the joint open. A small wedge was eased into the gap, then one of the archaeologists began to ratchet up a jack that would force the gap to open wider.

"They're opening it way too fast," Laura whispered, her voice panicky. "Let too much oxygen in there too quickly and everything could disintegrate." Rachel returned the pressure as she felt Laura take her hand and squeeze.

A second jack was applied to the other end and, centimetre by centimetre, a gap began to appear all round the two halves of the log. Rachel stood on tiptoe to see the coffin with her own eyes. There was definitely an opening, where the lid was being lifted from the base.

Dalton kept up a whispering commentary as his team worked at the opening, threading strong nylon webbing under the lid, working quickly but carefully to preserve what was within. A large winch was already in place alongside the trestles on which the coffin was supported, and a chain from the winch swung gently from side to side over their heads. One of the archaeologists attached the webbing to a large hook that hung down from the winch chain.

He gave the signal to pull.

A whisper went through the assembled crowd as one of the archaeologists pulled on the chain. There was silence, until all that could be heard was the rattle and clank of the winch chain as, slowly and steadily, it lifted the lid of the coffin. The massive half of an ancient tree trunk rose slowly into the glare of the arc-lights, casting a deep black shadow over the archaeologists standing below.

Rachel began to cry.

High up in the oak tree on the green, Gabriel, for the first time in his life, felt hot tears pour down his cheeks.

He could see the coffin clearly in his mind.

He could feel what Rachel was feeling and he whispered over and over again, "Don't worry, Rachel, this is meant to be. This had to happen. This is just the beginning of our story." And, as he sent his message out across the blackness, he felt a warm feeling of elation creep through his body, as the coffin was opened to the fresh night air.

Jacob Honeyman sat on the edge of a battered kitchen chair, his nose centimetres from the screen, holding the TV aerial over the set to get a better picture.

The camera edged towards the coffin and Chris Dalton continued his commentary.

"The lid is now off and once the team has made it safe, we can be the first to look inside…"

Honeyman stared at the screen, his mouth falling open.

"So we, the *Treasure Hunters* team, and you, the viewers, will be the first people in thousands of years to— Oh … my … God…"

"Oh, my God," Honeyman said.

*   *   *

The chatter and clink of glasses in The Star had stopped, and every face was turned to the TV set above the bar.

Celia Root held her hands to her face, barely able to look as the strong light on the camera pushed into the void at the bottom half of the coffin; as its ancient remains were exposed to view.

Blackened, and lying in a shallow pool of dark brown water, two figures were instantly distinguishable, their heads twisted back and their arms entwined.

The image was shocking and real: the bodies decomposed, but as fresh as if they had been buried months, not centuries, before. To the untrained eye, it could have been the scene of a murder rather than a burial.

"This … is … incredible," Dalton said. "We have not just one, but two bodies here in an absolutely amazing, *amazing* state of preservation. This has got to be a really significant burial. Instantly, we can see that these bodies are clothed in … some kind of woven fabric. At the top here on what looks like a female figure we can see quite a lot of hair, possibly braided … you can just see a bit of gold, or at least a gold coloured, hair ornament here…"

Rachel and Adam could not stand to watch was happening on the screen any longer, and crept over to where they could see directly into the coffin. Their mouths and eyes widened in wonder as they stared down upon the mortal remains of the figures from their shared visions.

The knight and the maiden.

Dalton's surgically gloved hand traced out the outline of the female head, mummified and wet as if it were made of old leather.

A twist of dark hair was just visible and a bronze grip held it to the blackened and shrunken ear.

"And if you just look down here…" The presenter pointed to the gnarled arms, twisted together. "You will see something very exciting indeed."

The camera tightened and revealed a golden glint. A delicate shred of metal, woven between the skeletal fingers of the two bodies.

The third blade of the Triskellion.

33

Gabriel had been waiting for them the moment the twins left the cottage. The morning was chilly and misty and Gabriel looked as if he were emerging from the vapour at the bottom of the garden path.

"Hello, stranger," Rachel said. "Where have you been?"

"Oh, I've been around, keeping an eye on things," Gabriel answered.

It was true, Rachel thought, he *had* been around. For the past two days his voice had become stronger and clearer in her head; guiding her and keeping her calm. Instinctively, she knew that the three of them had a date back at the chalk circle.

Their grandmother had been a little subdued over breakfast and looked as if she had not slept well. When Adam had asked her what she made of the discovery at the dig, she had smiled sadly. Had said that, although it was fascinating, some things were best left undisturbed...

Rachel, Adam and Gabriel tramped across the wet moor

into a scene that had changed still further in the two days since the sarcophagus had been opened. The location vans for the TV company stood on the misty horizon like grey blocks of stone and next to them, covering the circle and the surrounding area, a huge polythene tent had gone up to protect the dig from the elements.

It made the area look even more like a "scene of crime".

There were figures emerging from the tent, and Rachel and Adam stopped dead in their tracks when they realized that the shambling figure wearing a bobble hat, being closely followed by Chris Dalton, was Jacob Honeyman.

They watched as Dalton chatted and patted Honeyman on the back. The two men shook hands, then Dalton handed Honeyman something which he pocketed.

"Dalton's paying Jacob," Adam spat contemptuously.

Honeyman shambled across the moor towards Rachel, Adam and Gabriel and when, several metres away, he spotted them, he dropped his eyes to the ground. He waved, but stayed looking down until he reached them.

"Hi," he said.

Rachel and Adam mumbled a greeting.

"Amazing, isn't it?" Honeyman said. "The discovery. The blade … the bodies … *everything*. What an amazing night."

"So, where were you then?" Adam said, with characteristic bluntness.

"I watched on TV." The beekeeper tapped his nose conspiratorially. "Too many enemies out and about at night."

"Chris Dalton not being one of them," Adam said. "What did he give you?"

Jacob looked guilty. "Services rendered," he said.

"What services?"

"They paid me a few quid to film around the cottage and to borrow some of my artefacts, you know?"

"Oh, right," Rachel said, digging Adam in the ribs to silence him. "Well, see you around, Jacob."

Honeyman nodded, darting a look from one to the other, before pulling at the front of his bobble hat and shambling off.

The children watched him go.

"He's sold us out," Adam said. "He told them about the map, the blades … everything, I bet."

"That's unbelievable," Rachel said. "I thought he was helping us, not helping some TV company expose all our—"

"All *our* what?"

Rachel turned at Gabriel's question and saw that he was smiling. She realized that she – that they *all* – felt a strong degree of ownership over the circle. Over the artefacts.

Over the Triskellion.

"It's fine," Gabriel said. "This is what we've been waiting for. We needed someone like Jacob to get the ball rolling. We couldn't have done it. We needed someone else to dig up the grave."

"Why?" Adam asked.

"Well, apart from anything else, we didn't have permission, or the right machinery."

Rachel wasn't convinced. "Is that all this is about?"

Gabriel smiled, like he was trying to decide how much to give away. "We need to understand as much about our past as we can," he said. "It makes more sense of who we are, right? Now the third blade of the Triskellion has turned up, maybe the pieces of the jigsaw puzzle will come back together."

"What jigsaw puzzle?" Adam asked. He was looking to Rachel for help, but Rachel looked as if she already understood.

Gabriel continued, patiently. "The puzzle of who we are. Why you're here, why I'm here, and what has brought us together."

Before Rachel or Adam could say anything else, Dalton came strolling across. He was sipping from a Styrofoam cup of coffee and did not look best pleased to see the kids turn up. He seemed particularly uncomfortable around Gabriel.

"Hi, you guys. Did you watch the show? Awesome, wasn't it?"

"Totally awesome," Adam said, almost mocking.

"Anyway, not really much to see here now."

Dalton had moved a few steps to one side as he'd spoken, almost as though he were barring their entrance to the tent, or at least their view inside it. Rachel craned her neck and saw Laura Sullivan just beyond the entrance.

"Laura!" Rachel said loudly, hoping that once Laura had seen them, they'd be welcome.

The archaeologist poked her head out of the tent, looking pale and shaken. "Oh, hi, Rachel," she said.

"We were just wondering how things were going?" Rachel said.

There was a distinctly awkward silence. Dalton looked at Laura and shrugged, then walked away to where the production assistant was watching some of the programme's footage on a small screen.

"I thought you weren't having anything to do with this?" Rachel said.

"More of a damage limitation exercise, really," Laura said. "I couldn't stand by and let that clown mess up a find of this importance. My duty as an archaeologist overcame my personal pride, I'm afraid. And I think I may have found something … unusual here."

Rachel looked at Gabriel, who was staring off towards the trees as though he hadn't a care in the world.

"So, are you going to tell us?" Adam asked.

Laura glanced off to her left. Dalton was walking back towards them. She chewed her lip. "Listen, guys, this isn't really a good time," she said.

"Please," Rachel said.

Gabriel put his hand on Rachel's shoulder, "Come on, Rachel, we'll come back another time. It's not going anywhere just yet." He let his hand slide down Rachel's arm until his fingers became entwined with hers and he led her and Adam away.

Laura watched them walk disconsolately back across the moor, while she waited for Dalton to arrive back at the tent. She stopped him as he made to walk inside.

"Chris," she said, taking his arm. "Wait…"

"I'm waiting," Dalton said.

"Can you and Amanda come in and see this, and get one of the other archaeologists? I need someone to look at this properly…"

Within a few minutes, Laura, Dalton, Amanda and one of the archaeologists who had opened the tomb stood in the pale light of the tent that had been assembled round the sarcophagus.

A faint mist from a spray constantly played across the remains inside the wooden log to keep them from drying out. The bodies still lay in their twisted embrace, but Laura had put measuring tapes alongside them and a camera was permanently mounted overhead to record every detail.

"Some of these differences could be genetic," Laura said. "I know that, seeing as the corpse we're looking at is so old. But we all know three thousand years isn't so long in terms of evolution, and it doesn't explain this."

She pointed at one of the bodies and the others noticed that her fingers were shaking.

"Somebody please tell me that I'm not going mad."

34

A hooded figure presides over a burial, chanting and throwing handfuls of earth into a grave, its sides supported by green oak timbers. A mound of freshly dug earth by his side is garlanded with flowers and bowls of grain. Swords, arrows and shields are laid down in front of the mound.

A small group of villagers stands in tattered, woven clothes, their heads bowed.

Standing alone between the two groups of villagers are a young boy and a young girl holding hands. They are twins. They bear the olive skin and striking features that mark them out as different from the rest of the onlookers.

They stare blankly into the hole, uncomprehending.

Round each of their necks on a leather thong hangs a blade of the Triskellion.

The hooded figure nods towards an old woman, who leads the twins away. When he sees that the children have gone, the man in the hood steps towards a raised platform on which two bodies are laid in a hollowed-out tree trunk.

He lowers his hood, revealing pale, sunken cheeks and a hawk-like nose. He mutters an incantation as he leans over the bodies, removing the curved knife from the folds of his dark cloak...

Rachel looked up at the stained glass window. The meaning of the shocking images was beginning to come slowly into focus, but plenty was still puzzling.

"So this guy ... a traveller, a knight or healer or whatever he was, comes to the village and meets this girl. This maiden. They meet, they marry and they have kids."

"And then they die," Adam said. "And get buried just outside the village. Seems pretty straightforward to me."

"Straightforward?" Rachel looked at Adam as if he were mad. "Are you kidding? *How* did they die? I don't know about you, but I saw a knife."

"But they were already dead," Adam said.

Rachel shook her head. Nothing was making any sense. "They had twins, like us, we know *that* much. But why was their burial place so special ... and what about the shooting star? And the Triskellion? What does it mean?"

Adam plunged his hands into his pockets. "I've got another question for you. A big one."

"What?"

"How come every time we have one of these dreams or whatever they are, it looks like you and Gabriel? I'm never in them."

Rachel blushed. It was true. The knight and the maiden did look like her and Gabriel. She wondered if, maybe, that was just because, subconsciously, she wanted them to.

Adam leant across and patted the tomb of the crusader. "What I'd like to know is why they invented this Sir Richard de Whatever to cover up *this* guy's identity?"

"They must have had something pretty big they wanted to hide," Rachel said.

"How dare you?" The thin voice resonated about the church as Reverend Stone stepped out from the shadow of the side room.

Rachel gasped as the vicar's face moved into the light; it was the face of the hooded man from her vision.

"I am surprised you have the barefaced cheek to come in here, let alone question the authenticity of the tomb. You two started all this. How can you come back in here after what you've done?"

Rachel and Adam looked blank.

"You deny it?"

"Deny what?" Rachel asked.

"Theft." Reverend Stone's lips tightened: white against a face that was rapidly reddening. His hands balled into fists at his side. "I don't know how you have the gall to come back here. How dare you."

"I'm sorry, but we don't know what you're talking about," Adam said.

"You had better return what you stole immediately. There

are some very important people who will be after you for this. People who are very angry."

"What is it you think we've stolen?" Rachel asked.

Stone could bear no more insolence. His face reddened still further and he began to tremble. He reached forward and grabbed Adam by the arm, his bony fingers digging into the flesh. Adam cried out and wrestled his arm free.

"Get out," Stone screamed. *"Get out!"*

The vicar's voice echoed off the walls as Rachel and Adam ran out of the church and straight into the path of Chris Dalton and a concerned-looking Laura Sullivan.

"We were looking for you," Laura said breathlessly. "We need to talk."

Adam pointed back towards the church. "Well, I wouldn't go in there. The vicar's pretty mad."

"I know," Laura said. "Somebody stole something the other day. And I don't think he was too happy with the questions I was asking about the inscription on the tomb, either."

Dalton smiled. "Looks like we're *all* in trouble." He stepped across to Rachel, who was still a little shaky after the confrontation inside the church. He laid a hand on her shoulder. "Let's get a coffee," he said.

Having parked his black BMW on double yellow lines on the village High Street, Dalton commandeered the largest table in the Waverley Tea Room. The waitress silently took their order for scones and slices of toast and only spoke when

Rachel asked for a "latte". The coffee was instant, she said, but she could make it extra milky if that was any use.

"So, what do you two know about these gold blades?" Dalton asked.

Laura looked taken aback. "Hang on, Chris. Let's fill the guys in a bit first."

"I'm sorry," Dalton said, smiling at Rachel and Adam sincerely. "Listen, I know I'm a bit direct sometimes. It's just my TV training, you know? Trying to get to the heart of the matter. You probably think I'm a bit of a…" Dalton searched for the word. "Pillock. You know, with all this TV business."

Rachel and Adam had not heard the word before, but guessed its meaning and shook their heads out of politeness.

Dalton continued, his tone turning serious. "It's just that I really care about this stuff, you know?" He stopped and leant back in his chair as the waitress arrived. She laid the plates of scones and toast on the table. Three mugs of coffee and a hot chocolate for Adam. Dalton thanked her as she left and turned back to Rachel and Adam. "This is a really important discovery." He paused, letting what he'd said sink in. "I'm grateful you guys have been able to help us."

Dalton had never spoken so earnestly to either Rachel or Adam and they were flattered by his attention. Away from the camera he was actually a lot nicer than either had taken him for. His concern for the dig seemed genuine, and the twins began to relax.

"What else have you found?" Rachel asked eagerly.

"Let's just say that this burial is even more important than we originally thought," Laura said.

Chris coughed and looked hard at her, but Laura continued.

"We need help here, Chris." He shrugged, signalled her to carry on. "Look, we think there's a really good reason why these two bodies were buried outside the village. A reason why the chalk circle was made to mark the spot."

Adam bit hungrily into a scone. "So who do you think they were?"

Laura fixed him with an intense expression. "*That* we don't know. Yet. I should tell you why we were excited about digging in this area in the first place."

Dalton relaxed a little; he knew what was coming.

"About ten tears ago, a team of archaeologists were digging on a farm about thirty miles from here. The usual kind of thing: a standard round barrow burial, early Bronze Age, maybe four thousand years old. They found a body. A man. Nothing unusual in that, but exciting none the less. But like the bodies here, the acidity of the soil meant that enough bone and tissue remained to extract DNA from the body and get a genetic profile. You know what DNA is?"

Rachel nodded.

"Kind of," Adam said. "I've seen them talk about it on cop shows."

"OK. DNA is the chemical make-up that provides each of us with a unique identity. You will both have similar DNA inherited from both your mum and your dad. It's in your hair, in your fingernails, in your spit. All of your body's cells carry your DNA. This is how we trace and identify people. It's how they catch murderers who have left samples of their DNA at the scene of a crime."

"So these people *had* been murdered?" Adam asked, leaping ahead.

Laura shook her head, slurped at her coffee. "We don't know that," she said. "The team took DNA samples from the body they found on the farm. They also took samples from the farmer who owned the land now. And guess what?"

Everyone at the table was silent. Laura looked from one to another, then continued. "The DNA of the Bronze Age man was an exact match for the guy who was still farming that piece of land four thousand years later."

"Wow," Rachel and Adam said simultaneously.

"So, the farmer's family had not moved from that area in all that time. They'd stayed in the same place for four thousand years. This gives us a real insight into how we've developed. How people have changed over centuries, how certain illnesses or genetic characteristics stay within a local area."

"That is totally amazing," Rachel said. She sipped at her coffee, her mouth dry. "So how does this help with the bodies at the circle?"

"Well, it seems that people in this part of the world tend not to move too far from their roots. OK, your mum went to the States, but before that, her family, your *gran's* family, were here for generations. Which means there's a likelihood, if we can get DNA from these bodies, that we may be able to find the actual descendants of this Bronze Age couple."

Rachel's head was reeling with the new information, but before she could digest it, Dalton spoke.

"Trouble is, I think getting DNA samples from a village as buttoned-up as this, will be like getting blood from a stone."

Adam grunted his agreement, mouth full.

"We could start with you two, if you're willing?" Laura said.

Adam swallowed quickly. "But we're not really *from* here."

"But you *are*. Like I said, you will have some of your DNA from your dad who, I guess, is American."

"Right," Rachel said.

"But you'll also have your mum's, your gran's, your grandfather's, and all their ancestors, who have been around here for centuries."

Rachel started at the mention of their grandfather. He'd not been around in their lifetime. All they knew from their mother was that he hadn't been there when she was a kid either. It was something she had always spoken of with regret. She had hinted that her father had probably left soon after her birth, and that Celia Root had brought her up alone.

Rachel had often wondered if the lack of a father had been the cause of her mother's near permanent melancholy.

"So, if you two will give samples, maybe others will follow."

Laura looked at Rachel and Adam questioningly. "We just need to take swabs. It's very simple, honestly, and I promise it doesn't hurt." She smiled, then turned as the bell on the door rang and another customer swept into the tea room.

"Well, here comes another willing donor," Dalton said. He rose from his chair and the twins watched in horror as he greeted the man who had marched across to their table.

"Rachel, Adam ... have you met Hilary Wing?"

35

Hilary Wing dragged out a chair and sat at the head of the table. His smile showed a lot of teeth. "Yes, we have met…"

Rachel sat open-mouthed, while Adam visibly paled. They did not shake hands. Neither Dalton, nor Laura seemed aware of their discomfort.

"I was terribly sorry to hear about your scrape with the morris dancers," Wing said, looking straight at Adam. "The Green Men are usually a little better disciplined than that. One of the dancers was new by all accounts. I hope you're better now?"

Adam mumbled a nervous response about being fine, but could not shake the fact that he was sure that one of the dancers had been Hilary Wing himself.

"Hilary has been a great help in providing us with some of the background to the customs and rituals of the area," Dalton said.

"It's been my pleasure," Wing said. He took off a worn

tweed jacket that looked as if it might once have belonged to his father and hung it across the back of a chair. He rolled a cigarette and lit it; puffed out a thin stream of blue smoke with complete indifference to the people at his table or the groups of old ladies gathered at others.

Dalton cleared his throat. "Hilary has some really interesting ideas about the significance of the gold blades," he said.

"Or the *missing* gold blades," Wing said, blowing out another plume of smoke in Rachel and Adam's direction.

Dalton nodded. "Yes, the vicar has gone ballistic since that one was nicked from the church. I guess it can't have gone far in a place like this though."

"Somebody stole the *blade*?" Rachel gasped. Now she could understand why Reverend Stone had been so furious, and exactly what he had been accusing them of. "He thinks *we* took it."

Wing shook his head as though this were the most preposterous idea he'd ever heard. "All the same, you wouldn't know anything about it, would you?" His tone was gentle, *concerned*, but to Rachel's mind there were still a few too many teeth showing when he smiled.

"No way," Adam said indignantly. "We were nowhere near the church yesterday."

"What about the other one?" Wing asked.

Laura looked confused. "The one we found with the bodies, you mean?"

Wing stubbed out his cigarette in a saucer, staring hard at Adam. "No," he said. "Not that one. A little bird tells me that a *third* part may have been discovered, and I know you two have been doing a little treasure hunting."

"What little bird?" Adam asked.

"Well, an acquaintance of mine was having a friendly chat with our local beekeeper the other evening…"

Adam and Rachel exchanged a look. So Jacob *had* been the one to reveal the existence of the third blade.

"So?" Wing said. "About this other blade…"

Adam tried his best to return Wing's stare, but he could feel the blood rising to his face and looked away.

"Well, we didn't find anything," Rachel said. "We both had unfortunate accidents that day. Didn't you know?"

"Accidents?" Laura asked.

Wing wasn't about to give Rachel the chance to answer. "What day are you talking about exactly?"

Rachel opened her mouth and closed it again. She knew she had said too much.

Wing's grin widened and he raised his hands in mock confusion. "I never said anything about any particular day." He waited for a response and when none was forthcoming he shrugged, as though it was nothing more than a silly misunderstanding.

"You were going to talk about the Triskellion," Laura said.

"Of course," Wing said. He nodded politely towards Laura, then leant a little closer to Rachel and Adam. "As your treasure hunting chum Mr Honeyman will have told you, the gold Triskellion is a very significant pre-Saxon artefact. As the landowner on whose estate at least one of the blades was discovered, I do feel a little ... proprietorial about it."

"That's perfectly understandable," Dalton said.

Rachel had to concede that it was. Wing's interest in the Triskellion might simply be based on ownership. She could see how, as far as he was concerned, she and Adam were trespassers: searching for, and taking things found on his land. She wondered for a moment whether they might, in fact, have got Hilary Wing wrong. They had misjudged Jacob Honeyman, after all.

Perhaps they had got a lot of things wrong.

Hilary Wing took a piece of paper from the inside pocket of his jacket and unfolded it on the table. Everyone leant in to look. It was a photocopy of an old document.

At the top of the sheet, in a scratchy ink line, the three blades of the Triskellion had been drawn, laid out side by side and numbered. Below that was a diagram of the blades floating above one another, with arrows describing the direction in which each part was to be placed against the next. At the bottom of the sheet was a picture of the three Triskellion blades joined together, with a few lines of illegible writing scrawled underneath.

"This is a copy of an old manuscript kept up at the hall," Wing said. "It clearly shows that the three blades should fit together in a certain way."

"Pieces of a jigsaw," Rachel said.

Wing nodded. "Exactly." He produced a second sheet and laid it down. "And *this* ... is what I think it was used for."

The second document showed a drawing of the complete Triskellion and around it, pictures of stars and the moon.

"The position of the stars on this diagram relates exactly to the position they would be in around the chalk circle at the summer solstice." There was genuine excitement in Wing's voice as he ran a finger round the faded ink outline. "So, my best guess is that the amulet itself is some kind of early compass or navigational aid, used to take bearings from the stars."

Laura studied the diagram. "If you're right, it would be the earliest example of such a thing anywhere in Europe."

"So you understand?" Wing looked straight at Rachel and Adam. "It's very important that we find the missing pieces and bring them back together."

Rachel and Adam knew immediately what the other was thinking. They nodded their understanding to Hilary Wing, but both knew instinctively that he wasn't the person to be entrusted with the blade they had discovered in the woods.

"It's fascinating stuff," Laura said.

Dalton nodded. "*Really* fascinating..."

"I've made a few discoveries too."

"Really?" Wing said.

"This will interest you, Rachel. Remember the runes and

the other bits of inscription we found round the tomb in the church?" Rachel nodded. "Well, I emailed the pictures back to my guys in Perth. They love a puzzle like this and they've come up with a couple of blinding ideas."

Laura took a file from her bag and pulled out a page that was covered in digital photos of the inscription round the tomb. "OK, here are the runes we looked at. Thing with runes is that the meanings aren't hugely specific, but I don't think we're too far off with the bit we can actually read. They think it's probably an obituary, just like a gravestone inscription."

Rachel nodded again, but felt a shudder pass through her.

"They've come up with, 'The man who rides from the sun dies by the yew tree.' Make of that what you will…"

"Sounds pretty obvious," Rachel said. "Maybe this guy came from a hot country and died here of some disease."

Wing shook his head. "That's too literal. The *mannaz* rune, meaning man, can also mean mankind in general … and the sun rune can also be interpreted as the wrath of God." Laura nodded, acknowledging that what Wing was saying was true. "So it could also mean that some aberration was committed by these people."

"An aberration?" Adam said.

"Something outside the norm," Wing said. "Something unacceptable." He paused. "Something that meant that the wrath of God was visited upon them."

Laura looked impressed at Hilary Wing's authoritative knowledge of the runes. He had clearly done his homework.

"Interesting," she said. "But the other inscription's a lot less ambiguous." Laura took another piece of paper from her file, pushed it across the table so that Wing and the twins could all read it.

ᛈᛟᚾᚷᛖ ᚠᚲ ᚱᛟᛏᛘ ᛞᛖᛘᚱᛖ
ᛟᛘᚦᛖᚱ ᛒᚱᛁᛟᚷᛏᛟ ᚠᚱᚾᛏᛘ

Below the runes, Laura had scribbled a translation.

Wing and Root shall never bear fruit

"So why is this less ambiguous?" Rachel asked.

"Because it ties in exactly with this." Laura produced a blown-up photo from her file. "There's a small wall painting," she said. "High up above the nave."

Rachel stared at the picture. The detail showed a banner, flying from a small, pointed tent in the background of the scene. Magnified, Rachel could clearly make out an inscription on the banner.

wynnge & rote
yfeere never bryngen frute

"What language is that supposed to be?" Adam asked.

"It's Middle English," Laura said. "Say, 1300-ish." She traced her finger along the words. "Someone has already had a go at translating the runes and incorporated the inscription into the wall painting."

"So what does it mean?" Adam squinted at the picture. "That birds and plants can't make fruit?"

Hilary snorted in derision, but Laura was more sympathetic. "Yes, kind of, Adam. You often get this kind of warning in old inscriptions, that breeds mustn't mix, to maintain the purity of livestock, or corn crops, for instance." She stabbed at the picture. "But I think *this* has a more specific reference to families."

"Of course it does," Wing said. "The same inscription is carved into the fireplace in our dining room. The medieval spelling of my surname was *Wynnge*." He leant back and folded his arms as though it were all perfectly obvious.

Adam was starting to get it. "And maybe our mom's surname was originally spelled Rote?" he ventured.

"Top marks," Dalton said. "So, the inscription is a warning for the two oldest families in the village not to get together and have children. Makes sense too. Loads of these places bred among each other so much they've all got three heads and stand around at night shouting at the moon's reflection in puddles."

Laura and the twins were slightly taken aback by Dalton's rather brutal interpretation, but Wing agreed.

"Noble sentiments," he said. "Keep the breed healthy, keep the families apart." He flashed a nasty grin at Rachel and Adam. "I'm sure you wouldn't be too thrilled to discover that we were related, would you? However distantly…"

Adam was almost about to answer back, but Laura spoke

first. "What if they *didn't* stay apart?"

"What?" Rachel said.

Wing whipped round to Laura; spoke in an icy whisper. "Excuse me?"

"What if, at some point in the past, your family and the Root family ignored the warning and produced children? What would be the outcome? Maybe there was a genetic defect they were trying to avoid, or perhaps it was just territorial. I'm not saying they did ... but what if? I mean, I can't find anything in the parish records, but we probably wouldn't be talking about a marriage."

"You mean, like an affair or something?" Rachel said, concealing the slight thrill she felt at the idea.

"Sure," Dalton said. "Things like that have always gone on in places like this. Not much else to do in the country."

Hilary smirked, but Laura was following a different tack.

"Given that the village is so small, and that people didn't move around very much, it would be strange if a Wing and a Root *hadn't* got together at some time. It's a fascinating idea, don't you think?"

Laura looked directly at Hilary, raising her eyebrows, almost as if she was playing a game with him.

The smile evaporated from Hilary Wing's face and he turned slowly back to the twins. "If that were so ... and this is *purely* hypothetical, of course ... we would have to lay aside any differences, wouldn't we?"

Adam grunted. "Would we?"

"Of course," Wing said. "Because that would mean we were family."

36

"**W**hat was all that about?" Laura asked, as she and the twins walked away down the High Street. "He's got a bit of a problem with you two."

"Just a bit," Adam said.

"Clearly doesn't like people on his land."

"It's his dad's land really," Rachel said.

Adam looked back towards the tea shop, where Hilary Wing was still deep in conversation with Chris Dalton.

"He tried to kill us," Adam said.

"Adam," Laura laughed. She was about to pull Adam up for exaggerating, but one look at his pale face and his desolate expression told her instantly that he was not. Or, at the very least, that he truly believed what he was saying. She put her arm round him as they walked, feeling his narrow shoulders trembling under his shirt.

Adam suddenly felt like a small boy, his hands dangling by his sides and this older woman's arm round him. He slid his arm round Laura's waist, feeling her hip bump against him comfortingly as they walked. "I've got the other blade," he said.

Rachel gasped.

Laura stopped in her tracks. "What, the one stolen from the church?"

"No way. We wouldn't do that," Adam said. "Honest, Laura. It's another one. We found it fair and square. Hilary Wing locked me in his cellar and I tunnelled out."

Rachel nodded to confirm her brother's story. "He nearly died," she said.

"How on earth did you find it?" Laura asked, astonished.

"We had a map," Rachel said. "Jacob Honeyman helped us find the spot, but in the end we kind of found it by accident."

"I don't think it was an accident," Adam said.

Laura looked at him.

"Look, I know it sounds weird, but it was, like, the blade itself led me to find it. Underground. It was like I just followed a light."

Laura thought for a few seconds. "OK..."

"I think we were meant to find it and Hilary Wing wasn't. Otherwise he would have found it by now."

"You're right, it does sound a *bit* weird," Laura said.

"It's true," Rachel said. "Me, Adam and Gabriel found a tree, well, were almost guided to a big *yew* tree, and Adam just *happened* to be in a hollow underneath it. Came up from it, like the earth just spat him out..."

Laura looked from one to another. The story sounded ridiculous; a fantasy. But then, nothing could have surprised her more than what she had discovered a metre or so under the ground herself. "Who's Gabriel?"

"He's our friend. The dark-haired boy…"

"Rachel's boyfriend," Adam said.

Laura smiled as Rachel glowered at Adam and took another glance behind her towards the tea shop. Dalton and Wing had gone. "Is the blade in a safe place?" she asked.

"Sure," said Adam. "It's—"

"No, don't tell me," Laura said. "And for goodness sake, don't tell anyone else. For the moment you should forget you ever told me about it. OK?"

Rachel and Adam looked at each other. Decided not to tell her that Jacob Honeyman already knew.

"Wait till we need it," Laura said. "This could be our secret weapon."

Rachel looked at Adam. Did they need a weapon?

"Right," Laura said. "Shall we go and take these samples?"

"What, *now*?" Adam was less than fond of medical examinations. Even a routine check-up was enough to make him panicky. He'd already had enough excitement for one day, and it was still only lunchtime.

Laura laughed at Adam's wide-eyed, frightened expression. "Sure. It'll only take a few minutes, and it really won't hurt. We've got a temporary lab set up back at the church hall. We moved the coffin and everything there a couple of days ago for safekeeping…"

*   *   *

The hall was a large, single storey, wooden building set back behind the church on the edge of the green. *Treasure Hunters* had hired it for the duration of the dig as a place to keep their equipment dry and to store any important finds they made along the way.

Amanda had set up a temporary office in the far corner with a laptop and a phone, while Laura had sectioned off an area with heavy curtains of polythene sheeting, behind which the blurred, dark outline of the sarcophagus could be seen. Behind it, Rachel and Adam could just make out the shape of someone working round the sarcophagus and the faint hiss of the water spray that was still being used to keep the bodies moist.

In front of the curtains, several trestle tables had been assembled, on which lay the various coins, brooches, swords and shields that had been unearthed during the dig. One of Laura's fellow archaeologists was busy taking detailed photos of all the artefacts and labelling them. He looked up when Rachel and Adam came in; grunted a hello. Next to him another archaeologist, a woman, was working at something in clay on a potter's wheel.

"What's she doing?" Adam asked.

"We've been able to scan the skulls with some new infrared equipment we're trying out," Laura said. "Caroline is making up some sculptures based on 3-D scans of the skull shapes. Hopefully we'll be able to see what our Bronze Age friends looked like."

"Neat," Adam said.

Laura pulled back another thick layer of polythene. "Right, let's get this business over with. Nobody should be able to hear you scream from in here." Adam grinned, enjoying having his leg pulled, and the three of them stepped into another small, sectioned-off area equipped with a steel surgical trolley and a medical couch. Laura clicked on a floor-standing lamp and Rachel and Adam blinked in the stark glare of white, clinical light.

"OK, you guys," Laura said, taking a box of cotton buds from the trolley. "Open wide…"

Rachel and Adam looked a little taken aback, then did as they were told. Wearing rubber gloves, Laura took a cotton bud and wiped it round Rachel's mouth and gums, then dropped it into a polythene bag, which she sealed and wrote Rachel's name on. She then went through the same process with Adam.

Adam smiled and looked relieved. "That's it?" he asked.

"That's it. Unless you'd be kind enough to donate a little hair as well?"

"No problem," Adam said, eager now to please, and calmly pulled a clump from his head.

Laura laughed. "Just one or two hairs would have done," she said. Rachel obliged by plucking a couple of strands and handing them to Laura, who quickly bagged and labelled them.

"So you can extract our DNA just from that?" Rachel asked.

"For sure," Laura said. "That'll give us plenty. Mr Wing gave us some yesterday, and one or two others, so we'll be able to eliminate a few suspects straight away."

"Have you analysed the bodies yet?" Adam asked.

Laura suddenly looked awkward, and Rachel guessed that she was trying not to give too much away.

"Well, the DNA results are still being processed. But it looks like the female could be local … and the guy, well, it looks like he comes from a long way away. What we can tell, is what they'd eaten, and when. The contents of their guts – grains, pollen and so on – give us the approximate year of their death, about 1700 BC, and the fruit seeds give us an exact snapshot of the season. Looks like they died at the end of the summer."

"Like now?" Rachel said.

"Possibly. We're still trying to identify a few of the berries and grains."

One of the other archaeologists poked his head round the curtain and pulled down his surgical mask. He looked flustered. "Laura?" He glanced from one twin to another, trying to decide if it was all right to talk in front of them. Laura nodded. "Got a result on those berries from the bodies this morning. They're yew berries."

Laura and Rachel looked at one another.

"Yew?" Laura shook her head, as though trying to process this new information. The implications of it. "They're seriously toxic."

"Exactly," the archaeologist said. "Both guts contained significant traces of yew berries. These people were poisoned."

Oh, my God. The voice inside Adam's head was Rachel's and he knew that she could hear the same thought coming from him.

"That's not all." The archaeologist hesitated. "We've also established that the female was pregnant when she died." He looked at Rachel and Adam and cleared his throat. "She was carrying twins."

37

Laura walked with Rachel and Adam as far as the end of the lane that led up to Root Cottage. They walked slowly, and in silence. Each of them letting the latest discovery sink in.

"But they already *had* twins," Rachel said suddenly, breaking the silence.

Laura looked at her strangely. "What? How do you know?"

"I know how this will sound ... but I've seen them. In a vision, or a dream or something. I saw them getting married and having children, and then I watched them being buried. They had twins before they died."

"She's right," Adam said. "Twins who lived. I've seen them, too."

Laura looked at the twins in silence, but her face betrayed her thoughts; made it clear just how bizarre she found what they were saying. "OK," she said. "For the sake of argument, let's *assume* they already had twins. They're hardly going to kill *themselves*, are they? Not with a young family."

Rachel and Adam shook their heads.

"So maybe someone in the village didn't want them to have any more kids. We know yew was used to terminate pregnancies back then."

"But they were *both* poisoned," Rachel said.

Laura nodded. "Good point." She thought for a few seconds. "The only thing this has in common with any other Bronze Age burial I know about, is that if they were poisoned, then it may have been as a sacrifice to appease the gods. To assure the fertility of the land, of the crops, whatever. You see, usually people were only buried outside the village if they were considered bad luck. If they were outcasts." She thought about what she'd said for a moment. "That might also explain the state of the bodies."

"What do you mean?" Rachel asked. "What state?"

"The bodies aren't … complete. It's not unusual…"

Adam pulled a face. "Eucchh…"

Rachel stared at Laura, waiting for more, but Laura seemed reluctant to continue.

"Why would anyone have been an outcast?" Adam asked.

Again, Laura hesitated, as though she were deciding whether or not to share something.

"And if they were outcasts, why let everyone know where they are?"

"Right," Rachel said. "Why would they mark the spot with a big chalk circle?"

"Beats me," Laura said. "It's like 'X' marks the spot, or

something. Maybe it was so somebody could find them."

"Maybe so *we* could find them," Rachel said. "It's like a signpost."

Something dark passed quickly across Laura's face. "Or a warning."

Their grandmother was waiting at the door for them as they walked up the garden path and beckoned them in.

"Rachel, Adam. I wondered when you were coming back. Come in, we must talk." Celia Root seemed agitated as she wheeled herself back into the house.

The twins stood awkwardly by the fireplace while their grandmother manoeuvred her chair, positioning herself in front of them. "Darlings, there's been a terrible fuss about some blade or other," she said. "Do you know anything about it?"

Rachel and Adam tried hard not to look at one another. Tried and failed not to look guilty.

"Well, we saw that they discovered a blade at the chalk circle," Rachel said.

"Not that. Everyone knows about that, now. There's *another* one."

The twins shook their heads, but Rachel could see that this was cutting no ice with the old woman. "We saw one at the church," Rachel said.

"And what did you do with it?" Granny Root asked. "Please tell me, darling."

"We didn't do anything with it," Adam said. "The vicar showed it to us in a glass case."

"I see. And you thought you might like it, as a souvenir of your visit?" Granny Root smiled sadly, as if she had somehow extracted a confession from her grandson.

"No," Rachel said. "We looked at it, like Adam said. That's all." Rachel was trying to sound firm, but she could feel tears pricking at the corners of her eyes. To have been confronted in the church was bad enough, but to be questioned like this by their own grandmother was unbearable. "You're accusing us, like you think we're thieves or something."

"I'm so sorry, but I'm afraid your recent behaviour is against you." Granny Root's words and the tears in her eyes were a sharp reminder to Rachel and Adam of their ill-advised break-in at Waverley Hall.

"But surely you're on our side," Adam said. "Right?"

The old woman shook her head sadly. "It's not that simple, darling." She turned and shouted, "Gerry, you can come in, now. I'm getting nowhere."

From the kitchen, Commodore Wing stepped into the sitting room. He was quickly followed by Reverend Stone. It was clear that they had been listening to every word.

"I'm sorry, children," Granny Root said. "I gave you every chance to be honest with me."

Reverend Stone nodded. "Unfortunately we are going to have to do this another way."

The look her grandmother gave the commodore caused

something to flip in Rachel's guts. She had a horrible idea what this other way might be.

"You stole my map!" the commodore bellowed, abandoning any attempt at subtle cross-examination. "Now, what have you done with the blade?" The hot blast of his voice was almost enough to knock the twins back a step.

The weight of guilt and paranoia made Adam's head throb. He knew that one of the blades was only a few metres above their heads, hidden under a floorboard in the bedroom. It would be so much easier, he thought, just to come clean: to give them the blade, let them deal with Hilary. Then they could go home, forget all about it.

"There's another blade," Adam said quietly.

Rachel could have murdered her brother. Even though he was talking about the blade that they had found in the woods, the commodore and his lackeys would presume it was the one that had been stolen from the church. Adam's admission would convict them of something they hadn't done.

Rachel thought quickly, kept her cool and spoke.

"Of course there's another blade," she said. "Everyone knows that, don't they? In fact your son Hilary told us all about it, this morning. He showed us how it would fit together with the other two: the one from the church and the one they found at the burial site. It's just no one knows where this third blade is, right?"

The mention of Hilary's name seemed to take the wind

from the commodore's sails, and for a moment he was lost for words.

Adam saw what Rachel was trying to do. "That's right," he said. "That's what I was talking about…"

Trying to put her thoughts elsewhere, Rachel became aware of a low humming: the noise of a bee. She tried to look for it, but then the commodore stepped towards her, spoke quietly and menacingly.

"Are you trying to be clever, girl? Are you hiding something?"

Rachel suddenly felt her anger rising. She and Adam had been up in front of a kangaroo court of Triskellion dignitaries before and she remembered that going on the attack had been an effective tactic.

"You've got some nerve!" she shouted. "Talking about hiding things."

Celia Root gasped at her granddaughter's audacity. "Rachel!"

"No, I mean it. You people keep everything secret. It's like there's always something unspoken going on between you all. You whisper and you plot, and you've treated us like criminals ever since we got here."

"Now you listen to me…" the commodore said.

But Rachel wasn't listening. She could hear nothing but the blood fizzing in her veins and the low hum of the solitary bee. "Apart from anything else, it's bloody bad manners." Rachel was well into her stride and enjoyed spitting out her new, English swearword. Adam kept his head bowed.

"I don't think you know the meaning of manners," Celia Root said, in a trembling voice. "If you are keeping something secret, then you'd better tell us."

Rachel looked at her grandmother's twitching face. This woman was almost her nearest blood relative and in her eyes she saw what, at first glance, she took for hatred.

Rachel looked again.

What she could actually see was fear.

She glanced at the commodore and saw the same thing. She looked from one to the other and saw two old people, somehow smaller now than before, and bowed; shrunken suddenly by a secrecy that held them together but which also tormented them.

Where moments before they had been deeply scary, they were now just two, frightened old people.

Movement in the corner of the room caught her eye and she looked up to see the bee. Watched as it buzzed aimlessly around, butting into curtains and circling the dusty light fitting.

Zzzzz … dnk. Zzzzz … dnk. Zzzzz…

Rachel turned her attention back to the commodore, and followed a hunch. "While we're all talking about secrets, perhaps you'd like to tell us about the things that are written in the church? About Wings and Roots. About how they shouldn't … mix?"

Rachel's arrow hit the target squarely. Her grandmother

and the commodore stood in stunned silence, their faces drained of blood.

"You don't know what you're meddling with," Commodore Wing said quietly.

Rachel saw the expression on the old man's face and felt the look of defiance slip slowly from her own.

Reverend Stone stepped forward and broke the silence.

"Mrs Root, may I?"

The old woman gave a small nod, wiping a tear from her eye with a lipstick-stained tissue.

The vicar stepped towards Rachel, took a deep breath and yelled into her face. "Where is my blade?" Rachel flinched at the flecks of spittle that hit her cheek, but said nothing.

"Leave her alone," Adam said.

The vicar turned his gaze to Adam and put a finger to his thin lips. "Shush," he said. Then, from nowhere, his spindly arm swung wildly round and he slapped Rachel hard across the face.

Rachel screamed, and Adam moved, balling his hand into a fist and tensing to throw a punch at the vicar's scrawny throat.

Rachel's arm stopped him. "No, Adam," she said, choking away tears.

Then the bee landed on Reverend Stone's cheek...

He flicked at the insect, trying to remove it, but the bee's thorny feet held tight and it would not budge. Then another bee landed on his forehead, and another on his neck. Stone yelped as the first bee stung.

Rachel and Adam watched in amazement as a column of bees flew into the room from the kitchen. A dozen at first, then fifty … maybe a hundred, buzzing in through the open kitchen window, until the air in the room was black with the vibrating bodies and thick with their angry buzzing.

Celia Root's shrieks joined the screams of Reverend Stone as he was stung, again and again. The commodore was bent over the wheelchair, like a tweedy shell, heroically protecting the old woman from the insects yet, while bees crawled over the two of them, keeping them in check, neither seemed to sustain any stings.

Rachel and Adam stood frozen on the spot, horrified yet unable to take their eyes from the hideous spectacle in front of them.

Reverend Stone screamed until his voice was cracked and raw. He had fallen writhing to the floor, as every exposed inch of his flesh – his face, his eyelids, his lips, his ears and his hands – was covered with a throbbing layer of bees, stinging him repeatedly.

Rachel turned away, disgusted by the unearthly howl and the thrashing of Stone's stick-like limbs as the bees stung him to death. Astonished by the fact that neither she nor Adam seemed of any interest to the swarm.

That they had been left completely untouched.

Rachel stepped round the flailing body and ran towards the door. "I'll get help," she shouted, though even as she said it, she had no idea where help might come from.

She opened the door, hoping that the bees might fly out, but they stayed where they were, clustered round the adults in the room. She screamed for help, then saw two figures standing near the garden gate in the lane. She realized that it was Gabriel, and beside him, Jacob Honeyman, and she screamed again.

Neither Gabriel nor Honeyman moved from the other side of the fence, but as Rachel's scream died in her throat, the bees began to fly out of the door: a single line of five or six at first, then a thick phalanx, snaking off down the garden like black smoke.

Rachel turned back into the room, where one or two stray bees still darted and dipped around the ceiling rose. The bodies of hundreds of others – dead and dying after losing their stings – lay scattered across the floor. Celia Root sobbed, and Commodore Wing dared not move. She looked across at her brother. He was still rooted to the spot, staring down at Reverend Stone.

The vicar's head had swollen to the size of a football, purple and raw. His eyes had all but disappeared beneath eyelids that had swelled and closed completely. His sharp nose was now like an overripe strawberry, smeared across his face, and his puffed-up lips trickled with blood and drool and venom.

Rachel's hands flew to her mouth. "Oh, my God…"

From the end of his black sleeves, the vicar's once pale and delicate fingers protruded like those of inflated rubber gloves.

"He's dead," Adam said.

38

The twins sat shaking at the rickety table, while Jacob Honeyman put the kettle on. Adam picked at flakes of coloured paint that peeled from the table top while Rachel chewed at her knuckle nervously.

"Hot sweet tea," Jacob honked from the kitchen. "That should help."

Adam managed a grudging laugh. "Is there anything in this country that can't be solved by tea?"

The atmosphere in Honeyman's shack was not lightened by Adam's attempt at a joke. The single light bulb over the table illuminated everything with a stark, clinical glare, throwing dark shadows into the corners and making everyone look yellow and ill. In fact, Rachel *felt* ill; the sickening spectacle of the dying vicar imprinted on her mind's eye, and the deafening hum of bees still fresh in her ears.

It was seven o'clock. Three hours since Gabriel and Honeyman had whisked them away from Root Cottage with their grandmother's screams still tearing jagged holes in the afternoon air.

Gabriel sat slumped in Honeyman's battered old armchair staring at the floor. The light cast shadows under his eyes and made his cheekbones look sharper, his hair blacker. Rachel stared at him. He looked serious, and for the first time since they had met, Rachel felt a little scared of him.

Gabriel sensed her stare and looked up at her. "Well?" he asked, without opening his mouth.

"I can't believe you just stood by and let it happen," Rachel said. "I mean, the guy died in front of our eyes, in terrible pain. This is serious stuff. This is *life and death* stuff … not a stupid treasure hunt."

"You're assuming I had some kind of control over it," Gabriel said.

"Well, you did. Didn't you?" Rachel knew only too well what Gabriel was capable of. She had no trouble imagining that he had somehow controlled that swarm of bees.

Gabriel and Honeyman exchanged a glance.

"Maybe he had it coming to him," Gabriel said.

Rachel couldn't believe what she was hearing. *"What?"*

"Maybe it was just payback for something that happened in the past."

Honeyman nodded. "Something in the past…"

"Things catch up with people eventually." Gabriel shrugged, coolly, as if he were talking about a minor debt.

"So a guy gets stung to death because he's a nasty old

vicar?" Adam asked, shocked.

Gabriel smiled, but just for a second or two. "I'm not talking about him specifically," he said. "But perhaps someone *like* him did something bad a long time ago. He hit you, Rachel, because you tried to stand up to him, because you're strong-willed. A few hundred years ago, he would have burned you as a witch. A thousand years before that, he might have sacrificed you to please the gods."

"A thousand years is a long time," Rachel said. The vision of the knight and the maiden – of their final resting place and the hooded man brandishing the curved knife – flashed momentarily through her mind; an image rapidly replaced by a picture of the twisted, mummified bodies in the log coffin.

"Sometimes revenge *takes* a long time." Gabriel sat back in his chair. He looked almost pleased with himself.

"Whoa. I don't get this," Adam said. "You mean, he's taking the rap for something that happened in the past? Someone else did something bad and he pays the consequences? How's that fair?"

"Who said anything about fair?" Gabriel said. "Do you think people have been fair to you? We're all paying for stuff that was done in the past in some way or another. For things that were done by others."

"Yeah, well, you can't take it out on innocent people," Rachel said. "If everyone thought like that we'd still be fighting the grandchildren of soldiers who did terrible things in the Second World War." Adam nodded. They both remembered with horror the stories their father had told them about his grandparents being driven out of Poland during the war. How other family members had not been so lucky; how they had stayed and died. "We'd still be at war with people whose fathers and grandfathers killed members of our family in the concentration camps. It doesn't work like that, Gabriel. It *can't*. You have to forgive…"

"Not where I come from," Gabriel said, standing and looking from one twin to the other. "Where I come from, we get even." After a few seconds he grinned suddenly, as if the conversation had never happened.

"What?" Rachel said.

Gabriel reached into his pocket. He pulled out a glinting Triskellion blade and placed it on the table in front of the twins.

"*You* stole it from the church," Adam shouted. "Do you know how much trouble we got into because of that? They blamed us…"

"That's not the blade from the church," Honeyman said, putting cups of tea down in front of the twins. "It's the one you hid under the floorboards in the cottage. It wasn't very hard for him to nip in and grab it while you two were having a ding-dong with your nan. He was worried you'd spill the beans and tell them about it."

Adam felt himself redden. It was true, he almost had told them. "Talking about spilling the beans," he said. "You were the one who blabbed about the blade we found in the woods."

Honeyman looked at his feet. "I didn't have no choice," he said. "They'd already hurt me once. Who knows what Hilary Wing might have done?"

"It doesn't matter," Gabriel said.

"Listen, you need to do what he tells you," Honeyman said. "You've got to trust him." He looked at Gabriel, who smiled at him benevolently.

"I'm glad somebody thinks so," Gabriel said.

"You've got to stop blaming him or me, or worrying about what the old people think. None of it's important. This is bigger than all that, and we're nearly there now."

"Nearly where?" Adam asked, confused.

"Nearly at the end of it all," Gabriel said. "We've got different journeys home, but we all need the Triskellion back together before we can move on."

"But we've only got one piece of it," Rachel said, flatly. "The other one was stolen, remember?"

Honeyman took a quick slurp of tea, and began to fish in the deep pockets of his baggy trousers. "If you want to know who done the stealing from the church…" He pulled out a second blade, which he lay on the table next to the first.

Rachel and Adam looked open-mouthed at the blades which, seen together for the first time, looked brighter, more vibrant than either had done separately. They looked like new; *better* than new and their gleam seemed to give off more light than the single bulb that had begun to sway gently above the table.

"They're beautiful," Adam said.

The blades seemed to shimmer, then vibrate, rocking from side to side as if controlled by a magnetic force. Then slowly they began to spin, until they were positioned, point to point, their flattened centres overlapping.

Honeyman clapped his hands together, delighted. "See, they're finding themselves. Getting their bearings."

"Their bearings for what?" Adam asked, staring at the blades as they continued to hum softly against the wooden table top.

"We need the third one to find out," Gabriel said. "We know where it is."

"That's right," Honeyman said. "We know where it is all right."

"But there's only two people here who can go in and get it."

As Adam and Rachel returned the stares of Gabriel and Jacob Honeyman, it became very clear to them who those two people were.

39

As soon as Hilary Wing had closed the door of The Star behind him, Tom Hatcham threw the bolts and drew a curtain across the window. Wing studied the silent faces, the forlorn figures sitting at tables staring back at him.

Most of Triskellion seemed to have gathered in the small saloon: the Bacon brothers; the couple from the bakery, the greengrocer, the butcher and the old woman who ran the post office; the entire staff of the village school, the cricket team and the committee that maintained the green and the village's floral arrangements.

Hatcham went back behind the bar and poured a large glass of red wine. Wing took the glass, all but emptied it in one.

"Stone's dead," Hatcham said. "Toxic shock, the ambulance men reckoned."

"I know," Hilary snapped.

"Freakiest bloody thing. All those bees…"

Hilary turned to see his father sitting in the large armchair beneath the window, nursing a glass of whisky. Celia Root sat looking drained and traumatized beside him.

"There was nothing we could do," Commodore Wing said. The old man had tried to sound authoritative, but his voice sounded as frail, as empty, as Celia Root looked. In truth, the terrible events at Root Cottage had shaken them to the core, and both were riddled with fear and doubt. And worse, with guilt...

Was any way of life, any *secret*, worth dying for?

Perhaps they had held on to the past for too long, and now they were paying in blood.

Wing could see the uncertainty in their faces and, with it, his chance to seize control. He leant down close to the table so that no one else in the room could hear. "So we still don't know if they've got the blade?"

The commodore shook his head.

Wing turned round and addressed the room. "So where have these bloody children gone?" He looked from face to face. "Someone's sheltering them."

"All we know is that they've disappeared," Hatcham said.

"They're not with the telly lot either," one of the domino boys added. "We checked."

His friend nodded and chimed in. "They disappeared from the scene of a fatality, that's all we need to know. Perhaps this really is a police matter."

"Shut up, you moron," Wing barked across the bar. The

room fell silent as the man reddened, and Wing wiped away the smirk on Hatcham's face with one withering glance. "*Nothing* in Triskellion is a police matter." Wing stepped away from the bar, began to move slowly between the tables. "Things that happen in Triskellion are *Wing* matters and have been for centuries." He turned to look straight at the commodore. "They *used* to be handled by my father…"

"Still are," the commodore growled. He tried to stand, but Celia Root reached across the table and laid a hand on his arm.

"I don't think so," Hilary said. "You've lost control."

"That's not true…"

"I'm afraid it is." Hilary Wing raised his voice for all to hear. "There was a time when a TV camera wouldn't have got within miles of this place. There was a time when we paid no heed to outside opinion and ran the village by ancient rules." He turned his gaze to Celia Root. "And there was a time when bastard offspring wouldn't have been welcomed back here with open arms."

Celia Root took a sharp intake of breath. "Watch your mouth, Hilary," she spat. "These are my grandchildren here and they've as much right to be here as you do. I am as keen to preserve our way of life as anyone else here."

"Maybe that's because you have more to hide than anyone else."

"Shut up," the commodore said, steel in his voice again.

Wing pointed an accusing finger at his father. "Maybe

that's because both of you have something to hide. Because, actually, you have done more to damage this village than anyone else has *ever* done."

Some of the villagers began to murmur and to look from one to another in confusion.

"I think you'd better explain yourself, Hilary," Hatcham said.

The village greengrocer stood up. "That's right. You're going to start accusing people of something, you'd better tell us what you're on about."

Wing walked to the centre of the room. "How stupid *are* you people?" He looked at Hatcham, at the Bacon brothers, at all of them, knowing he was not going to get an answer, and spread out his arms. "This village is a special place. You know it is. You take it for granted that the crops around here never fail, that people don't get ill as often as they might. How many of your parents and your grandparents lived well into their nineties? How old are some of *you*? You think that's *luck*?"

The air of confusion in the room grew thicker. "What else could it be?" Hatcham asked.

Wing shook his head, like a schoolteacher losing patience with his pupils.

"This has always been a lucky village," a woman said. "Nobody from here died in the First World War, nor the Second."

"Blessed, that's what we are," another added. "Blessed by the ancient traveller, by the legend…"

"It's no legend," Wing said.

The women looked at each other, at Hatcham. "I don't understand," Hatcham said.

Wing swore under his breath, exasperated. "Why are you all here?"

"This business with Reverend Stone," Hatcham said. "It's not right, so we just thought—"

"He was murdered," Wing said.

"Now you're just being daft," the greengrocer said. "He was stung to death. The commodore saw it happen."

Wing waved his hand, dismissing the man's remark. "I don't care what anyone saw happen. Those children … the Roots and the … *other* one. They are responsible for this, and now they have stolen something that does not belong to them."

Hatcham nodded. "The blade from the church."

"There are three blades," Wing said. "The three blades that make up the Triskellion. These children already have two of them and thanks to that television show the whole bloody world knows where the third one is." He looked round, enjoying the reaction as his comments sunk in. "So, what do you think your precious legend has to say about *that*? Think this place will still be blessed if the sacred symbol of our ancient traveller is disturbed?" He glared at the villagers. "How much bad *luck* do you think that might bring?"

Tom Hatcham walked round the bar. He placed a hand on the shoulder of an old woman who looked close to tears;

nodded an assurance to several others who looked deeply disturbed by what they were hearing. Then he looked across towards the window. "What do you reckon to all this, commodore?"

Wing was not about to wait for an answer. "There's going to be a change around here," he boomed. "I am taking charge."

"You have no right," the commodore said. "Not until I'm dead."

"Watch me," his son said coldly. "Besides, we might not have too long to wait for that anyway."

The commodore lowered his head, the fight all but gone from him. Celia Root took his hand in hers and squeezed. Hilary Wing turned his attention to the rest of the assembly.

"We must find these children and restore what belongs to us before it's too late, by whatever means necessary. Then we'll deal with those television people, and with anyone else who does not have the best interests of this village at heart. *Anyone…*"

Wing looked round at the blank faces in the pub. He knew that most of these people had spent their lives keeping themselves to themselves, doing what had been expected of them and never questioning the way things were. Beyond the occasional dispute over a lawnmower or an unpaid bar bill, none of them had ever taken any sort of *action* in their lives. "Well?" he said. "Those who are with me, let's go. We need to find those brats *now*."

Tom Hatcham looked towards the commodore, waiting for guidance that did not come. No one else moved.

"You bloody fools!" Wing spat out the words angrily. "You inert morons. Your existence is threatened and you just sit here waiting for it to happen, like sheep."

There was a long silence, before the man from the dominos team finally coughed and spoke up. "Like I said, Hilary, what with the vicar and everything, I think this is a matter best dealt with by the police…"

Something like a growl began low in Hilary Wing's throat and, with a single movement, he took one large stride towards the bar and knocked the man off his stool. The rest of the bar gasped collectively. Now there *were* tears, and stifled sobs.

"Some of us make our *own* luck," Wing said. "And even if you're content to sit on your fat backsides and let everything you have get taken away from you, I'm not." He marched across to the door, staring at the corner table, his features widening into a grin when his father resolutely refused to meet his eye. "You'd all best order a lot more drinks," he said. "Drink and drink and drink until you're insensible and maybe you can forget what spineless idiots you've all been tonight."

He unbolted the door and turned away, speaking his last words out at the darkness before he strode off into it.

"Then pray that when you wake up tomorrow morning, your nice, lucky little world hasn't fallen apart."

40

It had almost turned midnight by the time Rachel and Adam had left Honeyman's cottage. They'd walked to the nearest phone box and rung Root Cottage to let their grandmother know that they were safe. There had been no reply. They'd also poured all their remaining pound coins into the box and put in a call to New York to tell their mother the same thing, but had only been able to leave a message on the answering machine.

"This is Kate. There's a beep coming, you know what to do..."

"Mom, it's us. Nothing to worry about. Just wanted to say, "love you", really..."

In truth, Rachel and Adam had felt that there was everything to worry about.

They walked towards the village across the freshly ploughed fields that bordered the beekeeper's smallholding. The ground sloped away, rough and rutted. The moon was full, but muted behind a thick layer of cloud, and with the torch that Honeyman had given them proving worse than useless, they both stumbled more than once as they made their way slowly across the fields in near darkness.

Adam slammed the torch into his palm in an effort to extract a little more light, but the thin milky beam only flickered, before dying altogether.

"Piece of crap," Adam said. "It's the only torch I've ever come across that seems to make things darker."

"It's been that kind of a trip," Rachel said.

They kept their eyes on the ground, picking their way carefully towards the distant outline of the church spire.

"Why us?" Adam asked.

"Why us *what*?"

"Why do we have to go and get this blade? Why can't Gabriel do it? We both know he could get it easily enough, right? He always seems to make stuff happen if he wants to…"

Rachel was glad that Adam couldn't see her blush in the dark. It was true that Gabriel seemed capable of making extraordinary things happen, but if he wanted Rachel to do something, all he had to do was ask.

"We've got all these pieces of a puzzle," Adam said. "The crusader's tomb, the stained glass window and the bodies under the chalk circle. But it still feels like there's a piece of the puzzle missing. The one that will actually show us what the picture is."

"I think we're the missing piece," Rachel said. "That's why

it has to be us. I think we were chosen."

Adam shook his head, none the wiser. "What does this Triskellion do, anyway? Even if we *can* get all the pieces together."

Rachel shrugged, then shivered, though it wasn't particularly cold. "I'm not sure, but I think we're the only ones that can make it happen. Kind of how you need the right sort of battery to make a light come on."

"Yeah, like this thing." Adam gave the torch another good hard smack and lobbed it into the bushes at the edge of the field. The effort caused him to trip slightly and he instinctively reached out for Rachel. She took his hand. "It doesn't make any sense," Adam said. "There's nothing special about us."

Rachel could tell when Adam was scared and trying his best not to show it. She squeezed his hand.

"I think there is," she said.

They moved towards the edge of the field and over a low wall, on to a narrow trail where the open space gave way to the woods. The going started to get easier, and they had just begun to pick up a little speed when they both stopped dead in their tracks.

A tall, dark figure was moving towards them fast.

Without a word they ducked into the bushes and crouched down, then watched, hardly daring to breathe, as a man they both knew to be deeply dangerous passed within a metre of where they were hiding.

* * *

Hilary Wing stomped into the woods, swatting aside branches and kicking leaves and clods of earth before him as he turned on to the muddy track and hurried towards the Green Men's encampment.

He muttered furiously under his breath as he walked, deciding that those idiots back at The Star deserved everything they got if they weren't willing to stand up and protect themselves. He could not be sure if their reluctance to follow him was simple cowardice or something else, but it didn't much matter either way.

He was content to follow his own path, as he always had.

He knew very well that most of those he'd grown up around didn't care for him a great deal, or were, at any rate, hugely suspicious of what he and his followers got up to when they gathered at night, deep in the woods. Actually, few in the village had really trusted him since he was a teenager; since he'd been expelled from endless schools and had begun running amok in the village and starting fires in the woods. He had never much minded what the locals thought, but his father's mistrust had been far harder to bear. It was when the rumours about the drink and the drug taking had begun, when the gossip about Hilary killing things for fun and sacrificing rabbits or worse in midnight rituals had become too much, that the old man had banished him from Waverley for good.

When he had been cut out of his father's life, of *village* life, once and for all.

The confrontation in the pub had certainly not improved his mood, but Hilary Wing had been seething all day, and, as he walked, his mind was still racing with dark suspicions and white-hot jealousies. Not only had he been obliged to grease up that idiot from the television to keep things sweet, but he also had been forced into an unwelcome closeness to the American brats. Now, to add insult to injury, that archaeologist woman was about to reveal that they were related.

In truth, Laura Sullivan's suggestion that Wings may have at one time or another bred with Roots, that they might have gone against the ancient warning spelled out in the runes, had hit painfully home. Now, someone had stumbled upon something that Hilary Wing had known for a long time; that he had hidden away in the back of his mind. It was something that he had always tried to deny.

Something that he was now going to have to confront.

He barely remembered his mother. She had died when he was three or four. He vaguely remembered an Air Force base; somewhere hot and dusty where his father had been stationed in the late 1950s. He remembered the big American car that his father had driven: the car in which his mother had been killed.

His father, too drunk to drive, had lost his leg in the accident, and the passenger in the back had suffered irreparable damage to her spine.

Celia Root…

Hilary Wing bristled, remembering how Celia, who had

been his father's Air Force secretary, had comforted the commodore after the terrible accident in which he'd lost his wife and they had both themselves been so badly injured. He'd always wondered if she had perhaps been comforting him for a lot longer than that.

In contrast to his mother, a dignified and somewhat aloof woman, Celia Root had always seemed a little … racy. Her lipstick was always brighter and more plentifully applied, and her uniform, as the photographs of the period showed, fitted rather better than most.

They had all returned to England a year or so after the accident. They had settled down. And then there had been the delicate matter of Celia's daughter, Kate.

The story that got trotted out was that Celia Root had been married overseas to a pilot who had been killed in action, flying with the US Air Force in Korea. But the maths simply didn't add up. Kate was several years too young for that. Besides, if she had been married, why did Celia mysteriously keep her maiden name? "Root" was certainly a well-respected old village name, but there might have been a little less gossip had she taken the name of her dead husband.

If there had ever *been* a dead husband.

Wing and Root shall never bear fruit…

It didn't take a genius to work out why Kate Root had got out of Triskellion and escaped to New York at the first opportunity. Growing up in a small village could not have been easy for her and she was almost certainly picked upon by some of the older villagers who had perhaps made a moral judgement on Kate's parentage.

Kate Root had been strong-willed, like her mother, and whenever the young Hilary had come across her during holidays from boarding school, he had hated her.

Wing and Root...

Now, as he tramped down the dark, narrow track into the woods, a horrible thought cemented itself in the mind of an older and wiser Hilary Wing. It made him hot with fury – at himself as much as anyone else, for failing to see it before. Not only did the very idea undermine his sense of who he was, but it threatened the inheritance that he was so grimly hanging on for.

For fifty years, Hilary Wing had considered himself an only child and sole heir to Waverley Hall, the estate and most of the village. However far apart he and his father had drifted, he had told himself that once the old man had fallen off his perch, it would all be his. He would finally be able to run things his way: to govern his personal kingdom.

But now, it was suddenly clear as day to him: that he and Kate Root shared the same father. That *she* was the poisoned fruit of Wing and Root.

Worse still, that his own father, Commodore Gerald Wing, was the grandfather of Rachel and Adam Newman.

Rachel and Adam weren't taking any chances. They waited until they could no longer hear Wing's footsteps crashing into the woods, before they came out of hiding.

"Where's he going?" Adam asked.

Rachel didn't hesitate. "He's looking for us."

"Oh, that's terrific." Adam began trudging away. He picked up a fallen branch and smashed it against a tree trunk. "Anything else we need tonight? A few landmines on the path, maybe? A small hurricane?"

Rachel jogged to catch her brother up and took his hand again. "It'll be OK, really. This feels like the right thing to do."

But Adam wasn't listening. "I mean, I know we're not his favourite people," he said. "I kind of figured that out when he locked me in a cellar then started shooting at you in the woods. But I'd really like to know what we've done to get on this guy's bad side."

Ahead of them, the church spire pointed black into the night sky, like a warning.

"It's not what we've done," Rachel said. "It's what we are."

41

Tom Hatcham paced up and down behind the bar, continuing to dispense drinks with the same ill-humour as he had done since Hilary Wing's exit. Though the immediate shock and hubbub had died down, Wing's words still gnawed away at Hatcham.

He knew he should have gone with him.

"Hilary was right." Hatcham raised his voice to address everyone in the bar. "What we've got here is far too precious to lose. Not to any TV company and certainly not because of a pair of American brats. I don't know about all this legend stuff and all the supernatural mumbo jumbo, but I *do* know that the life we've got here is worth protecting, and that somewhere along the line it's to do with that gold thing."

There were nods and grunts from assorted tables and someone shouted, "Go on, Tom!"

"It's our duty to make sure these people don't nick our village treasures. So I'm going after them." He paused, looked from group to group. "Who's coming?"

A murmur went round the bar, and finally the commodore spoke, summoning every last ounce of his former authority.

"I appreciate the sentiment, Tom, but don't let my son fool you. Hilary's not out to preserve anything. I'm afraid ... I'm *ashamed* to say, that Hilary is in it for Hilary. He thinks that by commandeering this artefact, he will assume some ... power over us all. But he's an idiot. He has no more idea than I do what the Triskellion is capable of."

Hatcham hesitated, then spoke. "With respect, commodore, whatever it is this thing does, we do know that if those kids have got it, it's in the wrong hands, and we need to try and get it back." The landlord grabbed his jacket from behind the bar and marched over to the door.

The commodore could do nothing but watch helplessly.

"Well?" Hatcham said, looking back at the expectant faces. A table comprising half the village cricket team, who were now quite drunk, stood on their feet.

"We're coming," said the burly fast bowler.

He was followed by three or four others in the team, by most of the parish council, men and women, by the dominos players and by the Bacon brothers, who had been lurking near the fruit machine in the back bar.

The group of a dozen or so, slapping each other's backs and egging each other on, staggered out into the night air, and off across the green, crossing the path that Rachel and Adam Newman had taken just moments before.

*   *   *

The pale rectangles of light from the windows guided Rachel and Adam across the graveyard towards the church hall. Dalton and the crew had moved out of The Star the night before and his BMW was parked outside, silhouetted against the purple night sky.

Rachel and Adam had dragged their heels across the wet grass of the churchyard. Its scattered and chipped gravestones were spooky at any time of day, but the voice in Rachel's head had urged her on.

Gabriel's voice – rhythmic, soothing, persuasive – had kept her calm.

"Take it, Rachel. Don't be afraid. You have the right…"

As they approached the 4 x 4, stacked high with Dalton's equipment, the door of the hall crashed open, casting a yellow wedge of light across their path. Masked by the shadow of the car, Rachel and Adam ducked behind the wheel and saw Dalton come charging out of the hall, quickly followed by Laura Sullivan. They were arguing, and as they approached the car, their voices became clearer.

"No way," Dalton shouted. "We need to sit on this thing for a few more days. I just need to get back up to town for a day or two, that's all, so I can manage the announcement properly. Just think of the news conference with all the major channels there. Just think of the headlines when I tell the world what I've found."

"Chris, this isn't all about *you*," Laura snapped. "This isn't about making news stories. It's far more important than that. Look … it's not a news conference we need, it's a controlled lab. Somewhere out of the way of prying eyes, with all the equipment we need, so we can make sure exactly what we've got on our hands here. *Then* we can decide whether we let anyone know what we've got. I mean … it might be safer *not* to, you know?"

"Are you joking?" Dalton spluttered. "This will make our careers."

"And what about the golden blade?" Laura's tone was calmer, more conciliatory. "Who are you going to hand that over to?"

"Who said anything about handing it over?" Dalton said. "Listen, haven't you ever had a present so good, so completely wonderful, that you just wanted to lock yourself away in a room all on your own and look at it?"

Laura shook her head and tried to speak, but Dalton cut her off.

"Well, this is *my* present. I found it. It's up to me what I do with it. It's a gift." Dalton gave Laura a smug smile as though there was nothing further to be said on the subject. "Now lock the bloody door and let's go. See if we can get a drink before the pub closes…"

As Dalton walked to the car, Rachel and Adam ducked down a little further. They watched as Laura reached into her pocket for the keys and then froze, peering towards the back of the car as though she had caught their movement in the shadows. As though she were looking right at them.

"Hurry up," Dalton shouted, firing up the ignition.

Laura shouted over the engine roar. "You're bloody mad. It's not ours to keep…"

Dalton ignored her and revved the engine.

Laura turned and looked towards the door of the church hall. She seemed to hesitate for a few seconds before turning back, then running to the car and climbing into the passenger seat. The car churned up clods of mud and grass as it lurched quickly away across the gravel of the church path.

Rachel and Adam spluttered, fanning away the exhaust vapour that had engulfed them as Dalton and Laura had driven off. As the rear lights of the car faded past the church, they took the few remaining steps up towards the darkened church hall.

Adam pushed open the door. "She forgot to lock it," he said.

"Maybe." Rachel remembered the look on Laura's face and couldn't help wondering if she'd left the door unlocked deliberately, for them.

Then Adam turned. "What the hell's *that*?"

The noise was coming from the woods: a terrible clattering and shouting that beat like the heart of something dark and dreadful as it drifted across the fields. Looking, Rachel and Adam could see the golden aura from a large fire rising above the trees.

They felt the hair on their necks prickle.

"Come on," Rachel said. She pushed past her brother and stepped into the chill of the church hall.

42

The Green Men chopped fresh wood every day and there was plenty to keep the fire burning. To stoke up its heat and its roar. The flames rose high above the treetops, and sparks crackled up in their wake: bright for just a second or two against the dark sky, before floating gently back towards the earth, like dying fireflies.

The huge fire blazed in the middle of a circle ten metres across; a ring of battered vehicles, of old oil drums, and of the Green Men themselves who walked in step round its perimeter, beating out a slow and steady rhythm as they waited for their leader.

Wearing dirty furs and strips of ragged leather, their head-pieces decorated with skulls and feathers, they beat with logs and metal pipes against the drums and tree stumps. Many of their faces had been blackened with earth, and their mouths, when they opened them to chant, were red and wet like animal guts in the glow from the fire.

"Tri-skellion… Tri-skellion…"

The rhythm got faster and the noise more intense as Hilary Wing moved slowly into the circle. His face was a mask, the blue eyes blazing in the firelight and standing in contrast to the black-painted flesh round them. He walked once round the fire, moving in the opposite direction to his men, laying a hand on the shoulder of each before he climbed on to the roof of his camouflaged camper van and held up his arms.

He waited for silence.

"We came together to celebrate earth and sea and sky," he said. "And to keep the ancient ways alive. We gather in these woods because we understand that the present is shaped by the past and because those that forget this have sacrificed their future. We are the memory of this place, and we are its *hope*."

The Green Men banged against the drums to show their approval, urging Hilary Wing on. He acknowledged their enthusiasm, nodding like a triumphant politician as he waited for the racket to subside.

"We are its only hope because only we have understood the threat to its existence. The attack on everything that makes us as we are, that makes our lives here so precious. We are its only hope because, ultimately, we are the only ones with the guts to fight back…"

There was more noise from the circle of figures that hung on every word, still as standing stones. And now the chanting began again; quieter this time, then growing louder as the excitement increased. The voices of the Green Men were a chorus of roars and grunted urges that lifted the words of Hilary Wing higher even than the flames.

"Tri-skellion … Tri-skellion … Tri-skellion…"

"Tonight is the most important night of our lives. Tonight, those that condemn what we do, that see us as little more than a joke, will have cause to thank us, and to regret their ignorant contempt. We have put on bells and danced on their village green. We have smiled and posed for pictures with children and with grinning visitors. We have played our parts very nicely, but tonight we will show those that dare to steal from us that we can fight as fiercely as any animal in these woods when it is threatened."

The chanting and the pounding grew louder still, and a small group peeled off from the circle and walked across the clearing to the great uprooted tree on its outskirts.

The small deer that was lashed to the trunk writhed against its bonds as they approached. Struggled in vain as one of them drew out a knife and went about his work.

When it was over, the creature was laid on a thick branch decorated with leaves and creeping ivy, and carried across to Hilary Wing as the noise from the Green Men rose to fever pitch.

Wing bent down to stroke the neck of the slaughtered deer, then raised himself up again and painted his face in streaks of the animal's bright blood. Once more complete again, the circle roared its approval and, holding his arms aloft, Hilary Wing was forced to scream to make himself heard.

"Green Men have gathered on this spot for centuries, and tonight we must embrace their spirits and the spirits of the creatures they have chosen to live alongside. We must harness their strength and their passion and their rage. We must take back what is ours by right."

On the fire, a huge log erupted into a cascade of sparks, as though the spirits that Hilary Wing believed still moved through the woods were signalling their support.

"We have danced and smiled enough," Wing said. "We are the guardians of the Triskellion – the chalk circle, the village and yes, even the amulet itself. We have a duty to defend ourselves, to defend what we stand for. Now … it is time to fight!"

And the Green Men cheered as Hilary Wing jumped down from the camper van; flailed their arms like wild animals when he ran across to a huge motorbike and started it up.

As the engine roared into life, a vast flock of crows exploded from the trees above him and rose into the glowing night sky like a black cloud as if they had been generated by the flames. The birds drifted, cawing as though they were in terrible pain, and following the procession of cars and trucks that trailed after Hilary Wing, out of the woods and towards the village.

* * *

In the all but deserted lounge of The Star, Commodore Wing limped behind the bar and reached for the bottle of red wine that Tom Hatcham had opened for Hilary earlier.

"Don't, Gerry." From her wheelchair at the corner table, Celia Root reached a hand out towards him. "Please don't drink any more…"

The commodore put the bottle down, moved back towards the table. "You're right. Drinking isn't going to help." He dropped into a chair next to Celia Root and let out a long and desperate sigh. "Nothing is going to help."

"What have we done?" she said.

"You know very well what we did."

She shook her head. "No, I mean, why is it so *bad*? It did-n't feel bad, at the time, did it?"

The commodore looked across at her and smiled. He had no need to answer that question.

"Anyway, isn't it all just a silly superstition?"

"Not silly…"

"Like something out of an old horror film?"

Commodore Wing knew that there was a lot more to it than that. Though he couldn't be sure *exactly* what would happen if the Triskellion were made whole again, he knew that it was what the boy Gabriel had come for.

He knew who Gabriel was.

And he knew why Celia Root's grandchildren … his *own* grandchildren would be the ones to find it.

It was a story he had heard from his own father, as his

father had heard it from his father before him: one that had been passed down through generations of Wings, going as far back as it was possible to go.

Back to the traveller and his bride. To their twin children. To the bodies whose recent desecration had signalled the beginning of the end.

"Gerry?"

He looked up, realized that he had been deep in thought. Buried as deep in the past as those bodies had been. "Sorry, I was miles away."

"What's going to happen?"

He tapped arthritic fingers against the top of his walking stick. "Probably nothing that any of us will see straight away, but things will change. It's special here, you know it is, we *all* know it is … and it's the Triskellion that has given us these … gifts."

"So if it goes, the gifts will be taken with it?"

"I'm afraid so…"

Celia Root nodded, as though the commodore were confirming her worst fears. She lifted up her face to his. "What about Rachel and Adam?" she asked. "What will Hilary do?"

"I've never known what my son was going to do."

"I won't let any harm come to them."

"Of course not…"

"Then we must do something."

The commodore shook his head. He needed that drink more than ever. "I can't stop it."

With a shaking hand, Celia Root reapplied her bright red lipstick. She snapped the compact shut and waved an arm towards the empty bar. "Those people needed your guidance, Gerry, and it wasn't there. You still owe them something. You still have a duty."

For a few seconds there was only the deep *"tock"* of the old clock above the bar, and the bells and beeps from the fruit machine in the next room. Then Commodore Wing rose slowly from his chair and began to push Celia Root towards the door.

"Let's hope we're not too late," he said.

They moved through the door and outside into the chill, began to move towards the commodore's car.

"It's funny," the old woman said.

"What?"

"How a blessing can become a curse."

43

Rachel and Adam spent five minutes looking for the light switches and then gave up. It wasn't *completely* dark inside the hall. Pale, blue-white work lights glowed from the sealed-off area in which the archaeological team had been working, pulsing softly from behind the curtains of thick plastic that had been hung in a layered square round the centre of the room.

The hall was surprisingly high-ceilinged, and even though they were whispering, the children's voices seemed dangerously magnified as they moved slowly through the eerie half-light.

"Could this place be any spookier?" Adam asked.

"I doubt it," Rachel said. Gabriel's voice was still there inside her head, telling her not to worry, but it was getting harder by the second.

"What's that?" Adam froze, and the urgency of his question made Rachel start.

"What?"

"That noise…"

They stood and listened. Coming from the other side of the room, from the part where they knew the bodies to be, they could hear a faint hissing sound. Rachel thought it sounded like a long, sad sigh.

Adam had read her thought. "Like a dying breath, more like."

Then Rachel remembered the tour that Laura had given them earlier, when she'd taken their DNA samples. "It's the sprinkler they use to make sure the bodies don't dry out. They must have it on a timer or something."

"I knew that," Adam said.

They moved slowly towards the first layer of polythene sheeting. The shadows that had been cast against the thick, creamy plastic by the equipment tables and by the sarcophagus beyond, seemed to shift and shudder as they approached. This time it was Rachel who knew what Adam was thinking. "It's probably just the spray moving across the lights," she said. "Or maybe it's the movement of the plastic sheets, you know? A draught from somewhere…"

"There is no draught," Adam said.

"Well, *something's* making me feel cold…"

They stepped closer and Rachel lifted a hand to push aside the polythene.

"Are we sure it's here?" Adam asked. "I didn't see it before."

"It has to be here."

"Well, if it is, they've probably got it under lock and key. It is gold, you know."

Rachel reached into the back pocket of her jeans, produced the chisel and the rusty screwdriver that Jacob had given her before they'd left. "Well, it shouldn't be a problem. They thought we were thieves before, right? Might as well live up to our reputation."

Adam held out a hand. "I'd best take them. I'm stronger."

Rachel handed them over, feeling a surge of affection for her brother, still brave – or still pretending to be – after everything that he had been through. "Let's get this over with," she said.

They moved inside the first layer of plastic sheeting. In front of them lay the long table displaying artefacts from the dig. Each one was labelled and had been carefully cleaned.

"It's not here," Adam said.

"You take a closer look," Rachel said. "I'll see if there's anywhere they might have locked it up." While Adam stayed at the table, Rachel moved on, skirting carefully round the edge of the raised platform on which the sarcophagus itself was laid. She pushed through another two layers of plastic sheeting until she had emerged at the far side of the hall. It was even darker here, but she could see that she was wasting her time. There was a low stage and an old piano. There were a few dusty bookshelves, some cupboards containing old parish newsletters, a tea set and hot-water urn.

There was nowhere secure enough to have stored the golden blade.

"Any luck?" Adam whispered.

"Not so far. What about you?"

Adam said something in response, but Rachel didn't really take it in. She had pushed aside another translucent curtain and moved back inside the cordoned-off area and was walking slowly towards the platform.

Towards the sarcophagus.

Gabriel's voice was still there inside her head, but fainter now, all but drowned out by a buzzing; by a low hum like the pulse of something electrical. Like a powerful current that flowed through her as she was drawn to the coffin. To the bodies...

She stepped up on to the platform, inched slowly to the edge of the sarcophagus and looked down.

It was her first real look at what had been found beneath the chalk circle. The images that she had seen on the TV screens could not do justice to it.

It was the heads that drew her. The faces...

At first she could not be sure if the faces – the bones exposed beneath tattered, leathery remnants of flesh – were preserved as masks of happiness or horror. A cap of some sort, almost fused to the male head and indistinguishable from the flesh itself gave the head a pointed appearance. Expressionless eyes stared hollow, their eyeballs long gone, but their lids dried into almond shapes, making the male figure look almost oriental. On the female, a thin row of dark lashes still framed the empty sockets, softening them, as did the remaining hank of chestnut hair that was twisted round her face. Desiccated lips had drawn back to nothing: thin-lipped holes exposing rows of browned teeth, which made the mouths look like those of chattering monkeys.

Were those grimaces or grins?

Seeing their arms still locked in an eternal embrace, Rachel had just decided that the expressions were closer to contentment than terror when her eyes dropped down to the torsos, and she quickly changed her mind.

She covered her mouth to stifle a scream, then called for Adam.

He came running, bursting through the plastic curtains and leaping up on to the platform beside her. "What? Jeez, you scared the life out of me…"

Rachel just pointed.

Adam leant forward and peered into the coffin, the milky half-light casting a pale glow across the bodies.

"What Laura said about them not being complete. She wasn't kidding…" Rachel could still hear Gabriel's voice, but now it was fractured and faint. It sounded as though he was crying.

Across the breasts of both bodies, the remains of the clothing had been carefully cut away. The rotting fabric had been peeled back from the bodies and laid aside, like tattered, dark wings, revealing the bones and the petrified flesh.

44

Jacob Honeyman had heard them coming when they were still a mile or more away, and, unable to remember whether or not he'd locked the gate after the children, had rushed out into the compound to check that everything was secure.

He had just fastened the padlock when he saw the lights. Dozens of pairs bearing down on him, like the eyes of night beasts. And when he realized how fast they were going, he guessed that he'd been wasting his time.

He knew that he would never be secure enough.

The convoy of vehicles accelerated as they rounded the final bend and roared towards Honeyman's land. He cried out, and threw himself out of the way as a large truck smashed straight across the low, wire fence and roared past him; dozens more followed, gouging huge tracks in the earth, demolishing a small coal bunker and crashing through several of his hives.

Honeyman picked himself up. There wasn't time to survey

the damage or mourn the loss of his bees. He knew he had to run.

They were on him before he'd taken half a dozen steps.

Two Green Men seized him by the arms and marched him across the compound to where Hilary Wing was calmly climbing off his motorbike.

The terror squirmed in Honeyman's guts like a snake.

"What are you running for, Jacob?" Wing asked. He walked slowly across to the beekeeper, shaking his hair loose and brushing clods of earth from his long, black coat.

Honeyman stammered and shook. "Look what you did. You're trespassing…"

"Yes, sorry about that, but time is rather against us, I'm afraid."

"I'll get the police," Honeyman said. "I'll have you arrested." He looked around. The old cars and battered trucks still had their lights blazing: a circle of them, blinding him. Aside from the men holding him, there were maybe two dozen more, half hidden in shadow. The skulls that many had fastened to their heads seemed to leer at him, and the black painted faces snarled and spat.

He knew that the police would be of little help.

"Where are the children?" Wing asked.

"I don't know what you're talking about."

"So why did you run?"

"I was scared. I *am* scared."

"Just tell me where they are and we'll be on our way.

I'll even pay for the damage."

Honeyman shook his head.

"That's a shame, because, like I said, we're in something of a hurry and this is what you might call an emergency." Wing stepped close to him, the streaks of blood on his cheeks dried brown and his breath hot on Honeyman's face. "I don't want to do any more damage than I have to."

"What are you going to do to them?" Honeyman asked.

Wing laughed. "Why would I want to do anything?" The smile vanished. "I just want what belongs to us, that's all. And you should want the same thing, unless you've already switched sides of course." He cocked his head. "You haven't sold us out, have you, Jacob?"

The snake in Honeyman's belly was coiling itself round his innards. He could barely breathe. He took a deep breath...

"I ain't telling you nothing," he said.

The rage flashed across Hilary Wing's face, but settled quickly into something like resignation. He signalled to one of his men, then turned away as Honeyman was frog-marched roughly to the corner of the compound and thrown into a rickety woodshed.

"You can't do this," Honeyman squealed.

Wing spoke quietly through a crack in the door. "I don't *want* to do this, but what choice do you leave me."

While two of Wing's men climbed up on to their trucks and passed down large metal cans, the others stood and watched. Beneath the earth that was smeared across their faces there was doubt etched round the eyes of one or two. And guilt.

But like Honeyman, they had little choice. Everything had gone too far.

Wing's men carried the cans over and began to splash petrol across the door and on to the sides of the old shed.

"Just tell us where they are and you can go back to bed," Wing shouted.

Inside, huddled in a dark corner among the logs and the spiders, Jacob Honeyman could hear the splashes of liquid and smell the fumes that crept under the door.

"I can't hear you," Wing said.

Honeyman began to scream.

In the church hall, Rachel and Adam were drawn away from the sarcophagus by a noise that grew louder in their heads. It made them dizzy, starting as an insistent buzzing, like that of the deadly swarm they had seen earlier, becoming high-pitched, squealing, like a badly tuned radio trying to find a frequency, before deepening into a terrible, echoing howl.

The frequency it had found was Rachel and Adam.

It was an unearthly cry for help that seemed to be coming from some distance away, from someone or something to which they had become attuned. Low and desperate. Rachel heard the noise and felt as if something were squeezing at her heart, wringing the blood from it until it was as dried up as the bodies lying behind her on the platform.

"Maybe it's an animal," Adam said. "Caught in a trap or something…"

They staggered over to a small window, holding their hands to their heads and peered into the darkness outside.

"I hope that's *all* it is," Rachel said. The fear squeezed tighter still, crushing the breath and the bravery from her. "I feel like my head's going to explode."

"Look," Adam said.

"Where?"

Adam raised his voice above the noise in his head, in both their heads, and pointed. *"There…"*

Rachel pressed her face to the dirty glass and craned her head skywards.

Electrical flashes illuminated dark purple clouds, which rolled and bubbled like boiling lead, moving fast overhead as if in fast forward. The clouds mushroomed and crashed across the sky in waves, so low that they appeared to be brushing the tops of the trees. Then another light, an orange one, lit the heavy, velvety clouds from underneath. An orange glow, another fire, this time from across the fields. The howl in Rachel's head grew stronger, more human.

"That's no animal," Rachel said.

They stared at the flickering light, and, as the howl in their heads changed into a scream, the twins knew that the cry for help was coming from the same place. Though Rachel had thought it many times since she'd first set foot in the village, she finally heard herself saying it out loud.

"Nothing will ever be the same again."

45

Hatcham and the other villagers could see the flames long before they got to Jacob Honeyman's place. The nearest fire station was nineteen kilometres away, but Hatcham put the call in anyway, as he and the others ran towards the beekeeper's cottage.

They stopped at the locked gate. Stared in horror at the overturned hives and the blaze that roared out of control, sending smoke into the purple sky that boiled overhead. At the crowd of Green Men that stood like statues in front of the burning building...

Hilary Wing marched across, stopping a metre short of the main gate. His eyes moved across the gaggle of villagers until they found Tom Hatcham. "Nothing to worry about here, Tom," he said. "Just a bit of a bonfire. Not a problem."

"I think we'll be the judge of that," Hatcham said. "The fire brigade are on their way and we'll take charge until they get here." He peered at Hilary Wing. He swallowed hard and spoke in a voice thick with apprehension. "You've got blood on your face," he said.

Wing dabbed at his cheek with a dirty finger. "Really?" he said.

"Where's Jacob?" Hatcham asked suddenly.

Wing took a few seconds to answer, then waved a hand dismissively. "He's around here somewhere, I think."

Hatcham and the others craned their heads, began to shout Honeyman's name.

"Probably gone wandering off," Wing said, casually. "We did warn him, but you know what the silly old fool's like."

Save for the roar of the burning shed and the wind hissing in the trees along the edge of the road, there was silence for a few seconds. It was broken by a scream that caused half a dozen of the villagers at the gate to step back in alarm. One woman looked as though she might faint, and others stepped up to comfort her.

Tom Hatcham felt the hairs prickle on the back of his thick neck; felt his legs begin to tremble. Days before, he had been party to scaring Jacob off, but this was in a different league. He leant against the gate for support and caught Hilary Wing's glance back towards the fire. Saw the smirk that passed like a shadow across his bloodstained face.

"Dear God, tell me you haven't," he said.

"Haven't what? You'll need to be a bit more specific," Wing said. He turned and strolled casually back towards the shed, swishing at burning cinders with a stick, letting his final remarks drift back over his shoulders with the wood smoke.

"I'll tell you this though, since you bring it up. It won't be God who saves this village…"

Hatcham clambered across the gate and dropped down heavily on to the gravel. With the Bacon brothers following at his heels, and the rest of the villagers not far behind them, he ran, panting towards the flames, screaming out Honeyman's name and looking desperately around for some way of putting out the fire.

Five metres short of the shed, he was beaten back by the temperature. Holding his hands up to protect his face from the heat, he shouted across to the Bacon brothers; told them to go into Honeyman's kitchen for water and buckets; told them to *hurry*.

The Bacons found the way to Honeyman's cottage barred by a trio of Green Men brandishing thick, wooden staffs. They turned back to Hatcham, helpless, waiting for further instructions, while another of Wing's men came running out of Honeyman's front door and handed a mass of papers to his leader.

Wing studied the documents and whistled quietly to himself as the flames climbed skywards.

Hatcham and the others could do nothing but watch, and weep, and cover their ears as another desperate scream exploded from inside the burning shed.

Huddled in the corner, with sparks and shards of red-hot wood flying about his ears, Jacob Honeyman moaned, and coughed, and waited for death.

The smoke was thick and black, and when he breathed it in, it felt as though hot soil were being poured down his throat.

He could feel the skin on his arms and legs beginning to blister.

He'd never really believed in too much, only stuff that everyone else thought was weird and freaky, but as he sank towards the floor he found himself hoping that there might be something afterwards. He thought about his mother who had died a few years before. He thought about friends that were long gone, and he worried about who was going to take care of his poor, poor bees...

He sucked in what he knew would be his final breath, felt it burning his lungs.

"That's touching."

Honeyman looked up at the voice and saw a figure walking towards him through the black curtain of smoke.

"Thinking about your bees, I mean."

"Sweet Jesus," Honeyman said.

Gabriel smiled. "It's getting pretty hot in here; I think we should be going, don't you?"

Honeyman was too stunned to speak. How could the boy have got into the shed? And why was he seemingly untouched, unaffected, by the fire? The smoke seemed to weave round him, as though he were moving inside some sort of glass case. The beekeeper watched, dumbfounded, as the smoke began to clear. It was almost as if it had become a living thing: rushing for the cracks in the sides and roof of the shed, towards the fresh air, as though being sucked out by some giant vacuum cleaner.

Gabriel held out a hand. "Up you get, Jacob…"

Outside in the compound, Hilary Wing, Tom Hatcham and the dozens of others watched in amazement as the flames sputtered and died. One or two of the older villagers crossed themselves and whispered thanks as the door crashed open.

Honeyman staggered out, his blistered hands stretched in front of him like a zombie, smoke billowing from his tattered clothing and his face blackened by the soot. He dropped to his knees and let out a volley of hacking coughs. Finally his lungs felt clear, and clean.

He stood up and turned round.

Gabriel was nowhere to be seen.

46

Rachel took a step back from the window and let out a long sigh of relief. The screaming in her head had died away. She turned to Adam. "Jacob's safe," she said. "Gabriel wants to meet us at the chalk circle when we've got the blade."

"I know," Adam said. "He talks to me too."

"Right. Sorry…"

Rachel drifted away from the window, back towards the centre of the hall. When she pushed aside the thick, plastic flap and stepped back inside the square of blue light, her eye was taken by two shapes on a table away to her left. Each was about forty-five centimetres tall and covered in a brown cloth. She remembered Laura explaining, and the woman who was working at the potter's wheel.

The clay heads.

Rachel walked slowly across to the table. She reached out towards the edge of the cloth and then hesitated. Did she really want to know? Or was it that she knew already?

She tugged at the cloth and it slid away, revealing the moulded clay head beneath.

"Adam…"

Adam wandered across, muttering about how they needed to find the blade and get the hell out of there. He stopped talking when he got close to Rachel; when he saw what she was staring at.

"Rachel…"

Rachel said nothing. She was looking at her own face.

The face of a young girl on her wedding day: the sunlight dancing across it, radiant.

Beaded in sweat, as she gives birth to a son and daughter: the pain and the joy indescribable.

Ashen in death. The expression frozen and unclear as she is laid in the ground next to her husband. As their hearts are torn out.

At her own face…

"It's amazing, isn't it?"

Rachel and Adam spun round at the same time, stared at the man stepping out of the shadows.

Chris Dalton.

"I mean, you could be sisters," Dalton said. "Most incredible thing I've ever seen. Don't you want to see what the other face looks like? You'll never guess…"

Rachel and Adam didn't move.

"Never mind. There isn't really time anyway." Dalton smiled at them, the strange light making his perfect teeth look almost luminescent. "I don't really need to ask what you're doing in here, do I? Or how you got in?"

"We were just looking round," Adam said.

"In the middle of the night?"

"We weren't bothering anybody."

"Looking for anything in particular?"

"No," Rachel said.

Dalton smiled again and raised his arm. He opened his fist revealing the golden blade. "Not looking for this?" Adam took a step towards him and the fist closed tight. "I don't think so."

"That doesn't belong to you," Rachel said.

"Right now, I'll think you find it does," Dalton said. "But it's no use without the other two, is it? You know what I'm talking about."

Rachel leant towards her brother and eased him towards the curtains. "Come on, Adam…"

Dalton bent towards the table where the tools had been laid out and in the next second a knife had appeared in his hand. When Adam took another step, Dalton held the knife out hard in front of him. "You're not going anywhere just yet," he said.

Rachel and Adam froze, their eyes on a blade that was rather less valuable than the one they had come looking for. The one Dalton still clutched tight in his fist.

"Now," Dalton said. "What was it that you were saying about the chalk circle…?"

*   *   *

Thin fingers of black smoke waved high above the village, drifting slowly across a sliver of moon, now all but eclipsed by the bruise-coloured clouds, rolling and bunching, low in the sky.

Roosting birds called out in alarm and gathered close together. Insects and small animals skittered towards their burrows. A couple out walking their dogs along the edges of the great moor stared at the heavens open-mouthed before hurrying quickly inside.

Once under cover, the dogs themselves took shelter beneath tables and chairs, sensing the change of atmosphere and tasting it, metallic on their lolling tongues.

The electricity in the air.

And something more…

47

By the time the commodore's Land Rover pulled up outside Jacob Honeyman's place, the beekeeper was wrapped in a blanket in his kitchen, talking to himself and being force-fed tea by one of the barmaids from The Star.

The Green Men had gone.

Commodore Wing helped Celia Root down from the car and into her wheelchair. He pushed the chair across the rutted ground to Honeyman's cottage, where half a dozen villagers were still gathered outside, staring at the smoking remains of the woodshed and muttering about Hilary Wing.

They all fell silent when they saw the commodore approach.

"What happened here?" he asked.

He asked the same question to several of the villagers by name, but nobody would answer. Nobody would so much as look at him. The smell of burning wood was almost choking.

Celia Root reached behind to lay a hand over one of Commodore Wing's. "Let's go inside," she said.

Hatcham and the rest of the villagers were packed into the tiny kitchen. Honeyman sat at the table, staring off into space and saying things that nobody could understand.

"What's been going on, Tom?" the commodore asked.

Hatcham took a deep breath. "They locked Jacob here in the shed, and set fire to it."

Celia Root's hands flew to her mouth.

Commodore Wing almost laughed. It sounded so ludicrous. "What?"

"It's true, commodore." Hatcham nodded solemnly. "They tried to kill him."

"Who did?"

Lee Bacon pushed his way across the kitchen. He was red-faced and snarling, carrying a wooden mallet that he'd snatched from the utensils drawer. "Them freaks from the woods. With blood on their faces and horns on top of their heads…"

Gary Bacon looked every bit as fired up as his brother. "Freaks is right," he said.

Suddenly Honeyman spoke up, looking intently at the commodore, his fingers clawing at the edge of the blanket round his shoulders. "The boy was in there with me," he said. "Walked straight through the fire and saved me, he did."

The commodore stared at him, then looked across at Hatcham and raised his eyebrows.

"He's been going on like that ever since he came out of that shed," Hatcham said. "I think the smoke might have, you know" – he tapped at the side of his head – "fused a few of the circuits."

"Straight through the fire," Honeyman said. "Like an angel or something."

Celia Root turned to Commodore Wing. "Which boy does he mean, Gerry?"

The commodore shook his head as though the question were unimportant, or else was one he didn't want to think about. He turned back to Hatcham. "Hilary?"

The landlord nodded. "It was Hilary who made the others put him in there, I'm afraid."

"No…" The commodore looked as though his legs were about to give way beneath him. A woman grabbed a chair and the commodore all but collapsed into it.

Hatcham licked the end of a finger and dabbed at a stain on his shirt front. "I'm sorry."

"Something's got to be done," somebody said.

Celia Root wheeled herself across to the table and looked hard at Jacob Honeyman. "Where did they go? Jacob?"

Honeyman raised his head to look at her. The wide eyes and broad grin shone through the soot that was smeared across his face. "He made the fire stop, you know. He *told* it to stop…"

"Where did Hilary and his men go?"

"You won't get any sense out of him," Hatcham said. He

stepped across to the chipped wooden counter top and grabbed the sheaf of papers that Hilary Wing had left behind; the documents he'd been studying before he'd jumped back on his motorbike and led his men away, unnerved by Jacob's miraculous escape. Hatcham pushed them across the table towards the commodore. "Here…"

Commodore Wing looked down at the ancient map, at the hand-drawn amendments and the spidery scribble. He tapped a finger at the point on the map where the chalk circle was clearly marked; where Honeyman had written: *This is where they must come together!*

Celia Root turned to look out of the small kitchen window at the hills that sloped away at the edge of the fields. She shuddered involuntarily, feeling the menace in the blue-black sky. "What's Hilary going to do?" she said.

The commodore looked as though he could scarcely bring himself to consider it, but Tom Hatcham had the only answer that any of them needed.

"Seeing what's happened here," he said, "I reckon he's capable of doing just about *anything*…"

Hilary Wing accelerated hard, urging the big motorbike up to sixty miles an hour as he tore along the winding, unlit lanes around the village. He knew these roads well and had spent many nights driving around them on the old Triumph. He enjoyed the speed, the night air on his face and the time it gave him to collect his thoughts.

Tonight, though, he had a job to do. A sacred duty to fulfil.

He'd left the rest of his convoy well behind. Several of those big old vans and trucks could barely get above thirty miles an hour anyway. Most had difficulty negotiating some of the tighter corners and had to pull over if there was anything coming the other way.

The motorbike, like its rider, gave way to nothing and nobody, and the adrenaline generated by the night's events made Hilary Wing feel invincible.

Up to sixty-five now, the wheels squealing against the road as he leant over to take a sharp bend. As he drove, the powerful headlight picked out the bright eyes of creatures in the undergrowth on either side, blazing for just a second and then gone: weasels, fieldmice, foxes. He felt an affinity with these animals, with the world that they belonged to, as he raced through the night. He drew strength, had always done, from everything around him that was untamed. Wild animals fought tooth and nail to protect their territory, their young, and when his father was gone, it would be down to him to do likewise – to protect the villagers.

From the threat of outsiders and of change. From themselves.

He would start tonight. He would take back the blades of the Triskellion and return them to the earth. It was the natural order of things and he would do whatever was necessary to make sure that those things did not change.

It did not matter that the enemies he must go up against

were children, or that they were his own flesh and blood. There was no room for emotion or sentiment. He accelerated still further, deciding that the Root children might even pose a threat to his own inheritance, and that if he was forced to take the strongest action against them, he would be killing two birds with one stone.

Or *three* birds, if he counted the other child. The outsider...

The wind lashed against his face as he drove on, and he could feel the streaks of deer's blood crusted on his cheeks.

It felt like armour.

The bike touched seventy, and he almost lost control taking two sharp corners in quick succession. He straightened up and breathed in the cold air. The chalk circle was only a few minutes away.

Suddenly, something howled away to his left and he took his eyes off the road for a second. When he looked back he saw the boy just a hundred metres ahead, spotlit and frozen in his headlight beam, like a flash photograph. Instinctively he put his foot on the brake, but then took it off again, flicked back his wrist and felt the bike lurch forward beneath him.

Three birds...

Fifty metres ahead the boy raised his arms, as though he was waiting. Hilary Wing leant down over the handlebars and drove straight at him. He screamed in rage and excitement as he bore down on the figure of the boy, until, a few seconds from impact, he felt the front wheel torn from his control. He clung on for dear life, but the handlebars jerked beneath his hands as though they had taken on a life of their own.

There was nothing he could do.

His last sight of the figure in the road was blurred and shrouded in terror.

But he could see that the boy was smiling.

Hilary Wing's scream grew louder as the machine veered away to the left and roared up on to a steep bank of grass at the side of the road. It smashed through the thick hedge and sailed high into the field on the far side, Wing's hands still clamped round the handlebars as the motorbike crashed down and exploded in a ball of flame and shredded metal.

Those creatures near by – foxes, weasels, mice – bolted for cover, alarmed by the noise. But the creature in the road did not move. Unblinking, Gabriel stood and watched as the flames climbed even higher than those over which Hilary Wing had stood, triumphant, just an hour or so before.

48

The sun was coming up faster and earlier than usual, though it was still hidden behind the blanket of thick, rapidly moving cloud, and the strange light seemed to change every few seconds as it fell across the moor. The damp couch grass that whipped round Rachel's knees turned from black, to brown, and finally to a dirty green as she pushed through it towards the chalk circle.

Adam was a few steps behind her, Dalton's knife pressed hard into his back.

"Get a move on," Dalton said.

Adam half stumbled and turned to glare at the man behind him, to spit out his defiance. "None of this is going to do you any good, you know. Gabriel's not going to give you the other two blades."

Dalton kept walking. "You'd better hope for your sake that he does," he said. "I've not spent all this time, money and energy to have my greatest discovery nicked by a couple of kids."

"It's not your discovery," Rachel said, tight-lipped, under her breath.

They walked over a small rise and Rachel could see the chalk circle a few hundred metres ahead of her, stark against the ground even in the half-light. There were several cows away to her right and a small flock of sheep just beyond them. But the animals were unmoving: frozen, as if waiting for something to happen, or pressed into the ground by the weight of the cloud that by now seemed to be just centimetres above their heads.

Rachel kept walking. Ahead of her, she could see Gabriel standing equally still in the centre of the circle. He was waiting in the place where she'd first seen him that first night from her bedroom window. She remembered the crack of the glass shattering. The terrible storm.

It felt like there was another storm coming. A storm that was bringing the end of everything with it...

"You won't do anything stupid, will you?" Dalton said. Rachel and Adam shook their heads. "This goes all right and your weird little friend there doesn't mess me around, you'll be back with your gran before you know it."

Rachel grunted.

"Having a nice bit of breakfast."

Adam grunted.

The twins could do no more than half listen above the conversation they were having with each other in their heads, above the panic and confusion and argument that had been passing between them telepathically since Dalton had marched them out of the village hall at knife-point.

"He's going to kill us."

"Don't be stupid."

"He's going to get the blades and then kill us anyway so we can't tell anyone."

"Adam, relax. He's the guy off the TV. He's not going to hurt us."

"You're joking, right? I'm being marched across a deserted moor at the crack of dawn with a knife in my back. Nobody knows where we are and the sky looks like it's about to come down on our heads."

Then Gabriel's voice, cutting loud and clear into both their minds.

"Stay calm…"

As they got closer to the circle and Rachel began to make out the expression on Gabriel's face, she could see that he certainly looked calm enough.

"Don't you trust me, Rachel?"

She wasn't sure that she *trusted* Gabriel. Not exactly. Not like she trusted Adam, or her mother. But she had some kind of strange … faith in him, and she certainly didn't doubt what he was capable of.

She thought about fire and bees, and slowed slightly as she drew closer to him.

"You've been ages," Gabriel said, when Rachel and Adam stopped at the edge of the circle. Rachel had not expected

Gabriel to be surprised of course. She knew that he would have been able to see them coming from a long way away. That he would have known what was going on before they'd even set foot on the moor.

She wondered if Gabriel had known that this moment was coming for a very long time.

Gabriel lifted up his hand; opened his fingers to reveal the golden Triskellion that was two-thirds complete. "I suppose you'll be wanting this then, to go with what's in your pocket."

Dalton just stared for a few seconds, then reached into his jacket for the single golden blade he was carrying. He let out a hum of contentment as he looked down at it. His expression changed in a flash when Gabriel took a step towards him and he moved quickly, grabbing hold of Rachel and pressing the knife to her neck.

"You stay where you are." His voice was trembling with panic. "I can do without any more of your magic tricks. Exploding coins, whatever…"

Gabriel stepped back. "Whatever you want." He held out the Triskellion. "Let Adam come over here and get it for you, then when you have it in your hand, you release Rachel. Deal?"

Adam shook his head, opened his mouth to protest, but Gabriel raised a hand to silence him.

Dalton took a few seconds, weighing it up. He licked his lips. "Just get the blades and get back over here," he said, pushing the tip of the knife into Rachel's neck. "I'm feeling a bit nervous to tell you the truth, and it could get messy if my hand slips."

Rachel squirmed as Dalton's grip tightened round her arm. "Don't give it to him. He's bluffing."

Dalton kicked Adam in the back of the leg, urging him across the circle towards Gabriel. "Only one way to find out," he said.

Rachel looked hard at Gabriel, spoke to him without saying anything. "Don't do this. You *can't*…"

"It's fine, really."

Adam took the final step, and held out his hand for the Triskellion.

"Not after everything we've been through to get it," Rachel said.

Gabriel smiled and held out the Triskellion for Adam to take. His voice in Rachel's head was perfectly calm and strong. "I told you to trust me."

It was all taking too long for Dalton's liking. "Come on, bring it here," he snapped. Before Adam had taken three steps back towards him, Dalton reached forward to grab the golden amulet, pushing Rachel aside as he did and stepping back to admire his trophy.

"I hope you think it's worth it," Gabriel said.

Dalton opened his mouth to speak, and it stayed open as the pieces of the Triskellion moved slowly towards one another as though pulled magnetically, gliding across his palm, the metal edges kissing softly before welding them-selves into one, perfect whole.

"That's … incredible," Dalton said.

Gabriel beamed. "I'm glad you like it. Not so sure it's going to feel the same way about you though."

Before Dalton could respond, the Triskellion began to hum and spin on his palm. Dalton moved to cover it with his free hand but the Triskellion was already rising into the air, drifting up and away until it was hovering, just out of his reach. He stood on tiptoe, trying to grab it.

"Nearly got it," Gabriel said. "Just another few inches…"

Dalton made one final lunge and as he did so, a beam of white light shot from the Triskellion, knocking Dalton sev-eral metres back through the air. He screamed as the bolt hit his chest, and was deeply unconscious by the time he crashed back to the ground, his limbs twisted like a broken action figure.

"Deadly in the wrong hands," Gabriel murmured as the Triskellion drifted back towards him, spinning gently back down on to his palm. "But in the *right* ones…"

Rachel and Adam watched as beams of bright light burst from each blade, shooting in straight lines as far as the hori-zon on three sides of them. Then, the lines began to blur and shift, and the beams moved down and around, sliding across each other, dancing and weaving like ribbons round a may-pole. Now they were more like water than light and, as the twins stared, the three beams flowed between and round them, gathering them in and easing them across the circle towards Gabriel.

Rachel and Adam moved without being told, without needing to look where they were going; guided by the beams that snaked round them on the moor, by the bright Triskellion of light that was pulsing and wrapping itself tightly within its own shape, carved into the earth many centuries before.

The chalk circle was suddenly brighter than the twins had ever seen it, and looking up they saw a thousand more beams thirty metres above their heads; a latticework of light bursting from the amulet that still spun in Gabriel's hand.

It hung above them like a dome, like a shield.

"Rachel, Adam..."

Gabriel had spoken with his mind, and Rachel and Adam were drawn still closer to him, watching as a constantly changing pattern of light began to move at incredible speed around him. It span in a complicated vortex. It curled in strings and fell in dazzling sheets and from within it Gabriel's voice began to sound different.

"I suppose we need to talk about a few things," he said.

Rachel and Adam held up their hands to shield their faces, but their eyes adjusted quickly to the light, and, as they stared into it, Gabriel began to change.

49

By the time the Green Men reached Hilary, it was almost light. Abnormally light...

All they could do was stand and stare at the blackened skeleton of the old Triumph. Its tyres were melted, the fuel tank had been shredded by the explosion, and a black circle was scorched into the field round it. Blackened springs showed where most of the big saddle had burned away, leaving tatters of leather round the edges like scraps of blistered skin.

They found Hilary's body in damp grass several metres away. The clothes were still smouldering, and two of his men took off their long coats and covered him to prevent the body from burning any further. The acrid smell of scorched flesh and burnt rubber hung in the chilly dawn air, so heavy that they could almost taste it. One or two retched at the roadside as the foul smell caught in their throats. Others began to wipe away at their black face paint with tissues and rags; the charade of dressing up suddenly seeming absurd and childish in light of the night's events.

Tom Hatcham and several of the villagers caught up with them soon after, having taken the same narrow lane from Honeyman's place towards the moor. Hatcham shook his head as he trudged through the wet grass and took in the grisly scene. He dutifully took out a mobile phone and called for an ambulance, though he guessed it would be far too late by the time it had driven from the nearest town.

The villagers and the Green Men shuffled about uneasily, throwing guilty glances at one another. It was as if they had all woken from a shared bad dream of which they were now all terribly ashamed.

Tom Hatcham could not meet anyone's eye. Instead he stared at the rolling grey clouds overhead, which began to disperse as a beautiful shaft of yellow light broke through and shone down in finger-like rays on to the moor.

It looked as though it was going to be a beautiful day.

Hatcham wondered who was going to tell the commodore what had happened to his son.

Jacob Honeyman was jerked from his dream by the crowing of the cock from a neighbouring farm. Bloody thing was early. It was normally regular as clockwork. He straightened himself at the kitchen table and took a deep breath.

He could still taste the smoke, and hear the crackle and spit of the flames around him and he knew that these were not the blurry remnants of his dream. They were memories, all too real and painful, and they would stay with him for ever.

He needed a hot bath, and a stiff drink.

They'd all left in dribs and drabs once the excitement was over, once they had figured out where they needed to go: Hilary Wing and his gang, whooping like monkeys in their trucks; Hatcham and his cronies. The commodore and Celia Root had been the last to go, the old woman reluctant to leave him, keen to make sure he was going to be all right.

"I'm so very sorry, Jacob," she'd said, as the commodore had wheeled her out of the shack.

Honeyman had watched the Land Rover pull away, feeling like the old woman had been apologizing for all sorts of things. For more than just what had been done to him that night by Hilary Wing.

He stood up from the table and walked across to the small, grimy window above the sink. He looked out at the sky and for once he was grateful to the cockerel and its infernal racket.

Today was a special day. It was one he'd long dreamed of but it was not one he would have wanted to dream away.

His buoyant mood was swiftly and brutally punctured as more of the previous night's events came back to him in horrifying detail. He saw the convoy of trucks and battered vans ploughing through his fence and rampaging across his land. He could hear the terrible crashes as the Green Men wreaked their destruction.

A moan rose up into Honeyman's mouth, and he forced himself to drag open his front door, to step outside and survey the damage.

He needed to see what had been done to his hives. What was left of his precious family of bees.

"What a glorious light," Celia Root exclaimed, as the clouds broke above the car and streaks of sunlight lit the road in front of them.

Commodore Wing folded down the sun visor above the windscreen and narrowed his eyes against the unusually bright sunrise. From Honeyman's cottage he had driven the long way, round the edge of the moor, which, unknown to him, had taken him away from the scene of Hilary's accident.

They were both silent for a moment, the events of the evening weighing heavy on their minds, then Celia spoke.

"Do you think, this … all this terrible business, people dying, behaving madly, trying to kill one another … do you think it's all our fault, Gerry? Because we…"

"Because we were in love? Because we had a child? I don't think so, darling." Commodore Wing gave her a sideways glance. Tears were pouring silently down Celia Root's cheeks.

"But we went against the legend. We mixed our two families; we knew we shouldn't, but we couldn't help it … and now I think perhaps we've cursed everyone."

"Don't think like that, Celia. This was bound to happen one day." The commodore coughed, uneasy at speaking his most private thoughts, even with his closest companion. "You know, the older I get, the more I see a shape in things. A destiny that we have no real control over. I think perhaps that we were *meant* to get together. That somewhere along the line, someone or something decided that the time was right for us to have a child. Someone guided us. There was nothing unusual about Kate, was there? You remember how beautiful she was?" Celia nodded. "But then the twins came…"

Celia Root paled at the memory. "Do you remember how spooked we were when they were born? It was as if the prophecy was being fulfilled."

"And perhaps their coming back here was also meant to be."

"But I was so terrified when Kate said she was sending them. I feel like I've treated them terribly badly, but I was so scared. I must get them back to Kate now. Gerry, I must…" A sob caught hard in Celia Root's throat.

Commodore Wing pulled the car over by a gate on the edge of the moor.

"Don't worry, darling. In time, they'll realize that you meant well, that we were just doing our duty trying to protect everything. We'll get them back to Kate and all will be forgiven. I promise. Look…" He pointed across the moor. Thirty metres away, standing in the chalk circle, three small figures were spotlit in the shafts of early morning sun.

A smile crept across Commodore Wing's weathered

features. "They'll understand, darling." He leant over and kissed the woman he'd loved for over forty years on the cheek. It was still wet from tears and her eyes were closed.

"Look, Celia, it's a wonderful sight. Celia? Darling…?"

But Celia Root's eyes remained closed, her face smooth now and honey-coloured: bathed in the warm, reflected light of the strange new sun.

50

Gabriel was becoming something else in front of her eyes but, as Rachel tried to follow the shafts and beams of white light that danced and flashed about her, she realized that she was completely calm about what was happening. The voice in her head was soothing her, guiding her thoughts.

While Gabriel was clearly changing, he still somehow remained himself. It was as if thin layers of molten wax were peeling away from him, so he looked less formed, foetal almost, covered in a thin membrane. Then the layers would regenerate, morphing and reshaping into a new version of Gabriel: the changes rapid and fluid, as if multiple versions of the same person were appearing at incredible speed. As if new images were being projected on to him.

The vision settled momentarily, as Gabriel became the knight from Rachel's dreams. It was still Gabriel, but this version was subtly different: the cheekbones a little higher, the eyes more slanted, the whole bearing more ... *foreign* somehow. The "knight" smiled, fixing Rachel with deep, black eyes, and she felt her heart jolt.

She turned to look at Adam who was watching, transfixed, frozen in a weaving vortex of light.

"Let my voice go with you," Gabriel said. He spoke to both their thoughts, his voice more resonant than before. "Follow my mind."

Both twins replied simultaneously. "We already are."

"Good…"

The knight held up a long finger, close to the pointed helmet that appeared moulded to his head, while the Triskellion, spinning somewhere above them, sprayed tiny droplets of light around the circle like a garden sprinkler. The amulet then dropped slowly, hovering lower and lower until it was almost touching the ground, before rising swiftly up again, the tiny particles of light weaving together, creating a human form as Adam and Rachel watched.

As the Triskellion spun away into the air, the figure of a girl grew up from the ground before their eyes; a figure at first made purely of light but which then fused and solidified until it appeared to be as real as the knight himself. Real and yet unreal, as if covered by a fine, translucent mist.

The girl took a step towards the knight, then turned to face the twins. Rachel gasped as she looked into the deep, brown eyes of her double; at the face she had seen moulded in clay on a potter's wheel. The girl smiled, and Rachel smiled back, feeling instinctively warmed by the presence.

"Who are you?" she heard the voice in Adam's mind ask.

"We are your ancestors," came the answer, though neither the knight nor the maiden moved their mouths. "You are descended from our children. Our beautiful twins. Our son generated the male line of this village and our daughter, the female."

Wings and Roots, Rachel thought.

"And Gabriel...?" Adam's thoughts ventured further.

"I am Gabriel," said the knight. "The Gabriel you know comes from me. From the same place as me."

Both Rachel and Adam felt reluctant to ask the obvious question, but their curiosity quickly got the better of them. "Where is it, this place?" their minds asked as one.

The knight looked at them benignly and raised his finger again, pointing skywards into the shaft of light which bathed them all.

The canopy of beams in which they were encased began to crackle and shift again, reworking itself; weaving different patterns until Rachel could see a new shape forming round them.

The chapel from the church...

It was as if the chapel was being holographically generated round them, there on the moor, in the middle of the chalk circle. Rachel and Adam stared in amazement. The chapel was complete in every detail, but glowing with a sparkling inner light.

The knight pointed towards the tomb, and Rachel saw

instantly that the stone effigy carved on top was not a crusader but the knight himself. The two figures walked slowly
towards the carved figure, the knight taking the maiden by
the hand. Rachel and Adam watched the knight slide open
the lid of the stone tomb as if it were no heavier than a sheet
of cardboard, and reach inside.

Rachel and Adam moved closer and saw that the stone
casket was lined with lead, and that something was resting
on the bottom, laid out on a small pallet of dried straw.
Rachel's first thought was that the two blackened lumps
looked like ancient lumps of coal, but then another thought
quickly took hold. A thought that was both shocking and
comforting at the same time.

"It's their hearts," she said.

The two figures turned and smiled at the twins while
reaching into the tomb. The knight took out one of the hearts
and the maiden the other. In their hands the two organs
began to glow, and they turned to each other and embraced
and, as they did so, the figure of the maiden melted into that
of the knight and disappeared.

The knight folded his arms across his chest and bowed his
head to Rachel and Adam. Then, as Gabriel had done before,
he began to change, layer by layer. The projection of the
church began to fade while the beams of light, darted
around, faster and faster; moving between them until the
three remaining figures were bound by a lasso of light that
wove round them in the shape of a Triskellion.

When the layers had peeled away for the final time, Gabriel stood before Rachel and Adam as a boy again. As he had appeared the very first time they had seen him, marching round the chalk circle in the rain.

"Does that answer some of your questions?" he asked.

"Yes," Rachel said.

"Good. I'm glad."

"But…"

"No," said Adam. "I want to know why…"

"Why what?" Gabriel's voice asked as he smiled.

"Everything," Adam said. "Where you come from, why you're here, why we're here."

"We needed to be together to make this happen," Gabriel said. "You were born to make this happen, and it was only when you were old enough that I could come and find you."

"But if we're related, and your ancestor … *our* ancestor came from…" Adam pointed skyward. "Then had kids with a girl from … *here…*" Adam looked at Rachel, trying to grasp the growing implication of his own words. "Then that means that we're, you know, part … same as you." Adam pointed at the sky again, his eyes widening, unable to say the word that would describe finally what he had clumsily pieced together.

The Triskellion dipped and hovered, spinning slowly between them as if to confirm Adam's thoughts.

"So is that what you came all this way for?" asked Rachel, looking at the floating amulet.

"No," Gabriel said. "But that was what made it possible."

Gabriel placed his hand flat on his chest. "I've got what I came for."

The hearts of his ancestors. Of their joint ancestors. Rachel felt her own heart lurch in her chest.

"Thank you," Gabriel said. And then he began to fade. This time, the layers seemed to melt and peel from him and he became fainter, almost transparent.

Now Rachel's heart felt heavy and she saw tears rolling down her brother's face. "Don't go, Gabriel," she cried. "We need you, we're scared."

Adam shouted through his tears, reaching out towards Gabriel, who was fading fast, the sunlight already visible through him. "It must be such a long way for you to go. You'll be lonely. You can't go alone…"

The fading outline of Gabriel smiled and held out his hands towards Rachel and Adam, the voice in their heads dropping to little more than a whisper. "I'm not alone," he said.

Then, as the network of light around them evaporated, Gabriel disappeared for the last time.

Rolling clouds cast a shadow across the moor as Rachel and Adam stood sobbing in the centre of the chalk circle.

Rachel looked down.

In her hands she held the complete Triskellion…

The moment was broken as Adam grabbed her arm and pointed into the sky at the edge of the moor. Out of the clouds, a dark silhouette was approaching, dropping low and moving quickly across the sky, coming their way.

Faster now, black and menacing...

The twins turned and started to run as the noise of the machine drowned out all other sounds, but they had barely gone a few steps before the wind from the giant blades knocked them flat and pressed them to the ground.

51

Rachel could barely lift her head from the flattened grass around them. The helicopter hovered directly above, manoeuvring this way and that, like a giant insect looking for a suitable leaf on which to land; the draught from its huge blades making the coarse grass thrash about the twins' heads. With tears streaming from her eyes, Rachel reached out and grabbed Adam's hand.

She squeezed it, finding solidarity with him, as if these might be their final moments.

The black skis beneath the helicopter dipped into their field of vision ten metres away, closer and closer to the ground but barely touching it, the huge rotors continuing to beat the air. Their vision blurred, Rachel and Adam saw two figures jump from the cabin of the craft and run towards them, ducking low beneath the whirling blades. Rachel squeezed Adam's hand tighter, and as the figures approached, they could see that they were men.

Men wearing white, protective jump suits and headsets.

Together, the twins tried to get to their feet, and when they could not, to crawl away, but the fear twisted in their guts and turned their legs to jelly, making escape impossible.

Then a third figure dropped from the helicopter. A woman. A tall woman in a puffa jacket whose red hair blew around wildly in the wind, almost obscuring her face.

Laura Sullivan.

The two men grabbed Rachel and Adam by an arm each and hoisted them to their feet.

"C'mon," one of them shouted from behind his plastic mask. "Let's go." He jostled the twins forward, forcing them in the direction of the waiting helicopter. Laura beckoned them towards her, shouting something urgent, her voice lost in the thwack of the blades.

Rachel and Adam fell into Laura's arms momentarily but she, too, shoved them forward, urging them to climb up into the hovering aircraft. Helped by the men in jump suits, Rachel and Adam put a foot on the skis beneath the helicopter and climbed up a small, steel ladder into the cabin.

Laura Sullivan hesitated, holding her hair away from her eyes, looking at the forlorn figure of Chris Dalton, lying on the wet moor several metres away. His hands were moving shakily towards his head. He was alive. Laura chewed her lip, as if she were considering helping him.

"Doctor Sullivan." The voice barked from behind her, and she turned to see one of the jump-suited men hanging from the helicopter by one arm, holding out the other to pull her in. "We've got to go…"

Laura took the outstretched hand and climbed aboard as the noise of the engine rose to an unbearable level and the helicopter lifted into the air.

The sudden upward thrust threw Rachel and Adam back against the bulkhead inside the cabin, and one of the white-suited men moved fast to steady them. He guided them down on to a thinly cushioned bench and fixed tight safety belts round their waists. Laura crowded into the tight space, pulling the hatch shut behind her, and as she sat down opposite them, clearing their line of vision, the twins saw that there was another person in the cabin.

Their mother.

Rachel and Adam sat and stared, their mouths open wide – the rush of emotion as dizzying as the rise of the helicopter. They looked to Laura, who grinned, then nodded, as though to confirm that it wasn't a dream. Kate Newman unclipped her safety belt and threw open her arms, a sudden lurch of the helicopter launching her across the cabin and on to her children.

She hugged them, smothering them with teary kisses. "My poor babies," she said.

The childishness of the phrase made Adam smile instinctively, but at the same time it released a powerful pang of longing in the heart of both twins. They returned their mother's hugs and kisses, bawling and blubbering, trying in vain to describe their feelings.

After a minute, Rachel put her hands on her mother's shoulders, steadying her, holding her slightly away in order to focus properly on her face.

"Mom, how did you…?"

"I knew something was wrong," her mother said. "And Jacob emailed me…"

"You know Jacob?"

Kate Newman smiled. "I've known Jacob since I was a little girl. And for someone like him to get it together to mail me, I knew I had to come. Then when Adam called…" She mussed her son's hair, her lip trembling, new tears forming on her eyelids, kissing him again. "You were being so brave, but I could hear it in your voice. I knew something had happened."

Rachel just nodded, taking it all in. She glanced at Laura Sullivan and her mother caught the look.

"Then Doctor Sullivan got in touch with me and told me what was going on. She even arranged my travel. She's been *amazing*."

Rachel reached out and took Laura Sullivan's hand as well. Laura smiled, then pulled away when a walkie-talkie crackled inside her jacket. She listened to a distorted message from the pilot that none of them could quite understand, then stepped through into the cockpit leaving the twins and their mother alone in the cabin.

Rachel glanced through the porthole at the shrinking landscape below.

At the tiny Land Rover on the lane and the old man standing beside it, looking up at the sky. At the flashing blue light of an ambulance that was tearing, too late, along the road into Triskellion. At the village itself, laid out like a model, and the vast moor that spread out beyond it.

Rachel dug in the pocket of her jacket, panicking suddenly that she had left something important behind. But there it was. It felt warm and comfortable in her palm suddenly; as if it were something she had been holding on to for a very long time.

The Triskellion.

The amulet that had been the beginning, the middle and the end of their adventure.

"So where are we going, Mom?" Adam asked. He ran the back of his sleeve across his wet face. His mother pulled him tight to her chest.

"We're going home, honey. We're going home."

Adam grinned across at Rachel, and she grinned right back. But as the helicopter banked sharply and doubled back across the moor and away towards the coast, Rachel looked down at the perfect chalk circle below, no bigger now than a coin, and knew that she was home already.

epilogue

The damage was not as bad as Honeyman had feared, and he told himself that he shouldn't really be surprised. The bee was a marvellously resilient little creature: the only insect that provided human beings with food and as tough in its own way as any one of them.

At this time of year he had upward of forty thousand bees in each of his two colonies, and it looked as though he hadn't lost more than a few thousand. Most importantly of all, both his fertile queens had survived. A couple of the hives were beyond repair, smashed into pieces by one of the Green Men's huge trucks, but the majority were undamaged. He was delighted to see that the three wicker ones, or skeps, that had been used by his great-great-grandfather nearly two centuries before, had escaped unscathed.

Honeyman reached into each hive, carefully removing the honeycombs one by one and checking for damage. He let the bees crawl across his hands and up his arms while he looked for cracks, gently laying aside those combs that were too badly broken to be of any use. Then finally, he removed any dead bees; gathering the tiny bodies in an old plastic bucket as he moved from hive to hive and muttering a few words of regret and thanks for every single one.

Each tireless worker. Each faithful drone.

He would probably lose no more than three or four pounds of honey by the time he'd sorted the mess out, but still, it was a lot of the colony's hard work gone to waste. It took the nectar of two million flowers to produce one pound of honey, with each bee flying the equivalent of one and a half times round the world.

Honeyman was trying to figure out where one and a half times round the world was, when the bees began to swarm.

He stepped back, alarmed for just a moment as he remembered what had happened to Reverend Stone, but he realized almost at once that the bees were not about to hurt him.

They simply had a message to deliver.

He watched as they began to dive and dart in numbers; moving together, then around, in three intersecting circles.

The hum getting louder as they gathered and span in the morning air: a living, buzzing Triskellion…

And Honeyman knew.

And jumped around for joy as the morning brightened across the village and the fields on every side. He performed a clumsy, joyful waggle dance of his own, because he knew that the mission had been accomplished. He knew that things were finally as they were meant to be, and that Gabriel was on his way home.

He wondered what would become of Rachel and Adam, and his answer came tearing across the sky towards him from the direction of the moor.

Black and buzzing; silhouetted against the buttery sun.

Honeyman covered his ears as the helicopter clattered above him, then stood in front of his shack and watched, his bees whirling around his head, as it grew smaller and smaller. Until it was no more than a speck on the skyline.

Zigzagging its way into the blue.

author's note

In 1997, archaeologists excavated the body of a man from a Bronze Age burial on a farm in Dorset. DNA testing on the body proved that the farmer who currently farmed the land was the direct descendant of the man who had been buried over 3,000 years earlier.

Read an exclusive extract from the second
book in the thrilling TRISKELLION trilogy.

Available spring 2009

Triskellion 2
prologue

The helicopter was banking slightly, moving across an area of flat, black ground, when Rachel heard the pilot pass a crackly message to Laura Sullivan.

She nodded and put away the notes she'd been reading.

Rachel looked across to her mother and Adam, pressed closely against one another in the seats next to her. Adam's cheek was flat against the window.

They'd been flying for about an hour, maybe more, she thought, and she'd watched the landscape waking up below her as they passed low above it. A patchwork of green and brown fields, loosely stitched together by threads of irregular lanes, had given way to clumps of terracotta houses, becoming denser and more tightly packed as they approached the city. Lines of traffic had built up and begun to snake slowly along the main roads. Lights had winked in the windows and then faded as the sun struggled up to bleach them out, and Rachel had watched it bathing the crush of buildings and the twist of the river as they'd flown over the centre of London.

Adam had sat forward, excited, and pointed out the London Eye, the Houses of Parliament and other landmarks familiar from films and pictures. Places they had seen but never visited.

Rachel yawned. Beneath the rattle of the helicopter blades, she thought she could hear a faint buzzing, just for a second or two, and wondered if a bee was trapped somewhere in the cabin.

Zzzzz … dnk. Zzzzz … dnk

She looked around and finally located the stowaway, slowly walking the glass circle of the porthole just above her head. With the sky behind it, the bee looked like a little man, exploring the surface of a new planet. She wondered if it had travelled with them from the village.

One of Jacob's, come to see them away safely.

Laura turned round, reached across and laid a reassuring hand on her arm. She signalled to Rachel's mother, told her that they would be landing in a few minutes. Rachel watched as her mother nodded and squeezed Adam's hand. She smiled, but it was thin and weak.

Her mother looked tired.

Rachel was exhausted too: her brain and bones aching in equal measure. The last few hours, the last few weeks, seemed like a nightmare she was waking from, wrung out, but at least she knew that it was over. That she'd feel better when they were on the plane, and better yet eight hours or so from then, when they were finally home.

From the window she could see the land stretching out to

one side, and if she craned her head, it was the same through the cockpit window: flat as far as she could see. Free of trees, free of anything.

She heard the men up front talking on the radio, its squawk like the noise of some angry insect as the helicopter turned again.

A complex of buildings came slowly into view ahead and to the left. It was single storey, and brown, and she could make out the line of a perimeter fence. She looked hard for aircraft, for a control tower, but could see nothing. It wasn't like any airport she'd ever seen.

"Laura? Where're the planes?"

They came down fast, the large "H" in the landing circle growing bigger as they descended. They hit it dead centre with a bump that made Rachel's teeth shake and she looked across at her brother to see if he was OK.

He gave her a thumbs-up.

Then everything happened very quickly...

Rachel was being pulled from the helicopter, out into the roaring wind of the rotor blades, turning to watch the same thing happen to Adam and trying to get close to her mother. But Laura was leading her mother away, putting some distance between her and the men who had emerged from a metal door in one of the smaller buildings.

The men who had come to take her children.

They wore headphones and sunglasses. They didn't speak.

Rachel tried to yank her hand away as she was led towards

the door, but the man escorting her only increased his grip. Adam cried out to her and they both cried out to their mother, but when Rachel turned to look she could see that her mother was sobbing and shaking her head, that Laura was doing her best to keep her calm, shouting over the noise of the engine as it died.

Telling her that everything was going to be fine.

Rachel watched, helpless, as Adam was ushered fast through a door, several metres away to her right. He shouted something to her which she couldn't catch, his voice lost beneath the wind and the sound of her own grunts as she struggled to free herself.

The nightmare hadn't ended. She hadn't woken up...

The last thing Rachel saw on the outside was a hazy line: the furious arc of the bee as it buzzed around her. She twisted her head to get a last look, to pass a last message, but then it too was shut out as the heavy metal door slammed hard behind her.

OPERATION RED JERICHO

"A must read!" *The Sunday Times*
"Makes an Indiana Jones adventure look half
asleep." *The Ultimate Teen Book Guide*

Shanghai 1920: While on board the *Expedient*,
Doug and Becca MacKenzie anxiously await news
of their missing parents … and stumble across
a mysterious secret organization created
to protect mankind from evil.

England 2002: Joshua Mowll inherits his
Great-Aunt Becca's archive of documents and
pieces together the events that took place eighty
years earlier: a story of two young people caught
up in an extraordinary adventure.

OPERATION TYPHOON SHORE

The explosive sequel to *Operation Red Jericho*

Celebes Sea, May 1920: Battered by a typhoon,
the *Expedient* is shipwrecked on a volcanic island.
No radio, no rescue, no escape.

Doug and Becca MacKenzie's search for their
missing parents must wait; but what part did the
mysterious Guild play in their disappearance?
Will the strange riddle Becca and Doug unearth
be the key to the dark secrets of the Guild
and a means of escaping the island?